State of Grace

John Sweene

Acclaim for this book.

"I couldn't put this book down. So much of it so close to what our nation is dangerously close to becoming. I remember reading about the eugenics policies of sterilization of women considered less than human. Prisoners being used as test subjects without being told about danger they were in. I highly recommend this book to anyone who would feels the need to learn about how the US helped spread the poison that is eugenics."

Jolyane Justice

5.0 out of 5 stars

It was a great read, very detailed accounts and as good as a lee Child's book.
You do not want to put the book down.
A must.

Australian Reader

5.0 out of 5 stars

State of Grace by John Sweeney is a fast-paced and intriguing espionage thriller that will keep you eagerly flipping through its pages. I thoroughly enjoyed reading State of Grace for its creative story and honest examination of racism in many countries in the interwar period. I would recommend this riveting story to readers interested in history or spy novels.

Titan Reviews

Historical Note

Although written as an espionage thriller, some of the events are factual, such as America's key role, especially the involvement of the Rockefeller Foundation and some leading academics and politicians, in helping Germany develop a eugenics policy that laid the foundations for the Holocaust.

Some of the characters are also real, such as Stefan George and his artistic circle who played a key role in fostering the aesthetic and cultural forces that persuaded the German people, of all classes, to vote for Hitler.

All the other characters are purely fictional and bare no resemblance to any persons living or dead.

To my children: Gwion, Megan and Iona.

The blood-dimmed tide is loosed, and everywhere

The ceremony of innocence is drowned;

The best lack all conviction, while the worst

Are full of passionate intensity.

The Second Coming - W.B. Yates

Those who don't know history are doomed to repeat it.

Edmund Burke

White supremacists are the "greatest threat" in America.

President Biden

Chapter 1

Halfway across Waterloo Bridge, Phillip Kumar stopped.

Should he go on? Who were they expecting? Did they know who he really was?

An icy wind rippled the river and the late November skies threatened snow. He caught the scent of the sea on the incoming tide, the swelling Thames reminding him of the Ganges whose riverbank had been his childhood playground. He gazed at the tugboats trailing black smoke as they dragged barges upstream, fighting the cross currents of the turning tide while a vessel's warning wail carried along the river. Why him? Why was he being summoned by the Foreign Office for a job he hadn't applied for? What was the job?

Like many others, he had lost his position a year earlier in 1929 when the financial crash caused the economy to collapse. British exports slumped by 50 percent and his job as a shipping clerk disappeared overnight. Since then he had applied for hundreds of jobs, but never got an acknowledgement – all because his name was Kumar. He only got the job in the shipping office because a friend's father ran the firm, but when the crash came and the company went bankrupt, he too lost his job.

For over a year he had barely survived on the two pounds ten shillings he got for being a volunteer in the Army Reserves, and now, out of the blue, a summons from the government to an interview he knew nothing about.

And why meet in the poshest hotel in London, The Savoy, where as soon as he entered they would know he was an outsider, someone who didn't belong, someone not pukka, not the genuine article – how they knew he didn't know: he was fair-haired, blue-eyed, light-skinned, looked European and spoke perfect English, but somehow they knew he was an imposter. He should turn back. But a permanent job, especially with the Foreign Office, was his only way out.

No, he would face them – he pulled up the hood of his red duffle coat and headed for the Strand.

Phillip stepped into the foyer of The Savoy Hotel and felt a frisson of fear as a man in black tails and bow tie made a beeline towards him.

The man stopped in front of Phillip and gave a small bow. 'Can I help you, sir?'

Was the sir delayed, spoken in a lower tone, signalling they knew? Phillip's words come out as if from another person, 'The Thames Suite, please.'

The man gave Phillip a conspiratorial smile. 'Straight through those glass doors and you'll come to a lift, sir. It will take you up to the suite.'

Phillip nodded without meeting the man's gaze and strode towards the doors, a faint trickle of sweat running from his armpit.

He stepped into a corridor where a man in uniform stood next to a lift.

The elevator clanked to the top floor and Phillip found himself on a landing with a door at one end, and at the other end a large window that looked out onto the Strand. Where should he go? There were no signs. He trod cautiously towards the only door, but before he reached it, it was opened and Captain Blakeney stood in the doorway, beaming. 'Hello, Phillip.' He stretched out his hand.

Phillip felt awkward shaking the captain's hand. Captain Blakeney was the commanding officer of the Territorial Army unit he belonged to and had only ever saluted the officer. 'Do come in,' Blakeney said, holding the door wide.

The room was cosy with a patterned carpet and French Impressionist paintings on the walls, along with scenes of British redcoats locked in battle. A coal fire blazed in the grate, giving the room a slight sooty smell. A window looked out onto the Thames. It was the back of the hotel, and just outside the window was a metal fire escape.

Next to the coal fire stood a man in his late thirties, five foot eight, plump without looking overweight, brown eyes and fair hair.

'This is Major Smythe,' Blakeney said.

'Did you bring the letter?' Smythe said.

Phillip crossed to the fire and handed Smythe the envelope containing the letter.

Smythe took the letter and placed it in the middle of the fire. He watched as the flames curled the envelope into brown ashes, and then poked the remains into the coals. He returned the poker to its stand. 'Tea.'

Smythe strode to a table with a silver teapot and two cups. 'I'm sure you must be cold. Tea will warm you up. Do sit down. Chair by the fire. I like your red duffle coat, makes you look like a student.'

Phillip had bought the coat on sale in Simpsons Piccadilly, just after he lost his job, thinking it made him look middle class and so would impress when he went for job interviews. He sat in one of the upholstered wing chairs, next to the fire. Captain Blakeney sat on an upright chair next to the door.

Smythe approached the fire with two cups and handed one to Phillip. He then eased himself into the other chair. 'Sorry there is no sugar. Don't use it, so forgot to order it.'

'That's OK. I … don't always have it.'

Smythe smiled and sipped his tea. 'Now, Phillip, you must be wondering what this is all about.' He leaned back holding his cup in front of him. 'Well, first off, we know a lot about you.

Phillip's heart sank.

'Don't look so concerned. All good stuff. Captain Blakeney here has filled me in,' he nodded to Blakeney. 'We know you are a patriot, ready to defend your country, which is why you joined the Territorials as a reserve, and you helped defeat the General Strike by volunteering to be a special constable in the Organisation for the Maintenance of Supplies.'

'Absolutely,' Blakeney said. 'Phillip's made of the right stuff. Knows how vital it is to fight the Bolshevik threat. And it's the Communists we're up against, Phillip. Germany is their next target, sure as day follows night. And then France, Spain, and then we'll be next. Plenty in this country ready to support a Bolshevik takeover.' He shuffled his shoulders. 'These days it's hard to tell where men stand. The Great War changed everything – old allegiances and beliefs scorned, and new loyalties and faiths embraced.' He stood up. 'Well, now I've introduced you I'll be off. Expected at my club for lunch.'

Smythe rose and showed Blakeney out.

'OK,' Smythe said. 'Before I say anything else, I need you to sign something.' He crossed to a large desk by the window. 'If you would care to come over.'

Phillip placed his cup and saucer on the table and joined Smythe. A document lay on the desk headed Official Secrets Act. 'As a part-time volunteer in the Territorial Army, you are automatically bound by the Official Secrets Act, but we though it prudent that you sign it officially.' Smythe flicked the pages of the document until he got to the final one. He held out a pen.

'Yes. Of course.' Phillip took the pen and signed.

Smythe gestured towards the fire.

'Now,' Smythe said, as he sat opposite Phillip, 'I understand from Captain Blakeney that you have requested six months' leave from the Territorials to return to Germany to complete a postgraduate degree in literature.'

'Yes, sir.'

'Why didn't you complete it first time?'

'I would have, sir. I was halfway through it when a friend of mine from university, here in England, wrote to me that there was a vacancy at his father's shipping firm and it was mine if I wanted it. Well, it was an offer too good to miss, sir, so I came back to England. But …'

'The crash.'

'Yes, sir. I've been unemployed for nearly a year and so I thought I would return to Germany and complete the course and get my master's, and then come back and look for a job teaching German in a school or college.'

'Don't you need some kind of teacher, training?'

'Not if you have a postgraduate qualification. Especially from the country whose language you'll be teaching. But …'

'But?'

'Well, teaching jobs are very scarce, sir. Teachers are staying put because of the job crisis.' He felt like adding that his name was also a problem and that he had applied for dozens of teaching jobs without getting a single reply and eventually learned it was because parents wouldn't want their kids taught German or French by someone with an Indian name. He was advised a master's degree from a German university would improve his chances.

Smythe placed his cup on the small table. 'Well, you could have a permanent job, in the Civil Service, waiting for you when you come back from Germany.'

'Really?'

Smythe smiled. 'Really.' He leaned back in his chair. 'What we need is someone like you Phillip, to travel to Germany and do an enormous service for this country. Something, so important, your country will be forever in your debt. And when you return, to show our gratitude, you will be offered a permanent post in the Foreign Office in Section V, which deals with counter espionage reports from our overseas stations. Some need translating and we need people we can trust to do the work. People like you, Phillip.

'You'll be employed by the Foreign Office as a Civil Servant with good pay, good prospects and a pension. These jobs are not advertised since we need to pick the right people, like you. And as you know Phillip, in these times secure jobs with good pay and prospects are like gold dust.' He patted Phillip's knee. 'And like I say, when you complete the mission, the job is automatically yours. And of course, this exceptional service to your country will be on record.'

Phillip found it difficult to hide his excitement. The perfect job. Secure employment, good income and lifelong career, and using his language skills. Also, he could blend in quietly and keep himself to himself.

'Now,' Smythe said, 'all that I'm going to say must remain a secret. You must tell no one. Not even your nearest and dearest, as they say.' He took a long drink of tea. 'I work for the Secret Intelligence Service, SIS, which is part of the Foreign Office. Well, to cut to the chase, we need someone to go to Germany and pick up a document. A very important document that must never see the light of day, and one you must swear never to read.' He looked down at his cup. 'I'm sure you're aware of the turmoil in Germany and it's going to get worse. Last month's elections saw the Nazi's come second and the Communist's third. The next election will be crucial. Either one of them could win. Both of them have paramilitary gangs roaming the streets killing each other, and anyone else they think is their enemy. This year alone, there have been over four hundred deaths. Two of our agents have been killed.'

Phillip felt his stomach churn.

Smythe stared at Phillip. 'It's vital we get the document so that it doesn't fall into the wrong hands. It could decide who wins the next German election, and the future of Europe.'

Smythe leaned back and gazed into the fire. 'The people who have the document are a bunch of amateurs who have never done this sort of thing before and think it's some kind of game. That makes it incredibly difficult dealing with them, and why we cannot use one of our agents. They have all these bloody go-betweens and have given us only vague instructions on how to make contact with them. And to top it all, we have to try to find them in Bayreuth in South Germany, not far from Tübingen where you studied. Perhaps you visited it. For the opera. Wagner.'

'Er, no. I did travel north to Berlin.'

'OK. Well, Bayreuth is a very small town, more like a large village, and so any of our men wandering around Bayreuth trying to find their contact would stick out like a sore thumb.' Smythe smiled at Phillip, 'That's why we need someone who would fit in naturally, a student. We would enrol you at Bayreuth Arts College doing what you did before, a postgraduate diploma in poetry, and pay all the fees and give you an allowance.'

Smythe gazed at Phillip. 'Also, if you take the assignment we will issue you with a passport in the name of Phillip Fitzwilliam.'

'My mother's maiden name.'

'Precisely. And when you return from Germany, if you want to, you can change your name to Fitzwilliam by deed pole.' Smythe smiled. 'It's not for me to say, but it might be helpful to your career.'

Phillip felt conflicted. Fitzwilliam. Not having to sign letters as Kumar would be an advantage, but dropping the name would hurt his father, who had loved and nurtured him all his life.

There was a long silence. A yellow gas flame hissed from a lump of coal.

'Can you shoot a revolver?' Smythe said.

'No. No I can't. I've only had some practice with a rifle.'

'Pity. We don't have time to train you. And if you're not used to handling one, it could be a real problem.' Smythe took a deep breath. 'Time is of the essence. The next election could not only change Germany, but also the future of Europe, and so time is of the essence, and if you accept the mission you will need to leave in one week's time.'

'I … I'm sorry, sir … but I don't … I don't think I can.'

Smythe stared into the fire. The coals settled like the crushing of insects' wings. Eventually he nodded. 'It's OK. It's a lot to ask.'

A flood of relief went through Phillip – Smythe wasn't going to pressure him. He didn't have to do it. He'd never fired a pistol and two experienced agents, who no doubt did have revolvers, had been killed.

Smythe stood. 'Well, think about it.' He wrote on the back of a card. 'This is the phone number to call if you change your mind.'

He handed the card to Phillip.

Chapter 2

Phillip froze as he entered the street where he lived.

A stray dog was in the road. Its half-starved body shivering as it loped along the street, its jaws hanging open as if ready to bite. Phillip turned and retreated the way he had come. As a child in India, a dog had bitten him and his mother had rushed him to the local clinic where they administered painful anti-rabies injections. He remembered how frightened she had been and didn't leave his side for days. Ever since he panicked when he saw one loose. He hurried back along the road and then slipped into a run-down teashop.

As he stepped into the café, he was hit by the smell of fried food and stale smoke. Men in grubby clothes lounged at tables with oilcloths covered in singe marks. An old woman, who sat alone with an empty cup in front of her, watched him as he went up to the counter, while the men squinted at him from under their peaked caps, greasy with handling. He knew he was out of place. He knew they judged him middle class. But he wasn't. He was just like them. He lived in the East End of London in a tenement and was unemployed.

If he told them they would sympathise and relate their own hardship stories, but then if he told the whole truth, that his father was Indian, they would immediately judge him as a 'half-caste', somebody beneath them and taking jobs that were rightfully theirs.

As in India, where working-class soldiers suddenly found that they had status because they were white.

Phillip carried his tea to the vacant table near the door, where he could sit and look out the window as if waiting for someone. Why couldn't he just be who he was? He was like an escaped prisoner on the run, always in fear of detection, of being exposed as an imposter. Even the double first he got at university for languages, philosophy and poetry, somehow felt it didn't belong to him, he didn't deserve it – it was a fluke.

Phillip sipped his tea. His father had his religion to give him succour and identity. What did he have? Nothing, not even his own self. Nietzsche said to become who you are, that it was the becoming that mattered, by growing you became yourself. But that took more courage than he had. Lacking the courage to express who he really was, he was trapped by the gaze of others, a prisoner of how others saw him.

Dusk shadowed the street, and the grey sky was seeping into molten lead. A lamplighter parked his bike by the side of the road and propped his ladder against the lamppost. Phillip got up and left the café.

He stepped into the hallway of his house and was greeted with the smell of curry. The four-storey house, like many in the area, was multi-occupied, and each floor housed one family. Phillip and his father had the ground floor, which comprised two rooms and a kitchen. Phillip had one room, his father the other, and they ate in the kitchen.

A family upstairs had once complained to the landlord about the 'stink' coming up from the Indian family on the ground floor. The landlord, a Russian Jew, had ignored the complaint, because, as Phillip later found out, his father paid the rent on time while the family who complained were always in arrears.

Phillip's father emerged from the kitchen. 'Ah, it is you. Food will be ready in one hour.'

'I'm not hungry.' Phillip took off his coat and hung it on the peg next to the door.

'You must eat at regular times, my son, or ...'

'I said I'm not hungry.'

'Well, I've made a nice vegetable curry, very mild, how you like it. I'm afraid it will have to last us for the next couple of days until pension day on Thursday.'

His father took Phillip's coat from the peg and draped it on a hanger. 'I'll hang it in the kitchen. It will dry properly there. Such a nice coat. You must keep warm in this weather.'

Phillip did feel cold and followed his father into the warm kitchen. His room would be freezing because it had no fire – they couldn't afford fires in unoccupied rooms.

The kitchen was where they had meals, and, during the cold winter months, where they sat and listened to the radio. It was clean and homely with patterned linoleum on the floor, and beige walls with black and white photos of India. Phillip sat at the kitchen table.

His father hung Phillip's coat on the kitchen door and smoothed the front of it down. Mr Kumar was five foot six, slim, with delicate features and large eyes that gave him a bird-like quality. He had a long grey beard that flowed down to his upper chest and a moustache that twirled sideways. He wore carpet slippers, an old baggy cardigan with stitched repairs to the elbows, dark trousers and a shirt with a frayed collar. His light-brown fingers rippled down the front of Phillip's coat. 'You look so smart in this new coat.'

Mr Kumar stopped grooming Phillip's coat and took a hanky from his cardigan pocket and wiped his nose. He then sat opposite Phillip at the table.

'How did it go?' his father said.

'What go?'

'The job interview.'

'How the hell did you know about my job interview?'

Phillip's father sat bolt upright, his eyes wide, like a startled bird in a nest.

'You read the letter!' Phillip said. 'I was the only one supposed to read it. It was top secret, from the government. You could be in trouble for reading it.'

'Oh. Top secret. Top secret. I'm sorry. Very, very sorry.'

'For God's sake.' Phillip slumped forwards, closed his eyes and put his hands to his throbbing temples.

'So sorry for reading the letter,' his father said, patting Phillip's arm. He then got up and went to the gas stove and put the kettle on. As he waited for the kettle to boil, he kept taking out his hanky and wiping his nose.

Phillip kept his head in his hands with his eyes closed.

'Phillip, I truly feel for you and know it is very hard getting a job at this time. But I ...'

Phillip raised his head and stared at his father. He wanted to say yes, it is very hard getting a job, but not only because of the economic times, it is because my name is Kumar. But he stayed silent; he loved his father and knew he was immensely proud of his Punjabi roots. His mother had been white English and his father, like most Punjabis, was light skinned and could pass as Greek or Southern European, but he insisted on having a full beard and wearing a turban which clearly marked him out as Indian. He said he wore it all the time out of respect for his religion.

His father crossed to the cupboard and took out a new tin of tea. Phillip knew what was coming. 'I met Mr Singh this afternoon and he insisted I take some of his best tea home with me. Darjeeling. The first picking.'

Phillip felt pain in his stomach. He hadn't eaten breakfast, which was usually toast and tea, and now his stomach felt full of acid from the tea he had been drinking all day.

His father spooned tea into the ceramic pot. 'You know Mr Singh is very keen to have you work for him.'

Phillip knew Mr Singh wanted him to work for him, and knew that his father and Mr Singh had agreed that Phillip should marry Mr Singh's daughter who was supposedly madly in love with him and would come with a huge dowry. But he would never marry

Mr Singh's daughter, no matter how big her dowry was, no matter what job he was given in her father's tea import business.

Marrying Singh's daughter meant giving up his freedom. He would have to conform to Indian culture and lifestyle and have his children brought up as Sikhs, and if boys, forced to wear turbans, and there would be nothing he could do about it. He had been brought up in his mother's religion, Catholicism. He had attended Catholic schools and observed the rituals of the faith up until his first year at university. Then he shed all notions of a personal god and accepted that all religions were simply codified beliefs reinforced by ritual; he vowed to live life according to his own beliefs, become who he was.

His father hesitated. 'It's just that … just that my savings have finished and we now only have my pension to live on.'

Phillip felt his stomach clench. He was relying on borrowing money from his father to finance his return to Germany to complete his postgraduate degree. But if his father had no money, that was impossible. His temples throbbed.

Phillip jumped up and rushed into his room.

He locked the door and slumped onto his bed. They had no money for him to go to Germany and get his postgraduate degree and become a teacher, and hardly enough to continue the meagre lifestyle they now led. Most of the two pounds ten shillings he earned for the one day a week he spent with the Army Reserves, went towards his share of the rent.

What if he did accept the SIS mission to Germany? He would be given a job in the Civil Service. He wouldn't change his name, but if he kept his head down he could lead a quiet life as a clerk and continue to write poetry. Just as T.S. Eliot worked in a bank and continued to write poetry, even after *The Waste Land* was published to great acclaim. Eliot, like him, totally believed in the British establishment and just wanted to fit in. But the mission was extremely dangerous. Two agents had been killed.

He was trapped.

Either he had to marry Mr Singh's daughter and submit to a lifestyle he rejected or accept the mission to Germany and risk being murdered.

A little after seven o'clock, the morning sun started to seep through the curtains. Phillip had lain awake all night, fully dressed.

He rolled over and stood up. In the gloom, the wardrobe mirror reflected his ghost-like image, and beneath it on the dressing table were two pennies, the last money he had, just enough to make a call to tell Smythe he accepted the mission.

Seven days after his first meeting with Smythe, Phillip strode into The Savoy Hotel, deliberately avoiding the stare of an elegant man in bow tie and tails. Looking straight ahead, Phillip crossed the foyer and pushed through the glass doors to the lift.

He took the stairs beside the lift. The one-week crash course on spy-craft, which he had just completed, said to always use the stairs since it gave you options if you needed to take evasive action. The course had also shown how to follow someone without being seen, and to know when someone was following you and how to evade them. He had also learned the code for communicating with SIS.

Although the course heightened his sense of anxiety, it made him proud to be part of an exclusive group who knew things the public didn't.

The door was opened before Phillip reached it, and Smythe beckoned him inside.

'Sorry, I forgot to order tea,' Smythe said, sitting in a chair by the fire. 'Do you want some?'

Phillip sat opposite Smythe. 'No, I'm fine thank you, sir.'

Smythe gave a half smile. 'Well, Phillip, tomorrow you leave for Germany. I'm sure you'll do very well. Just a few things to go over. We have just learned that Max Schneider, who has the document, sometimes uses the name Antonio Martini.' Smythe snorted. 'It's his stage name. Schneider, it seems, loves acting in musical stage plays. However, they insist you contact the go-between who will introduce you to Max Schneider.' Smythe shook his head. 'Rank amateurs. They think they're protecting themselves with these go-betweens, but it doesn't. It just makes things more difficult.'

Phillip felt a stab of fear. How dangerous was it going to be?

Smythe opened a package and took out a silver cigarette case. 'Not only do we not know who the go-between is, or what he looks like, this is their silly idea of how to make contact.' He flicked the case open and held it in front of him. Phillip saw it was packed with Dunhill cigarettes, their pale tips like hats on a line of soldiers, and on the inside of the lid an inscription, 'Always be true to thyself'.

'Their idea is that when you think you may have made contact with their go-between, you offer them a cigarette from this case. The man will decline and offer you one from his case, which should have the inscription, 'and as sure as night follows day'. You will then know he is their man.'

Smythe leaned back in his chair. 'They've obviously been watching too many spy movies.' He snapped the cigarette case closed. 'Their go-between will be in a nightclub in Bayreuth, very likely one called the Blue Lagoon. That's why we need someone like you Phillip who will pass as a student, and appears to be out in the clubs looking for the louche lifestyle that seems to be taking over Germany.' Smythe shook his head. 'Anyway, when you are at the Blue Lagoon, you ask for a White Lady cocktail. If someone then approaches you, you offer them a cigarette.'

'I don't smoke.'

'Learn. If you don't find him at the Blue Lagoon, visit the other clubs. There's only two or three in Bayreuth and so if you flash the cigarette case you should soon find him. Then, once you've made contact with the go-between, he will arrange for you to meet Max Schneider. When you've learned what Schneider wants for the document, make contact with us.' He got up and crossed to the window and stared out at the Thames.

Smythe sighed deeply. 'You must be careful, Phillip.' He continued to stare out the window. 'Trust no one. Germany is in such turmoil nobody expects their republic to last much longer and if the Communists get the document they could be elected to power and Germany will be lost.' He turned to face Phillip. 'So time is crucial. You understand?'

'Yes, sir.'

Smythe left the window and sat opposite Phillip. 'Now. This is vitally important Phillip. When you get the document it will be sealed, and remember, under no circumstances must you read it. Understood?'

'Yes.'

'Good. We've enrolled you in the Bayreuth Art Faculty as a postgraduate student studying German poetry. We've also found you somewhere to live.' He handed Phillip a package from the table. 'All the information you need is here, along with your train and boat tickets, one hundred US dollars and some Reichsmarks for expenses, and, of course, a passport with your new name on it. When you get to Hamburg you will need to buy train tickets to Bayreuth.' He leaned forward and touched Phillip's arm. 'There is no need for you to be in danger, Phillip, if you remember to act like a student at all times. Mix with the students and the local arty types and then when you go to the Blue Lagoon, or other clubs, you're just another student looking for the bohemian lifestyle.'

Phillip nodded.

Smythe handed Phillip a leather-bound book of Shakespeare's Sonnets along with a small codebook. 'You have been shown our variation of the Caesar Shift Cipher, so just give the sonnet number and the code.'

'Yes, sir.'

'Once you've made contact with Schneider, post an advert in the local newspaper, the *Volkischer Beobachter*, using the code. The ads are free, which means you can put the ad in the paper's letterbox at night. That way, nobody will know who placed it. Keep the codebook hidden at all times.'

Smythe looked into the fire and then stabbed the coals with the poker, creating a carpet of flames. He gave Phillip a quick look and then gazed back at the fire as the coals settled into tiers of white ash and red cinders. 'You must be very careful, Phillip, and, remember, trust no one.'

'Yes, sir.' Smythe was different from their first encounter. Had something bad happened in Germany and Smythe wasn't telling him? Should he say no, say he had changed his mind, the mission was too dangerous? But then he would have to live with his father and marry Mr Singh's daughter.

No, he would leave for Germany the next day.

Chapter 3

Bayreuth was as Phillip imagined – a small German town, with medieval houses and cobbled streets, just like Tübingen where he had studied five years earlier.

But Germany had changed.

As soon as he left the boat in Hamburg, he was struck by the multitude of flags portraying party loyalty, the number of posters demanding political revolution and the febrile atmosphere clamouring for change and an end to the status quo. His sense of unease was heightened when he saw a group of men wearing brown shirts with swastika armbands loitering on the opposite side of the road, staring at passengers as they filed out of the station. Were they looking for people who didn't belong in the town?

'Taxi?' said a voice.

Phillip spun round and faced a man in his early forties, overweight and wearing a peaked cap. 'Yes. Yes, please,' Phillip said.

They left the station and drove the short distance to the centre of Bayreuth, Prince William Square, which was bounded by medieval dwellings squeezed between tall neoclassical houses. They turned off the square, bumped down to the end of a cobbled lane and stopped in front of a house that faced up the alley, blocking it off. The dwelling looked medieval and had a slanting roof, tilting windows and inward-leaning walls, all offering mutual support. The driver hauled Phillip's case from the boot and dropped it onto the cobbles.

'How much?' Phillip said, clambering out.

The man saw Reichsmarks and American dollars in Phillip's wallet. 'Five dollars.'

Phillip gave him five dollars.

The man jumped into his car, turned it round and sped off up the alley.

The address Phillip had asked the taxi driver to take him to was number twenty-seven Rubenplatz, but there were no numbers on the door. He assumed the house in front of him was his lodgings. He tugged the chain that ran down the side of the front door and heard a bell chime inside the house.

The door was unlocked. A woman in her fifties with a broad face and blond hair tied back with a ring, gripped on each side by tortoiseshell slides that matched her blue-green eyes, stood in the doorway examining him. She continued to stare at Phillip without speaking.

'Excuse me, but is this twenty-seven Rubenplatz?' Phillip said.

The woman nodded.

'Erm. I'm Phillip K … Fitzwilliam. I'm looking for Frau Weiser. I believe she's expecting me.'

The woman pulled the door wide, and Phillip stepped into a dark hallway, with wood-panelled walls on which hung black and white prints of cathedrals and churches. A slanted staircase ran up one side. He rested his suitcase on the floor.

The woman banged the door shut which made Phillip jump, and then pushed past him and went up the stairs. Phillip grabbed his case and followed her, the stairs squeaking as he ascended. They reached a landing that ran from one end of the house to the other, with doors on both sides and large windows at each end. The woman unlocked a door and Phillip followed her inside.

The woman stood motionless in the middle of the room, her arms folded in front of her. Phillip wasn't sure what to do. Should he tip her? The room was small and neat, with a single bed pushed against one wall, beside which was a thin chest of drawers. Above the bed was an embroidered verse from the Bible in a glass frame, 'Seek and you shall find'. Next to the window was a washstand with a bowl and an enamel pitcher. A wooden wardrobe made up the rest of the furniture.

The woman frowned at Phillip.

'It's very nice,' Phillip said.

The woman shuffled her arms. 'The bathroom is at the end of the landing. If you want a hot bath you must let me know. You must book in advance.'

'Yes, of course.'

Frau Weiser handed him a key and left.

Phillip plonked his case on the bed and wondered if he had somehow upset the woman. Having noticed the rings on her fingers, he used the polite German term and called her Frau Weiser, but perhaps she was a widow and so he should have used another term. He would ask someone how to address her – he knew that in Germany it was important to use the correct form, depending on the person's status or profession.

He filled the wardrobe and chest of drawers with his clothes and then wrapped his codebook in a hanky and hid it under the washstand cabinet. The related part of the cipher, Shakespeare's Sonnets, he would carry with him since it fitted his cover of being a student. As instructed, he crossed to the window and surveyed the back of the house to see if he would be able to escape if the door was blocked. Smythe's room in The Savoy Hotel had French windows that led directly to a fire escape.

The drop to the gravel path below his window was about ten feet, which he thought he could manage. The rest of the garden was laid out with flowerbeds divided by mosaic paths, and at the far end stood a large willow, its drooping branches dappled with wizened leaves as it swayed in the wind like an oversized dress. The backs of the houses were intersected with alleyways, one of which ran alongside his garden. He would need to see where it led, but first he must locate the offices of the *Volkischer Beobachter* newspaper and register with the university. And before that, he needed a pee.

On the way back to his room, he saw a young girl struggling up the stairs with a large canvas. 'May I help?' Phillip said.

'Oh. Thanks,' the girl said, and rested the canvas on a step. She looked up, her smile lighting up her whole face, her liquid ebony eyes shining, her blue-black hair cut short so it framed her delicate features and pale skin. 'If you could get the other end, that would be great. It's not heavy, just awkward.'

A thrill of desire went through Phillip as he slid past her. He lifted one end of the canvas and the girl guided them to the door next to his.

Her room was larger but furnished the same. On the floor were cardboard boxes filled with leaflets and rolled posters, on the walls, placards and paintings without frames, and on the bed and wicker chair flyers for various shows. The girl stood the canvas against the wall and Phillip saw it was a painting of trees – defaced with a bright red swastika.

'Thanks,' the girl said. 'My name's Ruth. Are you staying here?'

'Next door. I've just arrived.' Phillip stared at the vandalised painting.

Ruth tilted her head sideways and smiled.

'Oh,' Phillip said. 'My name's Phillip. Phillip Fitzwilliam.'

'English?'

'Yes.'

'Well, you speak German very well for an Englishman. I thought you were Austrian.'

'My teacher was Austrian.'

'In England?'

'No, actually, in Tübingen. I was here five years ago studying, and now I've returned to complete my masters.'

'What are you studying?'

'Poetry.'

'You write poetry?'

'Well … not really.'

'Yes you do. You must let me read them.'

'Oh, I only had one or two published.'

'What, here in Germany?'

'Well, yes. But they're not very good.'

'I'm sure they are. You're just being modest.' She touched his arm. 'Well, you must come to a party, the day after tomorrow. I will introduce you to our leading poet, Stefan George.'

'Wow, *the* Stefan George?'

'The same.'

Although Phillip didn't really like or fully understand George's poems, since he used archaic words to express nebulous ideas, he was aware that Stefan George was one of Europe's most revered and influential poets and had a cult following.

'Would you like some coffee?' Ruth said.

'Er. OK. Thank you.'

'Don't worry, it's good coffee. My mother sent it to me from Berlin.' Ruth cleared a pile of flyers from the wicker chair and threw them on the bed. 'Take a seat. I'll just get some water.'

Ruth let her coat slip to the floor, and then lifted the kettle and turned, her dress moving in concert with her body. She stopped in front of him and Phillip looked up at her smiling eyes, her parted lips. He blushed as he turned his legs so she could pass. Ruth smiled and glided past him.

Her footsteps echoed along the passageway, and then a door slammed. Phillip felt embarrassed that she had caught him ogling her. What must she think of him; she, an artist who mixed with famous poets? But she did seem to be flirting with him, and she had invited him to a party. Perhaps she really did like him? He certainly found her attractive, especially the way she smiled; it reminded him of his mother. He wondered if she had a boyfriend.

He stood up and inspected the paintings on the walls. Each depicted a rural scene but the colours were mismatched with green skies and blue grass and orange-trunked trees with purple leaves. The style reminded him of a famous painter but he couldn't remember the name. They were signed R K. R was Ruth and he wondered what the K was for.

The posters were simple but effective, using block letters, a style he hadn't seen before, and advocated socialist programmes to be enacted by the SDP Government. From what he could gather, the SDP was like the British Labour Party, who, according to Captain Blakeney, had a lot of Neo-Communists in their ranks. Perhaps he should be careful what he said to her.

He glanced at the flyers that lay on the bed, most of which advertised concerts and shows. His heart jumped. One had the name Antonio Martini, the stage-name for Max Schneider. He grabbed the flyer and read that Antonio Martini was performing in a musical show called *Evil Flowers* – but there was no date or place.

Ruth came back into the room carrying the kettle. Phillip felt he'd been caught snooping. 'Just looking at all the … posters and things. Did you do all these?'

'Yes. They're not very good,' Ruth said, opening the door of a cupboard set into the wall, inside of which was a small gas ring. She lit the gas and plonked the kettle on the jets. Phillip wondered if he had a gas ring in his room, but didn't remember seeing a wall cupboard. Ruth stood waiting for the kettle to boil. Phillip jumped up. 'Please, you sit down. I can stand.'

'No. Sit, sit. I need to make the coffee. I can then sit on the bed. How long are you here for?'

'One year.'

'Oh, good. You'll be able to see our production of *Parsifal*.' She nodded to the canvas defaced with a swastika. 'Not as grand as Wagner performed in the Bayreuth Festival Hall, but ours is unique, which is why the Nazis want to stop it. They don't like the way the conductor is staging the opera, and so they tried to destroy the set.'

Phillip glanced at the vandalised image. How could someone act so violently towards a painted canvas? 'But it's just a set for an opera?'

Ruth laughed. 'Well, Mister Englishman, we Germans take our opera very seriously, and this production of Wagner's *Parsifal* has become political. The Nazis, National Socialists, want *Parsifal* to be a metaphor for Germany's need for a strong leader who will help us rise again and fulfil our true destiny.' She rolled her eyes. 'However, our production is the opposite. The conductor, Luigi

Conti, is staging *Parsifal* as a knight who learns that compassion is the true, guiding light for the world. Which is what I think Wagner was saying. It's his last opera, just before he died and when he was very interested in the Upanishads.'

Phillip had listened to his father talk about the Upanishads, the ancient philosophical texts that were the foundation for most Indian religions, and influenced Buddhism, and how important they were for leading a good life. It surprised him that Wagner, someone so German in outlook, could be inspired by them. Perhaps the Nazis had a point. But he stayed silent, not knowing very much about Wagner's operas, especially *Parsifal*.

'The conductor is thinking of having the actors in Indian turbans and flowing robes,' Ruth said, as she made the coffee. 'And that really upset the Nazis. We've all received death threats.'

'You're joking.'

'No. You are in Germany now. Every day people are being killed for what they believe in.'

Phillip thought of the two dead agents.

'You should go,' Ruth said, nodding at the flyer Phillip was holding with Antonio Martini's name on it. 'It's based on *Les Fleurs du Mal* by the French symbolist poet, Charles Baudelaire. Have you read him?'

'Yes. Some.' He hadn't read all of *Les Fleurs du Mal*, since the themes Baudelaire used were too pessimistic, and relied on finding beauty in the malignant and the obscene which he couldn't relate to since his favourite poet, Keats, used symbolism to show the unity between natural beauty and the unseen world. 'I would like to see it, but it doesn't have a date or place.'

'That's because it's a show put on by homosexuals and transvestites, which is against the law, so the date and place, usually a variety club, are filled in at the last moment to stop the police finding out where it's being performed. But I understand it's due on soon.'

'May I keep it?'

'Of course.'

Phillip tried to sound natural. 'Are there many variety clubs in Bayreuth?'

'No. Just two or three. The Cockatoo is the usual place. We're a small town and everybody knows everybody else, so it's often word of mouth. If the police find out where the show is they raid the club and arrest everybody. The police hate the shows because they mock politicians, especially the Nazis, and the police are all Nazis.'

There was a knock on the door.

'Yes?' Ruth said.

Frau Weiser entered. 'You know the rules about men in rooms.'

'Yes, but he lives here.'

'That makes no difference. Remember, I took you in when others wouldn't.'

'Yes. I'm sorry.'

Frau Weiser swept out of the room, banging the door behind her. Phillip jumped up. 'Sorry. I didn't mean to get you into trouble.'

'Don't worry. See you for the party, if not before.' She leaned forwards and kissed him on the cheek.

He was taken aback by her show of affection and blushed at the touch of her soft lips. Maybe young Germans were becoming more like the French.

Ruth smiled and Phillip quickly left the room.

Phillip put the flyer on the chest of drawers. Ruth said the show was soon to be performed in a Bayreuth club. If so, making contact with Max Schneider would be easy, and he could soon be back in England.

He lay on the bed, still tingling from Ruth's kiss. She was so attractive, and she had invited him to a party. She must like him. She was certainly left wing, but there was something wholesome and decent about her, her warm smile suggesting she wouldn't reject anyone because of their race or religion.

He gazed at the flyer for *Evil Flowers* and thought about the police raiding clubs. What if he was there when the police charged in? What if he was arrested and interrogated? They would find out he was an Englishman. What if they found out he was an SIS agent, a spy? What would they do to him?

He thought of the two agents who had been killed. Had they been shot for being spies, as happened during the Great War?

He had to urinate again.

Chapter 4

The printer of the *Volkischer Beobachter* newspaper was on Albert Street, a small cobbled lane tucked away from the main roads.

The building, an old coach house, still had the wide double doors, painted olive green. On one door, above the large letterbox, was written in gothic script 'Post for *Volkischer Beobachter*'. The building's discreet location meant he could post ads at night without being seen.

Phillip sauntered back to the main square.

The day was bright and still, with only a handful of people out beneath a pure blue sky and a cold sun that sparkled on the overnight snow. He then realised what was missing – posters and flags. Perhaps the town burghers banned them. Or maybe Bayreuth wasn't politically important and so was ignored by the major parties; it was little more than a large village built around Prince William Square, with low hills to the north and open fields to the south,

In the square next to the fountain, a man with one hand and no socks was sitting on a piece of wood, begging. A row of military medals shimmered on his tattered army coat and a soldier's cap lay open on the ground in front of him. Phillip's father had taught him to give to deserving beggars, and this man had clearly been brave and earned medals but couldn't work with only one hand. Phillip strolled up to the man and dropped an American dollar in his cap. The man jolted foreword and grabbed the note. He stuffed it in his pocked, and then, looking up at Phillip, nodded his head and saluted. Phillip wondered what the beggar would think if he knew he was an Englishman, someone whose compatriots had possibly caused his injuries.

Phillip crossed the square, heading for a small café he had seen in one of the side streets. Ruth, and the kiss she had given him, had never been far from his mind. What if they became close and then he was sent back to England? As he turned into the side street, a troop of Brownshirts came marching up the road towards him, their swastika flags held high as young voices in unison chorused the Horst Wessel song.

A man stepped out onto the street in front of the Brownshirts, holding up his hands and barring their way. 'Stop, stop,' shouted the man. 'The law forbids you to sing that song.'

The Brownshirts swarmed over the man like a pack of dogs that had caught its prey, punching and kicking him in a wild frenzy of fevered rage spurred on by a blood lust. The man burst from the melee and ran down the street without his trousers or shirt, blood streaming from his head.

The Brownshirts laughed.

A policeman on a bike appeared at the top of the street, stopped and rested one foot on the ground. The man with blood over him stared at the policeman. The policeman turned and rode away. The bloodied man hurried away down the street.

The Brownshirts reassembled into formation.

'Raise the flag. The ranks are tightly closed,' sang a voice. The rest of the troop joined in as they resumed their march.

'The SA marches with calm, steady step.

Comrades shot by the Red Front and reactionaries.

March in spirit within our ranks.'

Phillip watched as they marched past him to the top of the street, and then disappeared round the corner, their words becoming fainter.

'Clear the streets for the brown battalions,

Clear the streets for the storm division.'

Phillip hurried towards the café.

Inside he sat at a table and ordered Weisswurst, pretzels and a mug of tea. Nerves quivered through him as if some catastrophe was about to overtake him. He had seen fights in London, especially in his area of the East End, but nothing as savage as this. And the policeman had looked away. Smythe had said there had been over four hundred killings so far this year by paramilitary gangs. What if he were attacked?

His breakfast arrived. When he had been in Germany before, he had really liked Weisswurst, but now when he looked at the white sausages bobbing in the greasy water like naked corpses, his stomach churned and he felt nauseous. He waited till the waitress went out to the kitchen and then quickly wrapped the sausages in a napkin and stuffed them into his pocket.

Outside, he strode back to the town square. The beggar was still there and he handed him the sausages.

The beggar smiled up at him. He nodded to the side street where the Nazis had assaulted the man. 'Yeah, it does make you lose your appetite.'

Phillip smiled and nodded back, then turned and headed for the university, which was to the south of Prince William Square, adjacent to the Red River, so called because of the red mud that bled into it from merging streams. The Red River ran through the middle of Bayreuth, dissecting the town into north and south.

The area around the university, the cobbled alleyways, narrow streets and bookshops with clusters of young people talking and laughing, made him feel like a student again.

Stepping out from an alleyway, he was presented with a grand edifice with towers like witches' hats and stonewalls like a medieval castle – it was the university's Faculty of Arts and Science.

The school-keeper directed him to the third floor where Professor Muller had his office. As he made his way up the stairs, he saw that most students wore peaked caps of different colours with badges pinned to the side.

'Come,' said a high-pitched voice. Phillip took a deep breath and pushed open the door. Muller's office was sparse with big windows that looked out onto the park and the Red River. It had a large desk but no bookshelves. A man, in his late thirties with short black hair, large horn-rimmed glasses and wearing a jacket, shirt and tie, sat behind the desk. The man peered at Phillip over his glasses.

'I'm Phillip Fitzwilliam. I've been told to report to you, sir.'

'Ah,' Muller said, rising from his seat and extending his hand, 'our English student. Welcome to the faculty. I hope you enjoy your time with us.'

Phillip shook the professor's outstretched hand, which felt limp. 'Thank you, sir.'

Muller waved Phillip to a seat in front of his desk which was cluttered with books and papers and a half-written script on lined paper. 'So, you're Phillip Fitzwilliam from England,' he said, reading from a note on his desk. 'And you're here to write a dissertation on Poets in Our Time.'

'Sorry, sir. Could you repeat that, please?'

Muller peered over his glasses. 'Your dissertation will be a comparative study of modern German and British poets, and how they reflect the times we live in.' He took off his glasses and laid them on the table. 'One would assume you were aware of this.'

Phillip's hands were moist. 'Well, sir … it was somebody else who … who enrolled me.'

Muller leaned forward and picked up his glasses and put them back on. 'Mmm. Well, it's the only postgraduate qualification we offer in this university that's to do with European poetry. It focuses primarily on our Stefan George's *The Poet in Troubled Times*, and your T.S. Eliot's *The Wasteland*.'

Muller picked a sheet of paper. 'It says on your application form that you have joint degrees in languages, philosophy and poetry, and that you are fluent in German and French. Also, you have studied poetry in Germany before, at Tübingen University.'

'Yes, yes, that's true, sir.'

Muller took off his glasses and leaned back in his chair. 'Then you'll have no problem.'

Phillip felt annoyed with himself for feeling intimidated by Muller.

'You're right, sir,' he said, 'I'll have no problem.'

'Good.'

Phillip had read some of George's poems, but not studied them in depth. Holderlin had been the focus of his studies in Tübingen. Still, hopefully, he would have traced Max Schneider before he had to hand in the dissertation. He would have no trouble with T. S. Eliot's *The Waste Land*, even though he found it too Christian and defeatist. But that was his interpretation and was aware others thought *The Waste Land* was the old story of the Fisher King. He would have find out what Muller thought the poem was about. But Stefan George was a pain; he used unusual inflections at the ends of archaic words and was, overall, obtuse and deliberately vague.

'I also understand you were an active member of the Holderlin Association while you were at Tübingen.' He looked at Phillip and smiled. 'That being so, a colleague of my mine, Doctor Schmelter, would like to talk to you. She wondered if you could meet her on Friday morning. Her office is on the top floor, opposite the library.'

'Yes, sir.' Phillip thought it strange that Muller knew about the Holderlin Association since it was a drinking club that met to see who could drink the most and still recite Holderlin's poems without any mistakes.

'Have you registered with the university?' Muller said.

'Not yet, sorry.'

'Do you have your passport on you?'

'Er, no.'

Muller shook his head. 'I will need to see your passport before I can sign the form saying you are one of my students. You will then need to take the form to the registry to get your student card. I can see you in two days' time, on Friday. Bring your passport with you then. In the meantime you need to start work. I require an outline proposal for your dissertation by next Wednesday; one week's time.'

Phillip inspected himself in the mirror. What did people wear at nightclubs? During his previous time in Germany, he had only frequented inns and beer halls and so wore casual clothes. Now he was dressed in a single-breasted grey suit, white shirt and a blue-striped tie. He tugged the shirt cuffs to show the gold cufflinks his father had given him for his twenty-first birthday.

Hopefully, the patrons of the Blue Lagoon were not upper class, like in London nightclubs, where, from the pictures in the papers, the men all wore bow ties and dinner jackets. It was past nine o'clock; he needed to get going.

As he went out the front door, he noticed a wooden gate at the side of the house. It must lead into the alleyway he'd seen from his room. He pushed open the gate, and as he slipped into the alley, he banged into a dustbin. No lights came on and he carried on down the alley, and gradually his eyes adapted to the dark. The alleyway went past the back of houses to a main road called Hofer Strasse. He noted the name of the street and turned back.

A single lamp lit the lane from his lodgings up to the main road. Unseen patches of frozen snow made walking treacherous and he slipped twice on the cobbles. He had brought with him only a pair of town shoes. Perhaps he should buy some boots. In Prince William Square, the streetlamps spilled pools of mellow light onto the gleaming cobbles. It seemed enchanted, as if nothing had changed in hundreds of years and the past was ever present.

Some of the town houses had their ground floors converted to shops or offices while the upper storeys remained residential, their windows glowing with warm light that fell on the fountain that splashed in the centre of the square and the statue of a burgher from olden times that graced one corner. This feeling of gemutlich was what he loved about Germany.

Phillip began walking around the square, looking for the Blue Lagoon. If the go-between was at the club, he might be able to get the terms for the document back to SIS within the next few days, which meant he wouldn't have to write the dissertation. However, if he had trouble finding Max Schneider, the cover of being a student would be essential.

He arrived back where he started but there was no sign of the Blue Lagoon. The club's address said it was in the square. Phillip approached a man locking up a shop. A wry smile came onto the man's lips as he heard Phillip's request. He pointed to a narrow street on the other side of the square. 'Just as you enter, on the right.'

As Phillip strode into the street, he saw a blue, neon sign spelling out the Blue Lagoon. Underneath the caption was a glass arrow, flashing on and off, that pointed down the steps to a mysterious world.

Two women, one in high heels and the other in long, black boots, pushed past him and clomped down the steps. They waited at the club door. The woman in boots turned and stared up at Phillip, her heavy makeup transforming her into a painted doll that appeared and then faded in the pulsing neon light. The door unlocked and the woman in boots winked at Phillip and gave a loud, masculine laugh as she swept into the club. The door banged shut.

Phillip hesitated and then told himself he was being stupid and could always just walk out the club. He trod down the steps and tried the door handle which turned noisily, but the door was locked. The hatch at eye level squeaked open and then banged shut. Crimson light bloomed before him as the door opened and a man in an evening suit waved him inside.

Phillip stepped into a vestibule lit with a red glow that made things look disembodied, almost surreal. A woman, with permed hair that rose in coils above her head like blond sea serpents, lounged inside a kiosk. In front of padded double doors, a tall woman posed in a top hat, tails, black swimsuit, fishnet stockings and red high heels. She smiled and slunk towards Phillip.

'Welcome to the Blue Lagoon, my young friend. We have not seen you before.'

She spoke in a deep voice – Phillip saw she had an Adam's apple. 'Er, no. No. I've just arrived in Germany.'

'You are English. Yes?'

'Yes. I'm an exchange student.'

'How nice,' she said, as she took Phillip's coat from him, 'and so good-looking.' She stroked his red duffle coat. 'You must be our guest tonight.' She twirled round and gestured to the kiosk and then turned to the man in evening dress. 'Find a nice table for our new patron.' She patted Phillip's hand. 'You must enjoy your first night with us. And, it must not be the last.' She squeezed his hand.

Phillip nodded and blushed.

'So sweet,' the woman said.

'This way,' said the man in evening dress, opening one of the padded doors and sweeping his hand in front of him. 'Let me show you to your table.'

The club was larger than he expected. A quartet played American swing on a raised stage, in front of which was a dance floor filled with couples rotating their arms and legs to the beat of the Charleston.

Lamps on tables that circled the dance floor, lit the faces of the seated couples in half-light, like characters on a movie set. A blue smoke haze, enriched with the smell of perfume, wafted through the low-lit room. There was a slight buzz of conversation and several people turned their heads and smiled as Phillip was shown to an unoccupied table with a reserved sign on it. A waiter came up to Phillip's table. 'Drink, sir?'

Phillip was stumped. What was the cocktail he was supposed to order? He was about to say Pink Girl when he remembered. 'White Lady cocktail, please.'

The waiter bowed, turned and glided between the dancers, holding his tray flat on his hand at shoulder height. The music stopped and everyone clapped as the dancers made their way back to their tables. The waiter had accepted his order of a White Lady cocktail. Phillip's heart beat fast as he waited for someone to come up to him.

The waiter returned and as he placed the cocktail in front of Phillip, he said, 'It's on the house.'

'Oh. Thank you.'

The band burst into a high-tempo number and couples ran onto the dance floor. Some men were boogying with other men, while some couples looked as if they were man and woman. Phillip couldn't make out who were women and who men. A slim man with dark eyes, slicked hair and a thin line of lipstick for a mouth, came up to the table. 'Can I buy you a drink? Or would you like to dance?'

'Er, no thank you.'

'Waiting for someone?'

'Er. Yes.'

'What a shame. So young, so good looking.'

Phillip took out his cigarette case and laid it on the table. Smythe had said to make it obvious he had one. Sweat marks from his fingers glistened on the silver case. The sound of the loud, syncopated music unsettled him and he felt hot and sweaty. The cocktail tasted sweet with a bitter aftertaste. Dancers peered over their partner's shoulder and smiled at Phillip. He waited but no one came to his table. He needed to pee. He picked up his cigarette case and headed for the toilets.

Not seeing the step down, he tumbled into the toilets. A man in nylon stockings, high heels and a skirt hitched up to his waist was leaning forward with one hand on the wall and peeing into the trough. 'Yeah, you have to watch that step,' the man said, without turning round. 'Especially after a few drinks.'

Phillip went to the end of the trough and undid his flys. The man's eyes slid sideways and looked at Phillip's penis. Phillip couldn't pee. To avoid the man's eyes, Phillip read the poster above the trough. It was for a show called *Evil Flowers*, featuring Antonio Martini, Max Schneider's stage name. The same poster that was in Ruth's room, only this one had the place filled in, but no date. It said *Evil Flowers* was coming soon to the Cockatoo Cabaret Club.

The man next to Phillip went to the sink, washed his hands and left the toilet. Phillip still couldn't pee. He buttoned up his flys and went to the washstand, and as he rinsed his hands he peered at himself in the mirror – he would have to go to the Cockatoo Club if he didn't make contact with the go-between tonight.

A man with his back turned, watching the singer on stage, was sitting in the vacant chair at Phillip's table. Phillip's heart pounded. The man must be there because Phillip had ordered the cocktail. The go-between. Phillip sat down, took out his cigarette case, opened it and placed it on the table so the man, when he turned round, would see the inscription inside.

The singing stopped and the man swung round.

Phillip jumped.

The man wore a tin mask, and from the eyeholes, two mangled orbs like bloodshot marbles glared at him. The lower half of the face, not covered by the mask, was mutilated with scar tissue. 'The best they could do after the British shell exploded in my face,' the man said, his maimed lips lisping the words. The man looked at Phillip's cigarette case. 'English cigarettes.'

Phillip fumbled as he offered it up to the man, so the inscription, 'Always be true to thyself', could be clearly seen. The man took a cigarette, lit it and inhaled deeply, then blew smoke through the mask's nasal holes, like a horse snorting in winter. Phillip waited for him to offer his cigarette case with the related inscription, but the man just kept on smoking. He finished the cigarette, stubbed it in the ashtray and then put his hand on Phillip's. 'Like to dance?'

'Sorry. I have to go. I promised to meet someone.'

Phillip bounded up the steps. He then hurried across the main square, checking he was not followed. On the way back to his lodgings, he opened the top of his coat and let the cold air wrap around his neck. He had not found the go-between but he knew where Max Schneider was performing. If the police raided the Cockatoo Club while he was there he would be arrested, but the longer he stayed in Bayreuth the more chance there was of something happening that would expose him, as when the Brownshirts attacked the man and beat him because he wanted them to stop singing a song that was outlawed.

Bayreuth, no doubt like the rest of Germany, was in a state of lawless flux and anything could happen.

Chapter 5

The morning light from the window was in the wrong place.

Then it all flooded back. Germany, Bayreuth, the man being beaten by the Brownshirts, the Blue Lagoon. Phillip rolled out of bed and crossed to the window. The late autumn sky was silver bright, backlighting the black branches of the willow. There was a soft tap on the door.

'You look worried,' Ruth said, as she slipped past him into the room. 'What's wrong?'

'Nothing, nothing. I ... have to write this dissertation.'

'I know someone who can help you. She used to teach poetry and now lives in the artists' colony at Blue Ridge Farm. Come and see the sets we are building for *Parsifal*.' She stepped in close to him, her eyes smiling. 'You shouldn't be spending all your time in your room, alone.'

Did it look suspicious that he was staying in his room? 'Where is it?'

'Close to the university, in what used to be a church. We're building the set in the crypt.'

Near the university, and he would be inside, off the streets, doing something arty, just what Smythe had told him to do. Also, it was clear Ruth wanted him there. 'OK.'

Ruth steered Phillip down a wide street, at the end of which he could see the pointed towers of the university. They stopped outside an oblong building, which looked like a cross between a library and a museum. The entrance had big double doors and a portico with pillars and a flat roof, and Phillip could just make out the faint impression of a cross above the doorway.

Ruth unlocked the door and Phillip followed her inside.

'Used to be a church,' Ruth said, carefully locking the door behind them. 'An American heiress built it in 1901 to spread the Episcopalian faith to Catholic Bavaria. Needless to say it didn't take off, and when America joined the war against Germany, it was attacked by locals and closed down. After the war it was taken over by Bayreuth City Council and turned into a community centre.'

The building's stark interior, bare rafters, clear windows and plain walls were the opposite of the churches and temples Phillip had been in. The Catholic churches had stained glass-windows and walls and ceilings covered in murals, and the Sikh temples were decorated with rich carpets and ornate altars.

Rows of pews stretched to the chancel, a wooden platform on which stood a man with a baton. In front of him, musicians were sprawled along the benches. The man with the baton was tall, slim, with dark wavy hair, and though his tie was undone and his shirtsleeves rolled back, he looked elegant. He nodded and smiled at Ruth.

'That is our conductor, Luigi Conti,' Ruth said, quietly. 'We're really privileged to have him. He's an Italian Maestro and only agreed to do our production because of the way we are staging it. Also, because of this building. The Americans love singing hymns and so the acoustics here are superb. This way.'

Ruth led Phillip to a corner door at the back of the church. She pulled it open and then disappeared down steps. Phillip followed and found himself in a space as wide and long as the building above. It was the crypt. A row of naked bulbs ran down the middle of the ceiling, and two white canvases stood upright in the centre of the room, like starched shrouds. Propped along one wall, were thin canvases with swirling abstract forms in rich colours. 'Wow,' Phillip said. 'They're beautiful. They look like Indian Art.'

'You're familiar with it?'

Phillip felt flustered. He wanted to tell Ruth he was half Indian. 'There's a lot of it in British Art Galleries.'

'Because of the British Empire, no doubt. All the best stuff from the colonies was looted and taken to Britain.'

Phillip was stung and wanted to defend his country but stayed quiet.

Ruth touched his arm. 'Don't look so upset. All empires do it. The Louvre in Paris has the best Italian art, all stolen by Napoleon.'

Ruth pulled off her coat and wrapped herself in a smock, spattered with splodges of paint. The strains of rising violins drifted into the crypt.

Ruth gazed up at the ceiling. 'Ah, the overture. Perfect timing.' She picked up tins of paint and flipped the lids off with a screwdriver. '*Parsifal* is not much of a story. It's about knights who protect the cup that Christ drunk from at the last supper, and the spear that pierced him when he was on the cross. For Christians, the two top holy relics.' She arranged the paint tins from dark colours to light. 'In the opening scene, the leader of the knights, Amfortas, is being carried into a clearing in the woods to have his daily bath, which helps the incurable wound he got when an enemy of the knights stole the sacred spear and stabbed him with it. Only if the knights can get the spear back can the King's wound be healed. But the only one who can retrieve the spear is a "pure fool, enlightened by compassion". OK. It's the woods. What colour for the background?'

'You said it's in the forest?'

'Yes.'

'Then it will need to be green.'

She handed Phillip a paintbrush. 'Not necessarily. A king has yielded to temptation and lost one of the relics and as a consequence is tormented by an eternal wound. What colour do you feel that invokes?'

Phillip looked perplexed.

Ruth handed him an empty pot. 'Mix whatever colours you want. Just express yourself. There is no right or wrong. With Expressionism, everything is allowed as long as it reflects a genuine feeling.'

It then clicked that Expressionism was the style used in the painting he had helped Ruth take to her room, the one defaced with a swastika. He stared at the bare canvas.

Ruth laughed. 'Come on. Let yourself go. You can always paint over it.' She picked up a smock. 'Come on, take your coat and jacket off.' She held the smock open and then helped Phillip into it. As Ruth tied the strings round his waist, a sensual thrill ran through him. She smiled at him. 'Just listen to the music.'

The overture finished and then notes from the first act filled the crypt.

Phillip mixed pigments into his pot until he had a muddy red, which he applied to the whole of the canvas. Next, he made a vibrant green and slashed it across the canvas in irregular strokes. He stepped back, gazing at his work. Ruth inspected the canvas. 'Wow. You're a natural Expressionist. You ...'

The music stopped and there were shouts and banging from upstairs.

Ruth threw off her smock. 'Quick.' She grabbed her coat. 'Come on.' She ran to the back of the crypt where steps lead up to a trapdoor.

Phillip tore off his smock, snatched up his coat and rushed to the steps. Ruth wrenched back the bolt on the trapdoor and heaved it open. Daylight flooded in. They clambered out and Phillip found himself in the small cemetery at the back of the church. There was only one gravestone. Shouts and banging resonated from the front of the church.

Ruth slammed the trapdoor shut.

They trod through the overgrown grass and crept cautiously down the side of the church to the main road.

Brownshirts with swastika armbands milled on the road in front of the building, while two of their comrades banged iron bars on the wooden doors of the church. A plump man with half a nose, in a brown shirt and swastika armband, stood in the middle of the Brownshirts.

'Wow,' Ruth said. 'They must really think we're a threat. It's Rohm and his Brownshirts from Munich.'

Phillip assumed Rohm was the man with no nose. Beside Rohm were two young men Phillip had seen the previous evening, dancing together at the Blue Lagoon. So the Nazis tolerated homosexuals.

A small crowd on the pavement opposite the church were egging on the Nazis. Another group, some holding red flags, had assembled further along the street, and were booing and shouting slogans. A squad of policemen, with raised batons, charge up the street and attacked the crowd with the red flags.

Ruth grabbed Phillip's arm 'Quick. It's the Munich police. Run.'

Phillip and Ruth raced back down the side of the church, through the graveyard and into a narrow street as shouts and screams rent the air.

Phillip's heart was pounding as they hurried across the main square. What if the police arrested him? 'Why don't the police arrest the Nazis?'

Ruth laughed. 'Because the police from Munich are Nazis.'

'They got here quickly.'

'They were tipped off by Rohm.'

'But what about the local police?'

Ruth laughed. 'We only have three policemen in Bayreuth, and they are as bad as the Nazis.'

They reached the lane leading down to their lodgings.

'The church is not safe,' Ruth said, as they headed to the house. 'I'll move the set to the farm. It'll be safe there. Could you help?'

'Farm?'

'Well, the artists' colony. It's on land belonging to Blue Ridge Farm, a few kilometres outside Bayreuth, very peaceful and safe. Remember, I said someone lives there who could help you with your poetry. She's called Lena. She'd be happy to help you with your dissertation.'

They entered the house and stopped outside Phillip's door. He didn't care about the dissertation and wasn't sure Lena knew more than he did, but if the farm was outside Bayreuth in the countryside, and was safe, it would be better to be there till he met up with Max Schneider. 'OK. Sure.'

Ruth put her arms round him. 'Hey, don't look so worried. I'll look after you.'

Phillip circled his arms round Ruth, pulling her close, feeling the warmth of her body. He kissed her on the lips, their mouths opening to find each other's tongue, as if the intimacy and surge of desire had been waiting to happen. A door opened downstairs and

Ruth pulled away. 'Don't forget the Stefan George party tomorrow night.' She kissed him and went into her room.

Phillip lay on the bed and stared at the ceiling. The erection faded as he thought of the Brownshirts attacking the church. Had any of the police taken notice of him? He had planned to go to the Cockatoo Club tonight, to see if he could locate Max Schneider, but given the Nazi attack on the church, would the police be on the lookout for more trouble? He had to take a chance. He would have one drink and verify when Max Schneider, or Antonio Martini, was playing there.

He thought of Ruth. Was she the one? The one he could tell everything to and not be rejected? The one who could help him become who he was? But what if he found Max tonight and was then sent back to England within a few days? He would write to her. But what then? Once he was settled in the Foreign Office, would Ruth be willing to come to England?

The Cockatoo Club had a large facia above the entrance, featuring a strutting cockatoo in flashing blue and white lights. The doorman pulled open the glass door and Phillip stepped into a brightly lit foyer with a red carpet and walls full of photos of entertainers and posters for shows. One poster, with decaying orchids floating in a pool of murky water, stated that *Evil Flowers* was to be performed in four days' time. Perhaps Max Schneider was in the club tonight, rehearsing. Phillip deposited his coat and pushed through red doors into the club.

The room was packed with tables occupied by couples in a variety of attire; some wore full evening dress and had slicked down hair, while others sat in long gowns or sported flapper dresses. Everyone was heavily made up. Phillip was wearing a sports jacket and tie and felt out of place.

As he crossed to the bar, he noticed a curtain hung across a stage. He wondered if a show was to be performed, but no one had asked him to buy a ticket. At the bar he asked for a White Lady cocktail, but the barman had never heard of it. Phillip ordered a beer. Should he ask for Max Schneider or Antonio Martini?

The curtain dragged open and the talking hushed as a man in a top hat came on stage. He made a joke about money and politics that Phillip didn't understand, but at which the audience laughed. A man next to him at the bar asked if he could buy him a drink. Phillip said no thank you. He then offered the man a cigarette, holding the case open so the inscription, 'Always be true to thyself', could be easily seen. The man took a cigarette and held it, waiting for Phillip to light it. Phillip had no lighter or matches. The barman leaned over and lit the cigarette. The man blew smoke into the air and put his hand on Phillip's knee, then slid it up to his crotch. Phillip jumped up and headed for the door.

Phillip half-ran till he reached Prince William Square. The man was following him. Phillip ran across the square and down a side road. He strode past the lane that led down to his lodgings, and continued till he reached Hofer Strasse, which he knew would take him to the alleyways at the back of his house.

As he crept up the stairs to his room, his heart was pounding. Was the man following him a Communist, the German Secret Service, or just a homosexual who fancied him? At least he knew that Max Schneider's show was going to be performed at the club in four days' time. But how could he get to meet him?

Chapter 6

As Phillip strode up the cobbled lane from his lodgings, the morning sunshine made the previous evening seem miles away.

Were homosexuals always so fearless in making their desires known, or was it him? Homosexual men had always been attracted to him but never so up-front. At school and university when male classmates had approached him, it had always been discreet and open to being excused as a misunderstanding. Still, he now knew where Max Schneider would be performing, but would he agree to see him without the go-between? He had to.

Before meeting with Professor Muller's colleague, Doctor Schmelter, he would enhance his student status by getting a cap. All the students at the university wore them, often with ribbons or badges depicting the society or club they belonged to. On his last visit to Germany, few students had sported such caps but now it seemed they all had them.

He was still wondering why Professor Muller had suggest that Doctor Schmelter wanted to see him because he had once belonged to the Holderlin Association when he studied at Tübingen University. Tübingen was where Holderlin had lived in one room in a woodcutter's house, and where he wrote many of his best poems, and the students who studied him revered him as the greatest German poet ever. But what had that to do with the Holderlin Association, a student club that facilitated the consumption of vast quantities of beer.

The hat shop was on Woolfstreet, just past the Cockatoo Club. The shop assistant ran a tape round Phillip's head and then un-boxed a white cap with a black peak. It fitted perfectly. The assistant recommended a scarf in the colours of the Bavarian flag, now in fashion with local students, and so Phillip bought the scarf as well as the cap. On the way to the university, he re-arranged the scarf, letting it hang down his front and back, the way students wore it.

Just past the bus terminus, the beggar with the coat covered in medals was talking to a man. As Phillip searched in his pockets for change, the beggar waved at him. The man standing with the beggar turned and Phillip saw a flash of light. It was the man in the tin mask from the Blue Lagoon. The man in the mask headed towards him. Phillip turned and hurried off.

Phillip sped across the main square, aware the man in the mask was following him. He reached the narrow streets around the university, took a detour and then doubled back on himself. As he approached the entrance to the university, the man in the tin mask was nowhere to be seen. A hand on his shoulder made him jump. He spun round and was faced with two students smiling at him.

Both students looked to be in their final year and both had identical coloured ribbons around their caps, pinned with a woven badge. The one who had touched his shoulder was slim with a small moustache. 'Congratulations,' he said, lifting Phillip's scarf and pointing to his cap. 'You are now one of us. I'm Alex and this is Michael.'

'Oh, I'm Phillip. I'm …'

'From England and here to study poetry. Welcome.'

'Thank you.'

'Mmm, shame,' Michael said. He was tall, well built and had a serious air about him, but his eyes smiled.

Phillip stared at him.

'By shame, I mean I'm sorry to hear you speak German so well.'

'We were hoping,' Alex said, 'that we could help you with your German in exchange for you helping us with our English. We are studying English and have an essay to hand in by the end of the week.'

'No problem,' Phillip said. 'More than happy to help.'

'Excellent,' Alex said, slapping Phillip on the back. 'In that case you are invited to join our exclusive club.' He removed his cap and held it up so Phillip could see the embroidered badge.

The emblem depicted a beer mug and walking stick with a motto sewn into it that read *Durst wird durch Bier erst schön*, which Phillip translated as 'Thirst is only beautiful when accompanied by beer'.

'Our club,' Michael said, with mock gravity and adopting a Prussian upper class accent, 'believes only in the pursuit of beauty.'

'Therefore,' Alex said, 'to attain this lofty ideal, we go on long walks in the countryside to create a thirst and then find an inn so beauty can be called forth.'

Phillip smiled. 'Oh, right. OK.' It would be one more way of being part of the student fraternity.

'Actually, have you heard about Heidegger coming to give a talk?' Alex said.

Phillip knew Heidegger's book, *Being and Time*, which had come out three years earlier and was much praised by some of the members of the bridge club he belonged to. To try to impress his bridge-playing associates, he had struggled through it, and although dense and difficult, he gradually understood the ideas Heidegger was exploring and thought them profound. 'No, I didn't know.'

'He's coming to the university next week.'

'Oh, right,' Phillip said.

'Your tutor is organising it, Professor Muller,' Michael said. 'See if you can get us a seat. It's in the main lecturer theatre.'

'It's for the fourth year philosophy students,' Alex said. 'But there might be some spare tickets.'

'We think if we hear the great man speak,' Michael said, 'we might understand *Being and Time* more.'

'Yeah,' Alex said. 'It's one of those books you know is incredibly profound and important but is difficult to get to the bottom of.'

'It's because of the way he uses language,' Phillip said. 'He dumps all the traditional philosophical terms and invents his own. So he doesn't use concepts like epistemology, subjectivity.'

'Of course,' Alex said, putting his arm round Phillip's shoulders, 'why didn't I see that.' He cocked his head sideways and went cross-eyed.

They all laughed.

'Face it, Alex,' Michael said, '*Being and Time* is beyond you.'

'How dare you, sir. I challenge you to a duel.'

'Accepted,' Michael said, clicking his heels.

They both laughed. 'Come on,' Michael said, 'we'll be late for class.' He turned to Phillip, 'We will be in touch. We'll leave a note in your box.'

'Yes,' Alex said. 'Welcome to our club.'

As he climbed the steps to Doctor Schmelter's office, he checked that he had his passport with him; he needed to show it to Muller that afternoon so he could be registered at the university. It was in his case, along with an anthology of modern poets. He planned to spend the time before seeing Muller in the library cribbing the German introductions to Eliot's *The Waste Land* and George's *The Poet in Troubled Times*, and then combining them into an outline for his paper. Reiterating what the Germans thought the poems were about was essential in playing the academic game. Also, being seen working in the library would reinforce his status as a serious student.

He reached the top floor and saw a beautiful woman standing next to the library talking to a student. Her blond hair fell to her shoulders like threads of spun gold, framing the perfect proportions of her face, while the light from the windows bathed her in frail sunshine. Her lips spoke in soft tones as her blue eyes sparkled with intelligence. She turned and looked at him. Phillip blushed to be caught staring at her. He turned and went to the door labelled Doctor Schmelter and knocked. There was no sound from inside.

'You must be Phillip,' a voice said behind him.

Phillip turned. It was the beautiful woman who had been standing with the student. 'I'm Doctor Krystal Schmelter,' she said, extending her hand.

'Yes,' Phillip said, shaking her hand, her fingers as delicate as the body of a young bird.

'And this is Wolfgang Drexler,' Krystal said, indicating the student she had been talking to.

Phillip extended his hand but Wolfgang declined to shake it.

'Come along,' Doctor Schmelter said to Phillip. 'It's break time. I'll buy you a coffee. Or tea if you prefer.'

'Oh, thank you.'

'I'll see you later, Wolfgang,' Krystal said, and headed for the lift with Phillip following.

As they stood waiting for the lift, Phillip thought she was the most beautiful woman he had ever seen, just like the Roman Goddess Diana, whose image he had fallen in love with during adolescence.

'I understand you were in Tübingen a few years ago, studying Holderlin.'

'Yes.'

'Holderlin is the most German of German poets, and so you know who we are. The true Germans, that is, who are part of the true essence as expressed by Holderlin and now Stefan George and the National Socialists.'

What was she saying? Holderlin was nothing like George. George was nebulous enough to be adopted by the Nazis, but Holderlin was a broken soul who lived a hermit's life in a woodman's house and was out with the fairies most of the time, in an eternal land where peace and love reigned supreme, and was, most and foremost, religious and a Romantic. The savagery of the Brownshirts would be anathema to Holderlin.

They exited the lift on the second floor. Doctor Schmelter led Phillip into a large cafeteria full of students sitting at tables. She then guided him to an area partitioned off with lattice screens and found a vacant table. The enclosure was for university staff only and Phillip felt out of place. Professor Muller, who was sitting at a table with other people, smiled at him. Doctor Schmelter ordered coffee and tea from a waitress.

'Well,' Doctor Schmelter said, folding her hands as if in prayer, 'the reason I wanted to speak to you is to ask if you would help as a translator. I have documents to be translated from German to English. The translation must be of the highest standard since it is important to our eugenics programme.'

Phillip had heard people at some of the bridge games talking about eugenics, but it had all sounded rather abstract and often racist. 'I'm sorry, but I'm not very familiar with the subject.'

'That's not so important as your language skills. I can hear your German is excellent and I presume your English is even better.

As to the subject matter, it will be a chance for you to learn about one of the major threats to our European culture and all we have created. In fact, it was you British who started it. Your Doctor Galton invented eugenics forty years ago in 1883. He was inspired by his cousin, Darwin, who, as you know, wrote *On the Origins of Species* and taught us all about survival of the fittest. Doctor Galton then applied it to humans and created positive eugenics, which stated that superior members of society should only mate with those who have similar traits.'

Doctor Schmelter sipped her coffee. 'Our eugenics project aims to build on Doctor Galton's edict and keep our German blood pure through controlling those who are allowed to procreate and … other things, so the Aryan race can realise its true destiny.'

Phillip felt a frisson of unease. He remembered the last time he was in Germany that some students had talked about the Volk, the people born and bred in Germany from countless generations, being the only true Germans and the need to protect the purity of their blood line. But where did that put him?

Krystal smiled. 'I think you will be a real asset to our programme. Wolfgang was helping me but unfortunately his English isn't up to it and time is of the essence.'

That was why Wolfgang had given him a dirty look, thought Phillip. Doctor Schmelter was replacing him.

'By the way,' Krystal said, 'how tall are you?'

'Six foot one.'

Doctor Schmelter thought for a moment. 'One metre eighty-five. Excellent. You are the perfect Aryan. Tall, blond, blue eyed. I am doing a major study of the Nordic Races, and it is very hard to find a male to act as an archetype. Here in Bavaria there are too many Franks and leftover tribes that followed the Roman Empire, and so it's difficult to find really good Aryan specimens.' Doctor Schmelter smiled. 'So, what about your parents? What do they look like?'

'They're both dead.'

'Oh, I'm sorry to hear that.'

There was a long silence.

'It's OK,' Phillip said. 'It was a long time ago. I was born in India.'

'Ah, the Jewel in the Crown. Unfortunately, our attempts at colonisation have not been successful. Bismarck wasn't keen on them.' She smiled. 'But it is your ex-colony that is really exciting us. America. They are leading the world in developing race hygiene programmes to eliminate undesirables.' She leaned forward, her eyes sparking. 'In California they have passed legislation, endorsed by America's Supreme Court, to sterilise and eliminate undesirable populations – immigrants, people of colour, poor people, unmarried mothers, the disabled, the mentally ill, the indigent.' She leaned back. 'Yes, America is showing the way.'

Phillip was frightened and confused. He had never heard of an official programme for sterilisation. In India, his mother had said a woman who kept having mentally and physically disabled children, whose only future was begging, should be sterilised. But Doctor Schmelter had said people of colour and others. What did that mean? Americans who were black? Indians? Mixed race, like himself? Also, unmarried mothers and poor people. She couldn't mean it. But she said it was official policy in California and endorsed by the American Supreme Court.

'Now Phillip, I must go and get ready for my next class. I will leave the file to be translated in your in-tray. Please keep the document safe and do not show it to anyone else.'

Phillip nodded. 'OK.'

'How about we meet in my office next Monday at ten o'clock? Does that suit with you?'

Phillip hesitated. What should he do? If he said he wanted nothing to do with the project it would look strange, draw attention to him. 'Yes. That would be fine.'

'Thank you, Phillip. I think you're going to be a real asset to our work. See you next Monday.' She squeezed his hand. 'And remember, this is just between us.'

Phillip gazed after her as she left the refectory. She was the most beautiful woman he had ever seen, which, combined with her obvious intelligence, made her captivating, but the things she was saying filled him with deep unease. Perhaps he had misunderstood.

'Do you have your passport with you?' Professor Muller said, as Phillip sat in front of his desk.

'Yes, sir.'

Muller took the passport and then filled in a form and handed it to Phillip. 'Take this to the faculty office on the ground floor and they will register you.'

'Thank you, professor.'

Muller leaned back in his chair. 'So, how do you like Germany so far?'

'Really good, sir.'

'But not the coffee.'

Phillip smiled.

Muller peered over his glasses. 'You have your notebook?'

'Yes, sir.' Phillip rummaged in his briefcase and extracted a lined foolscap pad and a fountain pen. He wrote down a note to himself to ask about Heidegger's visit to the university.

'German poetry,' Muller said, 'at root, is about what it means to be German, part of the Volk, as your hero Holderlin so admirably expresses it. He is the spiritual forerunner of Volksgemeinschaft. Which is why the Holderlin Society endorses the National Socialists.'

Phillip wasn't sure what Volksgemeinschaft was. He would have to ask Ruth. But, the Holderlin Society endorsing the Nazis? That was unbelievable. Things had really changed. So that was why Doctor Schmelter thought he would be sympathetic to her eugenics project.

'A great deal of poetry is wishy-washy,' Muller said, 'all about flowers and nature. Real poetry, not all, but the best, George and T.S. Eliot, reflects a nation's search for meaning and its true destiny. Our poetry speaks of the Secret Germany that needs to be rediscovered by the nation, the Volk, the people. You must read Stefan George's book, *Geheimes Deutschland*, *Secret Germany*. It was published in 1922. There should be a copy in our library on the top floor; if not, the town library in the main square will have one. Or, you could buy one.'

Phillip nodded and pretended to make notes, but then decided to write verbatim what Muller was saying in order to brush up on his written German, which had suffered from lack of use.

'Interesting that Eliot's *The Waste Land* and George's *Secret Germany* were both published eight years ago in 1922,' Muller said. 'And both cry out for a new order to cure their nation's ills. You will contrast and compare the two works, as well as Holderlin's poems, which I understand you are very familiar with and echo much of what George and Eliot are saying.'

Bollocks, thought Phillip. Eliot's *The Waste Land* was open to interpretation but was generally seen as a call to resurrect an old order rather than invent a new one. Many critics thought Eliot was just moaning about a changed world where the elites, in terms of lineage, religion and culture no longer ruled, and so a cultured, learned man, such as Eliot himself, was no longer at home. And as for George being compared to Holderlin … Phillip wrote CUBE in his notes. It was an acronym for Complete Utter Bovine Excrement, a phrase he and his friends at university had created for books and statements they thought rubbish.

Muller waited till Phillip looked up and engaged his eyes. 'People must think with their blood and stamp out reason,' Muller said. 'One voice. One heart. One soul. One leader. In fact, we are witnessing a period of the New Romanticism, where poetry fuses with a certain political movement, the metaphysical and the concrete.'

CUBE – CUBE – CUBE, Phillip wrote.

Muller's eyes were shining. He leaned back in his chair. 'Now. I'd like a written outline of your approach to the dissertation by next week. I especially want you to concentrate on George's *The Poet Troubled Times*. You will see the symbol he speaks about is present in today's world. On the banner of the National Socialists.'

Phillip had skimmed through George's poem and thought of the lines,

'Master once more master – discipline once more discipline – he fixes

The true symbol onto the people's banner

Through the storm and horrible signals of the red dawn

He leads his loyal hoard to work

Of the wakeful day and plants the New Reich.'

Phillip nodded. Muller must mean the swastika. So Muller was a supporter of the National Socialists. Hopefully, he wouldn't have to hand in a paper, but if he did, he would create a sycophantic parody of what Muller had been spouting.

'I would also like you to do a critique of Stefan George's translations of Shakespeare's Sonnets.'

A jolt of fear went through Phillip. The Sonnets were part of his cypher code for communicating with SIS. Did Muller know something? No. It was more likely, as an academic, he wanted it as a piece of research that he could use in the future and no doubt claim as his own. 'Yes, professor.'

'Now, here's your library pass,' Muller said, placing a card in front of Phillip, 'so you can start work straight away. Now, off you go and get registered.'

Phillip picked up the card and stood up. 'Oh, professor, a couple of students asked if there were any places left for Professor Heidegger's talk.'

Muller smiled and shook his head.

The registry was on the right of the main entrance, through wooden doors without signs. Phillip found himself in a corridor with bare walls, no windows and neon strip lighting. Along one wall were in-trays with student names on them. He looked, but his wasn't there. A wooden counter jutted out from an opening in one wall. Through the opening, he saw people sat at desks. A middle-aged man rose from his place and sauntered up to the counter. 'Yes?'

'Oh, my name is Phillip Fitzwilliam. I've been told I need to register with you.'

The man looked at Phillip without speaking.

'My name is Phillip Fitzwilliam and I'm an exchange student, from England. This is my form signed by Professor Muller.'

The man read the form. 'Oh, there is a file for you from Doctor Schmelter.' He went back to his desk and returned with a closed box file. He slid it across the counter to Phillip. 'We haven't had time to put up your in-tray.' He then strolled to a shelf, took down a box file and extracted a brown folder. He ambled back to the counter. 'Passport.'

Phillip handed him his passport. The man flicked through it, wrote in the file and handed the passport back to Phillip. 'Certificates.'

'Sorry?'

'Your certificates. The academic qualifications you have that enable you to study here. They are not in the file. You cannot be registered as a student until we see them.'

Phillip's legs trembled. He didn't have the certificates. Smythe had handled it all. But he couldn't present his certificates because they were awarded to Phillip Kumar. 'Oh, I'll ... Sorry. I thought they'd been sent.'

The man shut the file. 'Well, you need to get them. Once we have seen them we can enrol you and then you can apply to the police for a residency permit. You must have a residency permit within four days of arriving in Germany or you cannot be here and your visa will be automatically terminated.' The man strode away.

As he hurried back along the corridor, Phillip's heart raced. This was his third day in Germany. He couldn't get the certificates in one day. If the police caught him without a residency permit, would he be arrested? Deported? Or even interrogated?

He must contact SIS immediately.

Chapter 7

Phillip retreated to the faculty library.

He would lie low till it was dark and then post the message to SIS.

As he placed Doctor Schmelter's file on the desk, he drew some comfort from the fact that he was doing work for a member of the faculty, but at the same time felt deeply uneasy about what the work involved.

Inside the slim box file was a note from Doctor Schmelter stating that the contents must be kept secret and that she would be pleased if he could make a start on the work as soon as possible. There were also some handwritten notes in English that he assumed were Wolfgang's. The notes contained many crossings out and lots of clusters of similar words in brackets, as if he was trying to choose which English word was correct. Phillip felt a pang of sympathy for Wolfgang, since the nuances of the English language often baffled native speakers.

He took out a brown folder. On the cover, written in German Gothic Script, was: 'Proposal for a Race Hygiene Centre at the Kaiser Wilhelm Institute for Psychiatry, Munich'.

He flipped open the folder and started to read the introduction.

'The identification of the need to protect the white race began in America in 1902 when Stanford University President David Star Jordan published his book, "Blood of a Nation". Jordan

revealed the fact that human qualities and attributes passed from one generation to the next through race and blood, supporting the original work of British scientist Doctor Galton, who invented eugenics.

Stanford University President David Star Jordan further identified the perfect human specimen, the master race, to be Nordic, possessing blue eyes, blond hair and white skin. We can now say that this superior race is Aryan and inhabits Northern Europe. It was noted that all the great advancements of the modern world came from the Aryan peoples.

Our aim in creating the Race Hygiene Centre in Munich is to duplicate and build on the work being done in America to eliminate that part of the population, deemed unfit to live, that is mongrelising the Aryan race.

It is widely accepted that the Aryan race, and all it has achieved, is in danger of decline. To prevent this happening we must act to keep the Blood and Race of the Aryans pure.

The first role of the Race Hygiene Centre will be to build the kinds of structures that have proven so effective in America.

Number one is to identify those whose seed must be exterminated so that they cannot continue to breed. To this end, America set up a special organisation to identify and record those peoples whose bloodline must be destroyed. This establishment was created in 1904 in New York at Cold Spring Harbor on Long Island, with funds from the Carnegie Institution. The Cold Spring Harbor institute created a data-file of index cards that recorded the details of millions of Americans from which the targeting and elimination of undesirables from society could be extracted.

At the same time, local charities such as the New York Bureau of Industries were used to identify those who needed to be deported, confined or subjected to forced sterilisation. These groups comprise such peoples as Jews, Italians and other immigrants from southern Europe who are not of the Nordic Race. This work was paid for by the Harriman railroad fortune.

We will also be applying for funding for the Race Hygiene Centre from the Carnegie Institution and the Harriman railroad fortune as well as the Rockefeller Foundation who is already the main supplier of funds for the advancement of the German Eugenics' programme.

Madison Grant, president of the Eugenics Research Association and the American Eugenics Society, has said in his influential book: "The Passing of the Great Race", publish 1916, New York, Charles Scribner's Sons, 'Mistaken regard for what are believed to be divine laws and a sentimental belief in the sanctity of human life tend to prevent both the elimination of defective infants and the sterilization of such adults as are themselves of no value to the community. The laws of nature require the obliteration of the unfit and human life is valuable only when it is of use to the community or race.'

'Here in Germany we are awakening to the truth of the danger we are in. We must ensure that the German people

understand that a nation is known through its blood. Blood is race, race is soul and soul is blood.'

The next part was headed:

International Support from Eminent People

'Academic Support

Race science is supported by some of America's most respected scientists. These include prestigious universities such as: Stanford, Yale, Harvard and Princeton. There is an opportunity, with American support from the Rockefeller Foundation and the Carnegie Institute, to establish a similar institution here in Munich: The Race Hygiene Centre. The Americans feel the way forward is to get rid of the lowest 10% when the opportunity arises, and continue doing so until you end up with the Master Race of blue-eyed, blond-haired Nordic types.'

The next part, under the heading 'Leading Thinkers', was incomplete. Phillip's eye was caught by the name George Bernard Shaw under the heading, 'Extermination of the socially incompatible'. He had seen many of Shaw's plays in London, which he liked for their wit and breaking taboos, but was surprised Shaw was involved in the eugenics movement. The notes said Shaw advocated the use of a chamber filled with gas to peacefully dispose of the unfit. Parts of Shaw's quotes were underlined: *'A part of eugenic politics would finally land us in an extensive use of the lethal chamber. A great many people would have to be put out of existence simply because it wastes other people's time to look after*

them.' George Bernard Shaw, Lecture to the Eugenics Education
Society, Reported in The Daily Express, March 4, 1910.

'Other leading thinkers to included,
Darwin
'If the various checks specified ... do not prevent the reckless, the
vicious and otherwise inferior members of society from increasing at
a quicker rate than the better class of men, the nation will
retrograde, as has too often occurred in the history of the world.'
Bertrand Russell
'Eugenics has, of course, more ambitious possibilities in a more
distant future. It may aim not only at eliminating undesired types,
but at increasing desired types. The time may arrive a little later
when the community as a whole must pay attention to the innate
quality as well as to the mere numbers of its future members.'
Maynard Keynes
'As director of the Eugenics Society for about seven years, Keynes
believed contraception was necessary to limit the growth of the
lower classes because they were too 'drunken and ignorant' to do it
themselves.'
Other famous people who support Race Eugenics to get quotes
about:
H. G. Wells
Helen Keller
Teddy Roosevelt – US president
Winston Churchill.
Alexander Graham Bell.

The next part was headed *Implementation and Applied Eugenics*.

Phillip closed the folder. A mixture of anger, fear and revulsion went through him. He felt his soul creep inside him as he began to realise the full implications of what was being promoted. There was no way he was going to make the translations. If necessary, he would say he lost the file. Or, he could destroy it. But there would be others, like Wolfgang, keen to translate the documents in the name of purifying the race. If ever such a programme took hold in Britain, he and his father would be in real danger.

He could feel his heart beating. It was like discovering someone you knew was secretly a murderer and you were in danger.

He sat for a long time seeing the light seep from the sky. Surely it must be just some fanatical minority amongst academics who were trying to make a name for themselves. Being provocative for the sake of it. He thought of handing the file back, but that would cause problems and attract attention to him.

Snubbing a doctor teaching in the faculty would be seen as reprehensible and rude. And if they learned he wasn't registered with the university because he didn't have the right papers he would be thrown out. And they would tell the police.

He would have to find a way of stalling Doctor Schmelter till he found Max Schneider and learned what he wanted for the mysterious document.

Chapter 8

When solid darkness masked the library window, he slipped out of the university, in his pocket the coded message asking for an urgent meeting with SIS.

He hurried towards Albert Street, desperately hoping he wouldn't encounter any policemen, or, worse still, roaming gangs of Brownshirts. To his surprise the streets were deserted. After sliding the envelope into the *Volkischer Beobachter's* letterbox, he headed back to his lodgings. The newspaper wasn't published at weekends so it would be Monday before the ad appeared.

The house was in darkness, hopefully Ruth had already left for the Stefan George party. He didn't think he should attend since he needed to keep a low profile, but he had been looking forward to going out with Ruth. The key slipped easily into the lock and the door opened quietly. Ruth was standing in the hall with two people; a young man in a German Army officer's uniform and a beautiful blond girl wearing a long satin dress and wrapped in a fur stole.

'Ah, there you are,' Ruth said. She smiled and kissed him on the cheek. 'We were just about to go without you. This is Phillip. Phillip this is Anna, my sister.'

Anna stuck out her hand and Phillip shook it. He was surprised that Anna had blue eyes while Ruth's were dark ebony, and Ruth had black hair while Anna's was the colour of hay.

'And this is her boyfriend, Captain Christoph von Allenbach.'

As Phillip stuck out his hand, Christoph clicked his heels and bowed, his head brushing Phillip's arm. 'Ah, you want me to kiss your hand?'

Phillip laughed, surprised at Christoph's old fashioned greeting. 'Well, if you insist.'

Christoph laughed, and reached out and shook Phillip's hand. He was a couple of inches shorter than Phillip. He had brown hair with an untidy parting on the left side, a soft face, flat nose and hazel eyes that sparkled when he spoke, giving the impression of someone who found the world amusing.

'Don't tease him.' Anna patted Phillip's arm. 'Poor boy. He's English.'

'Sorry.' Christoph bowed. 'I didn't mean to embarrass you.'

'No,' Phillip said. 'Not at all.'

'Don't worry. You will soon learn our little ways.' Christoph opened the door. 'In fact, we Germans and you English have much in common. We all come from the same tribes, the Saxons and Angles, blue eyed and blond hair. It's only down here in Southern Germany you get the dark-haired lot. The Franks.'

Phillip noted that Christoph had dark hair and brown eyes.

'Actually,' Ruth said. 'Phillip has been in Germany before. He studied poetry in Tübingen.'

'And even had poems published,' Anna said.

'Well … yes, but …'

'OK. Let's get going.' Christoph waved them towards the door. 'I need a drink.'

Phillip hadn't expected army officers to be at a gathering with poets. What if there were Brownshirts there? 'Well, actually. I do have a lot of work to do. My dissertation is …'

'Nonsense.' Christoph put his arm round Phillip's shoulders. 'It can wait till tomorrow. You are young, you must enjoy yourself. Too much studying dulls the brain.'

'You said you wanted to know when *Evil Flowers* was on,' Ruth said. 'Well, some of the actors from the show will probably be there. Madam Bernstein is a patron of the arts and funds all the unconventional stuff as well as the main theatre.'

What if he managed to meet Max Schneider tonight? What should he say?

'Yes, you must come.' Anna squeezed Phillip's arm. 'As a budding poet this is your chance to meet Europe's most famous poet, Stefan George.'

'The Master.' Christoph bowed.

'That's what his acolytes call him,' Anna said. 'The Poet Fhurer.'

'That's because he's the greatest living poet.' Christoph raised both arms. 'The oracle. The prophet. The leader.'

'Yes, well.' Ruth took Phillip's arm. 'That's what his followers think, but there are plenty who disagree.'

Christoph put on his spiked, officers hat, the gold crests glinting as he turned his head. 'You mean the Socialist idiots.'

'Enough.' Anna pulled Christoph out the door. 'Come on Phillip, you can meet George and decide for yourself. Also, Nanny Larsen-Todsen will be there to sing an aria from *Tristan and Isolde*.'

Christoph smiled at Ruth. 'Real Wagner, sung by professionals.'

Ruth stuck her tongue out at him.

'Tristan and Isolde is the next production at the Bayreuth Festival this July,' Anna said. 'You must see it if you are still here.'

'It won't be as good ours,' Ruth said.

Anna grabbed Christoph's arm as he was about to speak. 'Enough. Come on. We don't want to be late and miss Nanny Larsen-Todsen.'

They reached the top of the lane and Phillip felt safe in the company of Christoph, an army officer. And he might just meet Max Schneider. But how to approach to him? He would have to pretend to be a fan and find out what he could about him.

'So, who of our poets do you like the best?' Christoph said.

'Holderlin,' Phillip said.

'What about George.'

'Well … to tell you the truth, I find George rather obscure.'

'That's because he is,' Ruth said.

'No, no,' Christoph said. 'George is clear. He is a prophet. He sees the truth clearly; it is us who are at fault if we don't understand him.'

'Don't worry,' Ruth said. 'As I told you before, I know someone who will help you.'

'Aha,' Christoph said. 'Be careful Phillip, you are being drawn in. In exchange for help with your studies, dear Ruth will expect you to sing for your supper.'

Ruth put her arm through Phillip's. 'Actually, I do need help. What happened at the church has scared off most of the people who were helping with the *Parsifal* set.'

'Is Mr Conti OK? And the musicians?'

'Yes.' She moved in close to him and smiled into his eyes. 'Nice of you to ask. He got out all right. He's too important even for the Nazis to touch. But, like I told you, I'll be moving the set out to Blue Ridge Farm. There's an artists' colony there and I have one of the cabins. Anyway, the farmer, well, leader of the artists' colony, says I can use his barn to store and make the set. It would be really good if you could help.'

'OK.'

Christoph waved his hands. 'You see. You see. Wheeler-dealer. It's in her blood.'

Anna shoved Christoph.

Christoph ran in front of them and did some steps, which looked to Phillip like a Cossack dance.

Ruth and Anna looked at each other.

Ruth pulled Phillip close to her as they walked. 'My friend will help you even if you don't have time to help us.'

'Thank you,' Phillip said, not sure what was going on.

Christoph circled behind Anna and then linked his arm into hers. 'You know I love you. Even if you are an Israelite.'

Phillip felt less anxious; he was with people, one of whom was an army officer, going to a select gathering that no doubt included the cream of Bayreuth society, persons the Brownshirts wouldn't mess with.

They strode across Prince William Square, the house lights smearing a pale patina across the damp cobblestones, their footsteps echoing in the quiet night, to a grand, Neo-Baroque house that occupied the whole corner and part of the adjacent street. Christoph pushed open the ornate, iron gate and they trod along a gravel path with Art Nuevo lamps running along each side, then up stone steps to large double doors. Christoph pulled a chain and bells rang inside the house.

One door opened and a woman dressed in a flapper costume and waving a long cigarette holder, greeted them. 'Ruth, Christoph, Anna, darlings! Thank you for coming. In. In.'

They stepped into a large hall with a black and white tiled floor and a coach light hanging from the ceiling. Two men dressed in tails took their coats.

'This is Phillip,' Ruth said. 'He's over from England studying our poets. Phillip, this is Madam Bernstein.'

'Call me Helga,' Madam Bernstein said, kissing Phillip on both cheeks. 'How wonderful to meet you. Now,' she said, linking her arm into Phillip's and walking towards a large carved door, 'if you are studying our literature, you will be in good company tonight. Stefan has just published a book of poems he calls *Das neue Reich* -

The New Empire and is holding court. And of course, we have a special guest to sing for us.'

Helga stopped before the half-opened door through which they could hear a babble of voices. 'Ruth, darling, there are a couple of those National Socialists here and they are not happy with what you are doing with *Parsifal*.'

'I know. They've already paid us a visit and vandalised some of the set.'

'Oh, how dreadful.'

'Nothing that can't be fixed.'

'Good. Their funny little leader thinks Wagner is God, and he doesn't like the way your conductor is interpreting *Parsifal*. Anyway, I thought I'd warn you so you can keep away from them. They are wearing swastika lapel badges, of course.'

As they came into the room, they were met with a hubbub of voices, as if everyone were engaged in a competitive conversation. The guests stood in groups, with most of the women clad in flapper dresses and headbands, and brandishing long cigarette holders, some with unlit cigarettes, while the men wore evening dress, or sported check jackets with coronations in their lapels. Several army officers, in dress uniforms, were poised in a group. A polished piano burnished on the far side of the room, next to which stood a woman draped in white satin talking to the pianist.

A shoal of young men were clustered around a tall man with thin features, a mane of white hair swept back from his forehead, sparkling eyes and slender hands that wafted the air like pale birds.

'That's Stefan George,' Helga said, patting Phillip's arm. 'I will introduce you later. I'm sure he'll be interested in you coming to study our poets. Have fun,' she said, and floated off to join the group near the piano.

'I'll get us a drink,' Anna said. 'What would you like Phillip?'

'Oh, err … whisky. Thank you.'

'I'll help you,' Ruth said.

Phillip immediately regretted ordering whisky but couldn't think of anything else. Beer would be his choice but nobody seemed to be drinking it; they all looked to be holding cocktail glasses with sticks in them. Should he have ordered a cocktail? But the only one he knew was a White Lady, and that was a secret signal so he couldn't say it.

'So,' Christoph said, 'how do you like Germany?'

'Oh, it's good. Very good. People are nice.'

'Not like you heard in the propaganda?'

Phillip shrugged. As an adolescent he'd seen the posters that had been produced during the Great War and it wasn't until he lived in Tübingen that he finally rid himself of the distorted prejudice they had engendered.

'Don't worry,' Ruth said, as she joined them holding two glasses, one of which she handed to Phillip. 'We said the same things about you.'

'You only say that because you are a Communist,' Christoph said.

'I am not a communist. I am a Democratic Socialist.'

'Worse still, you support a bloody political party. At least the Communists, like us, want to kill this republic. What about you Phillip? Do you think our republic is a good thing, or a bunch of clowns destroying Germany?'

'Please,' Anna said, coming back with two drinks and thrusting one at Christoph. 'No politics. Not tonight.'

'It's not politics,' Christoph said. 'It's much more serious than that.'

'Political parties have worked for the British,' Ruth said.

'But we're German. We only thrive when we are one, when we are united, as in Bismarck's Empire, or Frederick the Great's, and so we need a third empire, a Third Reich. This Republic has splintered us. We need to become one again, under one leader and poets will show the way.' He raised his glass. 'As Heine said, "the poet's heart is the centre of the world". Only through the mystery of art can you glimpse the way to completeness.' He drank down his glass in one.

Anna waved to a young man in his early twenties dressed in a Prussian officer's uniform. 'The man of the moment,' Anna said, as the young man joined them. 'This is Berthold von Stauffenberg. And this is Phillip, a student from England studying our poets.'

Stauffenberg clicked his heels and bowed. Phillip bowed back.

Christoph laughed and slapped Phillip on the back. 'Well done, you bowed. We will make a Germany of you yet.' He placed his hand on von Stauffenberg's shoulder. 'Stefan George has dedicated his new collection of poems, *The New Reich*, to Berthold.'

The tapping of a glass hushed the room.

Everyone turned towards the piano as the opening bars of Wagner's *Mild und Leise* floated across the room. In perfect harmony with the piano, the voice of the woman in the white dress rose like a meadowlark and carried the crystal notes around the room. When she finished, Phillip clapped enthusiastically.

Ruth smiled at him and then leaned into him and gave him a peck on the cheek.

'I don't suppose any of the performers in the clubs are here?' Phillip said.

Ruth looked around. 'No. I don't see any. This seems to be a more select group. Possibly …'

'My dear Christoph, where have you been hiding this Adonis?' Stefan George said, as he came up and laid his hand on Phillip's arm. 'And I understand this cherub also pens poetry.'

George's high forehead and brushed-back hair emphasised his luminous eyes that seemed to fuse thought with emotion.

'I haven't been hiding him,' Christoph said. 'He's Ruth's friend. His name is Phillip and he's just arrived from England as an exchange student.'

'My God! What did they exchange him for?' George said, squeezing Phillip's arm. 'All the American gold on loan in the Reichsbank.'

'He's studying our poets,' Ruth said. 'Including you.'

'Well, so there is hope for our Anglo-Saxon cousins. Mind you, we wouldn't exchange such a gorgeous creature. Look, his skin glows pale gold like the snow on an alpine summer's evening, and those blue eyes like the cold sky. Are you cold, Phillip?'

'Cold? Well … no …'

'The poor boy is flustered. I play with you. But your fluster reveals the sensitive poet inside you. Who knows, you might write something that we could include in our collection of poems that express the true heart of Germany. The true destiny of a people is revealed in its poetry, just as your Shakespeare showed the frailty of monarchs.' He turned slowly with his hand raised as if performing the slow movement of a dance. 'We must now away on time's winged chariot, but Christoph, I charge you with the sacred duty of delivering this creature to us at our next gathering when I shall read from our latest publication *The New Reich*.' George turned and went off with his head tilted back and young men trailing after him.

Phillip watched George say goodbye to the guests, some of whom avoided going anywhere near him, and then leave with most of the young men in tow. The room was now half empty.

'Well, you've made a conquest there,' Ruth said, 'being invited to the next George reading.' She smiled at Phillip. 'Don't look so worried, it'll just be a gathering of poets and writers and academics, like yourself.'

Anna joined them looking upset.

Christoph was on the other side of the room standing in front of a man. Their heads were bent towards each other and they were deep in conversation. The man was small but stocky, with a shaven scalp and a thick red scar down the side of his face, as if hot metal had trickled down his cheek.

'He made it clear I wasn't wanted,' Anna said.

Phillip looked at Ruth.

'He hates Jews,' said Ruth. 'He's Major Drexler. He works for the Abwehr, the secret intelligence arm of the German army. Major Drexler knows everything that goes on in Bayreuth. And he's a Nazi, but he pretends not to be because members of the armed forces are not suppose to be in political parties.'

Phillip turned away. Drexler mustn't see him or know he was an Englishman in Bayreuth. What if he asked to see his residency permit? And Wolfgang Drexler, the student at the university whose job he had been given, was he a relative? 'Actually,' he said, turning to Ruth, 'I really do need to do some work on my dissertation.'

'No problem,' Ruth said. 'Now George is gone this is likely to degenerate into a shouting match.'

Anna gripped Phillip's arm. 'Please don't go.'

'I must,' Phillip said.

'I'll come with you,' Ruth said. 'Too many Nazis in one room.' She kissed Anna on the cheek. 'Tell Christoph you have a headache. He'll be only too pleased to get out of here now George has gone.'

They went quietly up the stairs and stopped outside Phillip's door. Ruth reached up and kissed him, the naked warmth of her lips thrilling him as she pulled him into her. A deep joy went through his body. He was being cuddled, hugged and lovingly enfolded by another human being; not since childhood had he experienced such affection. Ruth kissed him open mouthed, deeply, lusciously, her tongue flickering sensually behind his lips, then withdrew, opened her door and went quietly inside.

Phillip got ready for bed, his erection making it difficult to put on his pyjamas. Ruth mustn't have a boyfriend. She had taken him to a party and shown affection for him in front of others. And now kissing him like that. He felt a rush of certainty that she was special, maybe the one.

There was a knock on the door. It was Frau Weiser, dressed in a nightgown and knitted cap. 'This letter was delivered this afternoon. They said it was urgent.'

Phillip took the letter and closed the door. It must have been delivered while he was at the university. He opened it and read, 'To thine own self be true, and as sure as night follows day … Be at Saint Mary's church at twelve noon tomorrow.'

It must be from the go-between. Who? How? The man with the tin mask he'd met in the Blue Lagoon? He remembered the man chasing after him when he saw him with the beggar in the square. He must have been trying to make contact. Now he had and they were meeting tomorrow.

He had already asked to meet SIS urgently, and so the assignment could be over within a few days. But what about Ruth?

Chapter 9

Next morning at eleven, Phillip left his lodgings and headed for the Church of Saint Mary.

The thought that he could be back in London within days and perhaps never see Ruth again plagued him. Would Ruth care? He would ask her to write to him, but would she? Would he lose her? There was something special about her, her self-assurance, never judgemental, honesty, kindness, and her beauty and sensuality. He'd never met a girl like her. But it was her honesty that captivated him, humbled him. If only he could be as strong.

He crossed the Red River and then stood scanning the compound in front of the church. It was deserted. One of the church's double doors was slightly ajar. He strode to a shop adjacent to the church and pretended to look in the window while watching the bridge. A bus crossed, along with two or three pedestrians who kept on walking. He waited till he felt sure he wasn't being followed, and then made his way to the church.

As he entered, he instinctively dipped his hand in the font of holy water and made the sign of the cross. The Baroque frescoes, the ornate sculptures and the blaze of candles in front of the statue of the Virgin Mary, brought back memories from his childhood, when he had been an altar boy. He wished he still believed.

The man with the tin mask was kneeling near the statue of Mary, fumbling his rosary beads. The only other person in the church was a man in ragged clothes asleep in a pew. He looked like a beggar. Perhaps the church was a warm refuge for those without shelter. Phillip sat behind the man with the mask and waited, but the man continued to stare at the statue of The Virgin Mary, chanting softly as he twiddled his rosary beads.

The church was very warm, and as the man in the mask continued to pray, Phillip started to feel nervous and began to sweat. He took off his coat and draped it on the back of the pew. The click of a door disturbed the silence and a woman clattered out of the wooden confessional box. She walked up to the statue of Mary and lit a candle. As she passed down the aisle she smiled at Phillip.

'Go into the confessional,' whispered the man with the mask.

Phillip felt flustered.

The man turned to face Phillip. 'Go. Quickly.'

Phillip clambered into the confessional and knelt down. In the gloom he could just make out a male profile behind the grille. The priest made the sign of the cross and Phillip saw the flash of a large ecclesiastical ring, worn by Catholic bishops and cardinals. Phillip made the sign of the cross.

'Oh, you're a Catholic?' said the voice behind the mesh.

'Yes, your Grace.'

'Where are you from?'

'I'm ... I'm from England.'

'How sweet. And what is your name?'

'Ku ... um Phillip Fitzwilliam.'

'Now Phillip. Don't lie. This is a confessional.'

Phillip felt his stomach churn.

'We must trust each other, Phillip.'

'Kumar. Phillip Kumar.'

'Ah. And they gave you the cover name Fitzwilliam.'

'It was my mother's name, Your Grace.'

'Ah, so not quite a lie. Well, I absolve you, Phillip.' He took off the bishop's ring. The grille between the penitent and priest opened slightly and then stuck. 'Here. A present for you. It is too small for me.'

'But ... Your Grace ...'

'I'm not really a bishop. But I like dressing as one, and I especially like hearing confessions. I write music shows and there is nothing like the confessional for stimulating ideas. Please, take it.'

Phillip drew the ring through the narrow opening.

'Put it on. Put it on,' the man said.

Phillip put the ring on his third finger left hand. It fitted perfectly.

'Show me. Show me,' said the voice behind the grill.

Phillip raised his hand.

'Ah,' came the voice. 'Perfect. What beautiful hands you have. You must keep the ring always Phillip, in memory of me. Promise?'

'Yes, Your Gra ... sir.'

'You're very sweet, Phillip. Anyway, I want a British visa and two hundred American dollars. They must be American dollars. Here is the name and photo to go on the visa.' He began to push a thick envelop through the narrow opening in the grille, but it got stuck.

The priest's door was yanked open. 'Quick. Out,' said a voice.

The man behind the grille banged open the confessional door and rushed out. Phillip scrambled out and saw the man in the tin mask running towards the sacristy with an overweight man dressed as a Catholic bishop.

They both disappeared into the sacristy.

Phillip looked around. The church was empty. He began to panic. He rushed to the pew to get his coat. It had gone. He raced into the sacristy and then out an open door that led into the graveyard.

The cemetery was blocked off with high walls all round. The only way out he could see was down the side of the church.

As Phillip reached the front of the church, people were gathered around a man lying in a pool of blood. The man on the ground was the tramp who had been in the church and he was wearing Phillip's red coat. Whoever attacked the tramp must have thought it was him. Phillip's legs wobbled.

A woman said to get the priest. Another woman said it was too late, the man was dead. Phillip's stomach tightened with fear. Then he remembered the envelope stuck in the confessional grill. Could the police trace him from it? He had to get it. But what if those who killed the tramp were still around? Watching him. Were they also the ones who killed the two SIS agents? He had to get away. But he had to get the envelope. Police sirens sounded. He had to act. He ran into the church, raced down the side aisle, reached into the confessional and wrenched the envelope from the grille, ran into the sacristy, out the back door and into the graveyard. Police sirens now sounded in front of the church. He scrambled over the high wall and jumped down into an alleyway.

Phillip lay on his bed, trembling, the envelope on his chest. They had tried to kill him. Just like the previous two agents. He had to get the envelope to SIS and then back to England before the killers found him, but the ad he posted the previous day would not appear till Monday; two days' time.

Chapter 10

Church bells rolled across Bayreuth, calling the faithful to Sunday morning worship.

Phillip gazed out the window of his bedroom and wondered if Saint Mary's would hold a service for the tramp murdered the previous day, perhaps a Requiem Mass. The knock on the door made him jump. Was it the police coming to arrest him? Someone had recognised him as being at the church when the man was killed and knew where he lived.

It was Ruth.

She pressed a finger to her lips and slipped into the room. She put her arms around him and kissed him on the lips. 'Hey, don't look so worried. Come on, I'll take you to breakfast and show you the best café in Bayreuth for coffee. I have to meet Maestro Conti and arrange things for *Parsifal*, and then in a couple of days we'll move everything out of Bayreuth till the actual production.'

Phillip released himself from Ruth's arms.

Ruth stepped back and stared at him. 'Has anything happened? You look really worried.'

'No. Nothing. Just ... getting to terms with the course.'

'I told you someone at the artists' colony could help you, remember? When I move the sets to the farm, you can come with me.'

Being in the countryside would be safer than staying in Bayreuth. 'OK. Yeah. Sounds good.'

Ruth slipped her arm into his. 'Excellent. Come on, my treat.'

Phillip wasn't sure about going outside, but it might look suspicious if he spent all his time in his room.

The café was warm and smelled of freshly ground coffee. Phillip always thought the smell of coffee superior to its taste and preferred to drink tea. Art Nouveau posters adorned the walls and red gingham cloths covered the tables, which were occupied by people arguing and trying to talk above each other. A La Pavoni espresso machine was mounted on the counter, its Art Deco casing like an American locomotive. Beside it stood a samovar, gently puffing steam.

The clientele didn't look like churchgoers and so were not likely to have seen him at the church. But what about the killers?

Ruth ordered two coffees. 'This is the only place in Bayreuth you can get espresso coffee,' Ruth said. 'Do you have espresso coffee in England?'

'I'm sorry, I don't know. I've never seen it.'

'We have it in Berlin.'

'Is that where you are from?'

'Yes.'

'What brought you to Bayreuth?'

'I came here to study, and then after I graduated, I was lucky to get a job as a graphic designer. But because of the economic conditions I lost my job. Now I'm freelance.'

'And your sister?'

'She moved here because of Christoph. His regiment is based here.'

Two coffees in plain white cups with saucers were placed on the counter. Phillip was pleased the coffee had cream on top. He reached into his pocket.

Ruth stopped his arm. 'No, I'll pay.'

'No, really. Please. Let me pay. I have …' he was about to say expenses, 'an allowance'.

'Ah, rich parents.'

'No. No. Not really. It's just … '

Ruth smiled and paid.

They carried their coffees to the only unoccupied table, and as Phillip placed his cup down, some of the coffee spilled into the saucer – his hands were slightly trembling. A brown circle formed at the base of the cup. He quickly slipped a napkin under the cup while Ruth looked at someone who had just entered the café.

A tall, elegant man, wearing a black coat with an astrakhan collar and a red fedora hat, greeted them by bowing at Ruth. It was the conductor of *Parsifal*, Luigi Conti.

Conti carried his coffee towards their table, and Phillip saw on his lapel a large silver badge depicting an eagle carrying a bundle of sticks. Conti gave a little bow. 'May I join you?'

Ruth gestured at the vacant chair. 'Of course.'

Conti settled himself onto the seat. 'You are the young man who came to help with the set for *Parsifal*.'

Phillip nodded.

Conti raised his cup in a toast. 'Most kind of you.'

'I'm sorry about the Brownshirts,' Ruth said.

Conti patted her hand. 'Don't be silly. Not your fault. Mind you, that kind of raucous behaviour would never happen in Italy. El Duce keeps order, and order is all we need.' He sipped his coffee and then sat back in his chair. 'The main reason I agreed to come from Milan to Bayreuth is this café. It's the only one in Bavaria that serves real Italian espresso coffee.'

Ruth feigned indignation. 'And I thought you came for the chance to conduct *Parsifal* as Wagner intended it and the chance to work with a talented set designer.'

'Well. Maybe. But the coffee was the clincher.' He placed his cup back in the saucer. 'Now, it's too dangerous to rehearse here in Bavaria with all these bloody Brownshirts, so I am moving the orchestra to Berlin. We will rehearse there till three days before the production. The head of the Bavarian police, having been contacted by a government minister, has promised full protection for the two days before *Parsifal* opens and during the performances.'

'Good,' Ruth said. 'Phillip has agreed to help me move the set to the artist's colony at Blue Ridge Farm where I have a cabin, and the farmer who runs the colony, says we can use his barn to create and store the set till the production.'

'Excellent,' Conti said. 'We mustn't let these Nazi thugs intimidate us.'

'Oh, no,' Ruth said, looking over Phillip's shoulder.

Phillip's heart jumped. Had the police arrived?

Ruth shook her head. 'Bluum. Now we'll get a lecture.'

A man turned from the counter and headed for their table. He was average height, looked to be in his late twenties, thickset with jet-black hair, dark eyes and a set expression, and moved as if totally contained, as if nothing in the physical world touched him. Without speaking, he placed his coffee on the table and sat down.

There was a long silence and Phillip felt uncomfortable.

Bluum slammed his cup into the saucer. 'So, still think you belong here?'

'This is Phillip,' said Ruth, waving her hand towards Phillip. 'He's from England and is helping us with the sets as well as studying our poetry.'

Bluum slapped the table. 'Grow up. This is not a joke. You see what happens when Jews try to engage with German society.'

Ruth shook her head. 'It wasn't because we are Jews. The Nazis don't like the way we are staging the production.'

'Don't fool yourself. They know who is conducting it and creating the sets. Jews belong in Palestine.'

Ruth slumped back in her chair. 'Now you sound like a Nazi.'

Bluum's eyes blazed. 'Yes, that is what the National Socialists believe, and yes, we Zionists agree with them. Yes. Yes. Yes. We agree there is a Jewish Question; there always has been, and always will be until Jews have their own country. We agree the final solution to the Jewish Problem is a Jewish state. In Palestine.'

Silence.

'There is no Jewish Question in Italy,' Conti said. 'We Jews have been part of Italian culture since Roman times. Why should I want to live in a desert, in a country I have no affinity with? For your information, in Italy many leading Jewish families support the Fascists. We needed Fascism to keep order.'

Bluum glared at him. 'How long before they turn on Jews in Italy? Italians, like all nations, are prejudiced against Jews.'

'My dear boy. We all have prejudices. As a Milanese I am prejudiced against those thieving Sicilians who are descendants of Greek bandits. Stealing and brigandry is in their blood, which is why the Mafiosi flourish there. But our great leader, Il Duce, is dealing with them and is crushing the Mafioso. When we were united as a country, it would have been better if Garibaldi had left Sicily to itself.'

Bluum snorted. 'All Europeans are anti-Semitic. The German fascists are being honest. Soon your fascists will turn on Jews.'

Conti brushed some fluff from his sleeve. 'Your fascists are not in power and never will be, old boy, and besides, they are Nazis, not Fascists.'

'They are the same.'

'No they're not.' Conti pulled his lapel forward to show the silver eagle clutching a bundle of sticks. 'Fascism is being bound together for strength and order. Just as you bind sticks together, fasces, to get extra strength, the symbol of the old Roman Empire, so in Italy are we all bound together under a ruler who keeps order, order that permits progress. Your Nazis believe in blood and soil and the Volk, that you can only be a German if you are somehow Aryan. Which is rubbish.'

Bluum lowered his voice. 'You belong in Palestine.'

'Why would I go to Palestine?' Conti sighed and leaned back in his chair. 'There is no musical culture there.'

'We will build it.'

'What with? The Jews have no culture. We take it from the countries we are in. And often, I am proud to say, we add to it. You Zionists and Orthodox Jews have no culture. You have only laws and practices. A shtetl, Jewish village mentality, restless and vigorous and any state you create can only look forwards, never back.'

'We can do both.'

There was silence.

Ruth stood up. 'Come on, Phillip. We need to see about the set.'

Phillip stood up and followed Ruth out of the café.

'I've given my notice to the Frau Weiser,' Ruth said, as they reached the top of the lane that led down to their lodgings. 'When we've moved the set to the farm, I'll be staying there.'

Phillip held her gaze. 'Oh, so when are you moving out?'

'Day after tomorrow; Tuesday.' She leaned forward and kissed him. 'Come with me. I have my own cabin.'

Phillip took her in his arms and gazed into her eyes, pools of liquid ebony bathed in warm light. She was inviting him to move in with her. A thrill of anticipation coursed through him.

Ruth smiled and withdrew from his arms. 'I'll take that as a yes. OK, I must go and start making the arrangements for the move.'

Chapter 11

Early next morning Phillip slipped out of his lodgings and bought the *Volkischer Beobachter*.

Luckily the weather had turned mild and he didn't feel too cold without a coat. On the way back to his lodgings he flicked through the pages and saw his ad. Hopefully there would be a reply from SIS tomorrow.

He spent the morning at home and then headed for the university. The envelope with Max's terms was in his briefcase. He thought of hiding it under the washstand but suspected his landlady went into his room and poked around. He had once found his case, which he had pushed under the bed, the wrong way round. It was probably that she was just nosey, but he couldn't take the chance.

As he stepped into the faculty foyer the school-keeper stopped him. 'Doctor Schmelter asked if you would call into her office.'

'Yes, of course,' Phillip said.

On his way up the stairs he met Michael and Alex.

'Aha, Phillip,' Michael said. 'Just the man we've been looking for.'

'To take you on your initiation ceremony,' Alex said.

'That's if you are free?' Michael said.

Phillip hesitated. He didn't want to expose himself to being stopped by the police and asked for his papers, but that was less likely if he was out with fellow students drinking, which would fit his cover. 'Well, yes. OK.'

'Great,' Alex said. 'See you after classes. Say four thirty in the foyer?'

'Fine,' Phillip said.

He stepped into Doctor Schmelter's office and was struck by the sharp sunlight that poured into the room from the two large windows. The light bounced off the white walls, beige carpet and pine desk, creating the sterile brightness of a hospital, reinforced by the posters depicting the human body. Phillip felt his stomach turn.

'Thank you for coming, Phillip,' Doctor Schmelter said, indicating a chair in front of her desk.

Phillip sat down,

'I'm pleased to see you are reading the right newspaper,' Doctor Schmelter said.

He realised the *Volkischer Beobachter* was sticking out of his jacket pocket. 'Oh, yes. It helps with my German.'

'And other things, I'm sure. You are clearly in tune with our views. You must get tomorrow's edition. It has an article about our work, which you will find most interesting and will put into context what we are aiming to achieve.'

Phillip nodded. He would need to hide the fact that he bought the *Volkischer Beobachter* from Ruth since it was clearly the mouthpiece of the Nazi party, its features and editorials zealously promoting the party's racist ideology and violent methods for achieving power. He wondered if SIS had chosen the paper knowing its political views or just because the ads were free. Or both.

'Would you like some coffee?' Krystal said.

'Actually, I've just …'

'It's real coffee. Brought from America. You must try it.'

As Krystal busied herself with the percolator, Phillip examined the posters. They displayed the human body from different angles and stated the lengths of limbs and distances between body parts. There were also images of heads of all different sizes and shapes, along with annotations and clarifications.

Skulls gleamed in a glass case marked Deutsch-Südwestafrika, German South West Africa. He thought of what he had read in the file Krystal had given him and felt repulsed. Where had the skulls come from? Dug up from graves? Or worse?

Krystal placed a cup of coffee in front of Phillip. 'The human skull is the key,' she said. 'The ones you are looking at are from the Namibia tribe, and we also have skulls from Rehoboth Basters, children of white settlers who had sex with natives. Rehoboth Basters are the most disgusting animal in the world. We even have them here in Germany. The French have African negroes in their army and deliberately placed them in the Ruhr, which they occupied up until this year, and some German women have gone with the French negroes and produced Rhineland Bastards who actually claim they are German. But we have plans for them. The Americans have shown the way.'

A sense of danger grew inside him.

Krystal sat down. 'How's the coffee?'

'Oh, good, thank you.'

Krystal nodded at the skulls in the glass case. 'Craniometry is my area of research. We need to know the inherent characteristic of the true Aryan. Again, the Americans are ahead of us, and so are the British; your Thomas Huxley has done some ground-breaking work, work that is vital for the future of the Aryan race and the civilised world.' Krystal smiled and sipped her coffee. She leaned forwards, holding his gaze. 'What I would like to do is measure you, all of you. Especially detailed measurements of your head.'

Phillip didn't know what to say. He wanted nothing to do with her programme, but he couldn't upset her. If he did spurn her and she turned against him and then found out he didn't have the right papers, she would have him thrown out the university and no doubt tell the police.

Krystal leaned back. 'My special interest is on finding scientific and biological facts to determine who is Aryan and, even more important, to identify those who look Aryan, but are not, such as the Jews.'

It chilled him to think that he and his father, and Ruth, who he felt sure was Jewish, were seen as some kind of enemy who had to be eliminated.

Krystal clasped her cup with both hands. 'We need to cleanse our population, like the Americans. Three years ago, the US Supreme Court voted to allow states to sterilise the unfit.' She pointed to a framed script: *'If it's good for the community's physical health to be vaccinated against diseases, then it must be good to cut the fallopian tube for the nation's social health.'* US Supreme Court Ruling 1927.

'So, Phillip, I just wanted to check you got the file and to see how the translation is going?'

'Ah, well. I've had a quick look.' He took a quick sip of coffee. 'I can see how important a correct translation needs to be. There were some of Wolfgang's notes in the file and I'm afraid … I think I will have to start from the very beginning.'

'Oh, dear. I thought that might be the case.' She sipped her coffee. 'Professor Rodin has just returned from the First International Congress of Mental Hygiene in Washington with promises of money from the main American funders of eugenics who are keen to establish a Race Hygiene Centre in Munich. Professor Rodin will be the director of the centre and wants me to join him. But we need more funds, that's why the translations are so important.' She stood up. 'Well, I'm sure you will do your best.'

Phillip realised he was being dismissed and put his cup on the tray and hurried out.

Just before five he joined Michael and Alex in the foyer.

They headed north out of Bayreuth and Phillip soon found himself in a wooded area that looked more like a park than a forest, with mature oaks and sycamores standing in their own space surrounded with swards of grass, and tall fir trees as bare as telephone poles except for their tops, which were alive with chirping sparrows.

'I like your case,' Alex said. 'My family make leather goods.' He felt Phillip's case. 'Nice leather and hand stitched.'

He looked at the engraved initials on the case. 'PK? So it's not yours.'

'Er … no. My uncle's. Phillip Kemp. I was named after him and so I was given it when he died.'

'Well, it's nice to see something handmade coming from England.'

They walked along the path.

'Why does Wolfgang Drexler hate you so much,' Alex said, looking at Phillip.

Wolfgang Drexler, the student who Doctor Schmelter had snubbed in favour of him. Was he related to Major Drexler of the German Secret Service? Phillip's stomach churned.

'Wolfgang hates everyone who isn't a Nazi,' Michael said. 'But he's upset with you Phillip because his goddess cast him aside in favour of you. Drexler's in our English class and was bragging that he and Doctor Schmelter were friends and she had given him important papers to translate from English to German, but then you arrived and she dropped him.'

'I'm not surprised,' Alex said. 'Drexler is thick. He's useless at English.'

Phillip felt deep unease. If he was related to Major Drexler and he hated him …

'Wolfgang worships Doctor Schmelter as an Aryan goddess,' Michael said.

'Well,' Alex said, 'I wouldn't mind being Dionysius and coming across her in the woods. I'd ravage that Aryan goddess anytime.' He ran down a grassy slope and stood in front of a massive oak tree, its limbs like a giant pyramid of the natural world. Alex hugged the trunk and then turned and spread himself against the tree. 'I am the tree, the tree is me and we have both been born and nurtured in the same soil. I can feel it.'

'Now you sound like a Nazi,' Michael said.

'Rubbish. I voted for the Centre Party. They are the only ones who support the German Volk against bloody Manchesterisation. No offence Phillip.'

'What's Manchesterisation,' Phillip said.

'Making everything with machines,' Alex said. 'Like they do in Manchester and other industrial cities. There can't be any cabinet makers left in England with all the furniture parts being churned out by machines and then put together in mindless repetition by the workers.'

'Now you sound like a Communist,' Michael said. 'The Marxist Theory of Alienation.'

'Well it's true.' He leaned against the tree and posed.

Michael laughed. 'Now you look like Hitler. All you need is the lederhosen.'

Phillip smiled. He remembered seeing a photo in *The Daily Telegraph* showing Hitler in the Black Forest posing in lederhosen, while lounging against a tree. Everybody in the shipping office had poked fun at it, saying Hitler looked homosexual in his leather shorts and knee-high, white socks.

'Come on,' Michael said. 'We have a long way to go.'

As they ambled along the path, Phillip reflected that while mechanisation had come late to Germany, it had expanded rapidly and now Germany was one of the leading industrial nations. An accountant in the shipping office had predicted that if Germany kept up its rate of industrial expansion, it would soon lead Europe and be second in the world, just behind America.

After another couple of hours walking, the gloom started to collect amongst the trees.

'Ah,' Michael said. 'Twilight of the Gods; time to pay homage.'

'And bring forth beauty,' Alex said.

They turned left along a wide path and minutes later were on the southern outskirts of Bayreuth.

'Valhalla,' Alex said, gesturing towards a hostelry that looked medieval with a sign that said Oak Tree Inn. Next to the door was a stone drinking trough with metal rings for tethering horses.

A blazing log fire greeted them as they stepped into the dark interior of the pub. Long benches with wooden forms stretched the length of the room, and the air smelled of stale hops and strong tobacco. In one corner, a group of young people were seated round a table talking earnestly.

Michael went to the bar and ordered three beers.

Phillip watched the bartender fill the mugs, scrape off the foam, top up the beer, and then repeat the procedure till he had three glasses with a small head of foam crowning each. Phillip had always thought the process pretentious and a waste of beer, but perhaps they used the dregs for other things.

Michael handed Phillip a mug, picked up the other two and they crossed to the table where Alex was seated.

'Cheers,' Alex said, and they all clinked glasses. He then downed half his mug in one draft. 'Elixir of the Gods,' he said, banging his mug on the table.

'Ah, here he comes,' Michael said, as a young man left the group in the corner and came over to them. 'Uncle Joe's messenger boy.'

The young man, who looked to be about the same age as Alex and Michael, pulled up a chair and sat down at their table.

'This is Joachim,' Michael said, 'local secretary of the Young Communist League and this is Phillip, a student from England studying our poets.'

Joachim stuck out his hand and Phillip shook it.

'You're taking a chance having a meeting here,' Michael said. 'The Nazis are all over Bayreuth.'

Phillip felt uneasy.

'Been getting a lecture about the Volk?' Joachim said, turning to Phillip. 'Walking in the woods and hearing about the airy-fairy world of ideas, and how the German Geist from the spirit world will show us the way.'

'Don't listen to him, Phillip,' Alex said. 'He's a bloody Marxist. He doesn't understand Germany, he thinks it's all … dia … something materialism.'

Joachim laughed. 'Dialectical materialism.' He turned to Phillip. 'Karl Marx studied under Hagel, but like all great students, Marx turned his master's ideas on their head. Instead of the dialectic of change being the spirit of history, it is here in the material world of manufacturing and hired labour. Hence, dialectical materialism.'

'Good god,' Alex said. 'I've actually understood what dialectical materialism means.'

'I'll drink to that,' Michael said, and they both drained their mugs.

Alex picked up their empty mugs. 'Drink up, Phillip, we need to replenish the amber nectar that brings forth beauty. And then we have a ceremony to perform.' He nodded at Joachim. 'If you don't mind.'

Joachim shook his head and then stood up. 'Phillip, you must come to one of our meetings. Our movement is much more developed here in Germany than in England, and you could learn a lot.' He nodded to Michael and went back to the table where his friends were.

Alex returned with three foaming mugs which he placed on the table. 'Now,' said Michael, as Alex sat down, 'it is my sacred duty to present you with this insignia and welcome you into our most illustrious society.' He handed Phillip a woven badge with the beer mug and walking stick embroidered on it.

'Thank you very much,' Phillip said. 'I am most honoured to ...'

The doors of the tavern banged open and Brownshirts with swastika armbands, burst into the pub. A man standing at the bar hurled his beer mug across the room towards the Young Communist League, and the Brownshirts charged at them and started punching and beating them.

A Brownshirt picked up a smashed mug and slashed it across the face of one of the young communists. Blood sprayed like crimson mist over the heaving bodies locked in combat. Phillip felt sick with fear.

Michael grabbed him and they ran out the door.

'Best to split up,' Michael said. 'In case they think we are part of the Young Communists. Alex has escaped out the back.'

Phillip tried not to walk too fast as he hurried back to his lodgings.

Phillip lay on the bed as dusk thickened into night. His mouth still dry from fear, he rose and filled the kettle. As the blue gas jets spurted into life, panic shot through him – he'd left his briefcase in the pub. It had papers that could identify him, and Max Schneider's terms for the document.

Phillip stood at the top of the road and looked at the inn. The coach lamp above the tavern door spilled a pool of light onto the cobles and all looked normal. But what if the police were inside taking statements? What if the pub owners point him out as being there when the fight took place? A man came out of the inn and strolled up the road. He passed Phillip without looking at him.

Phillip sauntered down the road and passed the inn on the opposite side of the street. As he went by, he tried to look through the pub's windows, but saw only the reflected street. He turned back and stood across the road, opposite the inn. A man approached the pub and as he pulled the door open, Phillip peeked inside. There were no police.

Phillip stepped into the pub. Several people were sitting at tables speaking animatedly and laughing, some with swastika armbands. He expected everybody to stop talking, but they acted as if they hadn't noticed him. The table he had sat at with Alex and Michael was unoccupied. He searched around it and underneath it, but there was no briefcase.

He went up to the bar and asked if a briefcase had been left by mistake. The barman went up to a woman at the end of the bar who sat smoking.

The barman strolled back to Phillip. 'Sorry. No briefcase has been handed in.'

Chapter 12

The knock came again.

Phillip opened his eyes. It was ten o'clock in the morning. He must have dropped off. He'd been awake all night thinking about his briefcase. The knock came again, more loudly. Who was it? Major

Drexler with the German Secret Service? They had his briefcase and were here to arrest him.

He leaped out of bed and ran to the window. He was fully dressed except for his shoes. The knock came again and he heard Ruth's voice whispering his name.

Ruth ran her eyes over his crumpled clothes. 'Frau Weiser is downstairs. She wants to see you. Remember, I'm moving out today. To the farm.' She gave him a meaningful look.

'Oh, yeah. Of course.' Were the police with Frau Weiser? Waiting for him downstairs. He put on his shoes and followed Ruth out the door. She went into her room and he approached the top of the stairs. There were no voices from downstairs.

He stepped slowly down the stairs, his heart racing. What if the police were in her room, waiting for Frau Weiser to identify him, point him out? Should he bolt out the front door and hide till SIS could smuggle him home? As he reached the bottom step, Frau Weiser emerged from her front room. Phillip steadied himself. 'You wanted to see me.'

Frau Weiser studied him. 'Someone brought a briefcase here. They said it was yours.'

Phillip stared at her.

Frau Weiser glared at him. 'What initials are on the case?'

'Initials?'

'Yes. The case has initials on it, but they are not yours.'

'Oh, yes. Yes. PK. My uncle. Phillip Kemp. I got it from him. I'm a student I can't afford my own.'

Frau Weiser turned, went into her room and came out with Phillip's briefcase.

Phillip grabbed it. 'Thank you. Thank you. Oh, it has my dissertation in it. It took me a lot of work.' He rushed back up the stairs. As he stepped into his room he tried the catches on the case. They were still locked. He released the catches and dumped everything on the bed. It was all there; his papers and the envelope with Max's terms. He welled up and had to stop himself from crying. There was a knock on the door. Had Frau Weiser given him the case and then told the waiting police? He scrambled everything back into the briefcase and threw it under the bed.

The knock was repeated and he heard Ruth's voice. 'It's OK, she's gone out.'

Ruth smiled at him and put her arms round him. 'Don't look so worried. You really are in a state. Anything wrong? Can I help?'

'No. No. I've … just been up all night completing the first part of my dissertation.'

Ruth smiled at him. 'I told you, there's someone at the artist's colony at the farm who can help you. You mustn't worry.'

He burst out with a nervous laugh and then grabbed her and held her close. He needed to get the *Volkischer Beobachter* and see if there was a message from SIS and then … he had no idea what would happen after he handed over Max's terms. 'Of course I'll help you move the sets, but I've a few things to do first.'

'That's OK,' Ruth said, and kissed him on the lips. 'I'll meet you here this afternoon at four o'clock. That's what time the transport will be here.'

The message from SIS said to meet today in the town library at one o'clock and have a copy of Holderlin's poems in front of him. Smythe must have told the operatives that he had studied Holderlin on his last stay in Germany. It was ten o'clock and he thought of having breakfast but didn't feel hungry.

Along with the envelope with Max Schneider's terms, his case held his academic papers and so he might as well go straight to the library and work on them, just in case there was a delay in getting him back to England and he had to continue the role of student. Doctor Schmelter's file was in his room; he couldn't bear to have it on him.

Now that the weather had turned cold, he wondered if he looked odd without a coat. Clothes were expensive in Germany, as with most other things, but if he was going back to England soon he could buy a new coat there.

The reading room of the library had a classical atmosphere; its ceiling adorned with sages dispensing knowledge; its walls covered with shelves of leather-bound books; its windows fashioned with stained glass panels; its floor laid with multi-coloured marble, on which stood mahogany desks with orange lamps shaped like flames.

Just inside the library entrance was a wooden counter behind which sat a woman with flame-red hair going through a box of index cards. He strode quietly up to the counter. The red-haired woman stood up. 'Yes? May I help you?'

'Yes, please. I would like the *Collected Poems of Holderlin*, please.'

'Complete this form.'

Phillip took the form and wrote his request.

'I will bring it to your desk.'

'Thank you.'

He chose a desk in the corner so he could see the whole of the room, and then spread out his notes and the newspaper so no one would sit near him. The front page of the *Volkischer Beobachter* had the article Doctor Schmelter had told him to read. It reported a visit from America of a delegation led by Charles Davenport, who was here to foster and support Germany's expanding Eugenics Programme.

There was a photo of a group outside The Kaiser Wilhelm Institute of Anthropology, Human Hereditary, and Eugenics in Berlin. The Berlin institute was the centre of the Germany's eugenics programme and was being supported by American funding, including the Rockefeller Foundation.

The leading American eugenicist, Charles Davenport, was standing in the middle of the group, which included Harry Laughlin, superintendent of the Eugenics Records Office in New York; Henry Goddard, the renowned psychologist; Madison Grant, the internationally famous conservationist; on the end of the group was Doctor Schmelter, and next to her, Eugen Fischer, the director of the Kaiser Wilhelm Institute.

The article thanked America for its support in building a eugenics programme here in Germany, and said they especially appreciated, in these bad economic times, the funds from the Rockefeller Foundation, which enabled the building and running of The Kaiser Wilhelm Institute, the cornerstone of Germany's race-hygiene project.

Next to the photo was a quote by Adolph Hitler from his book *Mein Kampf*: *'There is today one state in which at least weak beginnings toward a better conception are noticeable. Of course, it is not our model German Republic, but the American Union, in which an effort is made to consult reason at least partially. By refusing immigration on principle to elements in poor health, by simply excluding certain races from naturalization, it professes in slow beginnings a view which is peculiar to the folkish state concept.'*

This was followed by a new quote from him: *'Now that we know the laws of heredity, it is possible to a large extent to prevent unhealthy and severely handicapped beings from coming into the world. I have studied with interest the laws of several American states concerning prevention of reproduction by people whose progeny would, in all probability, be of no value or be injurious to the racial stock.'*

Phillip folded the newspaper and threw it to one side. How could this be happening? He just couldn't get it straight in his mind. He had always been aware of racism, but this was in another league. Were they serious? What if the Nazis did come to power at the next election? Smythe had said the secret document that Max Schneider had was about stopping the Communists. But what about the Nazis?

The library clock said there was still thirty minutes before the SIS agent was due.

He opened the book of poems by Stefan George and turned to the one he had to study, *The Poet in Turbulent Times*.

Who will break the chains sweep order

Onto fields of rubble – flog home those gone astray ...

A book was placed beside him. It was *Holderlin's Collected Poems*. He looked up and smiled. 'Thank you.' He watched the red-head walking back to her place, noticing her slim figure and pert bottom, and realised he had no desire for her. Ruth was the one.

He finished reading George's poem and tried to envisage Stefan George at the head of a parade of poets marching through the streets behind a banner. They were hardly Brownshirts. And what if the Communist paramilitaries attacked them? Maybe the army officers, like Christoph and his friends, would help, but that would be anarchy. Was *The true symbol onto the people's banner* really the swastika, as Professor Muller thought? And if so, what did that say about the poem?

There was a cough and Phillip looked up into grey eyes with pinpoint pupils. The man sat down opposite Phillip. He wore a heavy brown coat, a trilby hat with the brim pulled down, a scarf that hid his mouth and thick, horn-rimmed glasses. The man turned the book of Holderlin's poems so he could read the title and then pushed an open cigarette case in front of Phillip.

Phillip looked inside at the inscription: 'To thine own self be true …'

Phillip had left his cigarette case at home. He picked up a piece of paper and wrote on it: 'Then as sure …' He slid it across the table to the man who read it and shook his head. 'Always keep your cigarette case with you,' the man whispered. 'Have you made contact with Max Schneider?'

Phillip nodded. He positioned the envelope from Max to his left and then gently nudged his books, pushing the envelope to where it was within the SIS agent's reach. The man picked up the envelope and, to Phillip's surprise, opened it. As well as the note, there were two photographs. The man read the note. 'Tell him yes.'

'What?'

'Tell Schneider we agree his terms.' He pushed the note back to Phillip. 'They will be ready for you to collect in a few days' time. Look for the ad in the paper. We will meet somewhere else, not here.'

'But I can't stay in Germany. I need my academic certificates from England in order to register with the university and get a police residency permit.'

'What?'

'I need my academic certificates to register with the university. But my certificates are in my real name, Kumar, so I can't use them.'

The man shook his head and clenched his lips. 'Idiots.'

There was a long silence.

'I can't stay,' Phillip said.

'You must. Think about it. You will be stopped at customs and without a residency permit they will detain you. And if you don't help us, we will deny all knowledge of you, which means you don't exist.' He leaned closer to Phillip. 'I'm sure I don't have to spell out what that means in a country like Germany.'

Phillip's stomach fell away. He was being forced to stay in Germany with no proper papers.

'Don't look so scared,' the agent said. 'You must have known what it would be like. This isn't a game. The stakes are sky high. Europe is in turmoil, and war is coming. Sooner or later we either fight the Germans who want their lands back or the Russians who want to dominate continental Europe.' He leaned back. 'You and me, my friend, are small fry and highly expendable.'

The agent held Phillip's gaze and smiled. 'Not like the movies, eh? There are no good and bad guys, only national interests.' He leaned forwards. 'OK. You need a new passport and papers. We can give you those, but only when you get the document. You now know who Schneider is, find him. Bayreuth is a small place. When you do, and you get the document, we will give you a new passport and a ticket home. And from what I hear, a job.'

Silence stood between them, like thick glass.

Phillip's stomach churned.

'You have good cover,' said the agent, 'a student. You fit in. Just don't get stopped by the police. Let me know when you've got the document.' He rose and then nodded. 'If anything changes, we'll let you know. Keep an eye on the ads in the paper.'

Phillip watched the man walk down the line of desks and out the door.

Phillip gathered up his papers. He was now in Germany illegally. What if the police picked him up? Would SIS help him or leave him to his fate?

He stood up. Should he look for Max straight away, or wait till *Evil Flowers* started at the Cockatoo Club? Whatever he did he had to lie low and avoid the police and the Nazi Brownshirts.

It was safer outside Bayreuth.

Phillip carried the last canvas up the steps from the crypt and handed it through the trapdoor to Ruth. He then climbed out and flipped the door shut, his fingers tingling with cold as gusts of snow eddied around the graveyard. Someone had placed yellow flowers on the solitary grave and tidied the grass around it.

He stood in front of the gravestone and read the inscription, the letters, strong and simple like an English newspaper headline, stated that Elizabeth Patterson lay beneath, her work done on this earth, and now in everlasting peace. Was death the only way to experience peace, to escape the anxiety he carried like a cancer? To never able to be who he really was; to say here I am, this is me, not the image people have of me and that I deserve my academic success.

He felt nervous as walked down the side of the church. What if the Nazis had discovered they were moving the *Parsifal* set, and were waiting for them? What if the police then came and asked for his papers? He forced himself to keep walking, and even when he came to the road and saw no one near the church, he still felt afraid.

A canvas-covered wagon stood in the road. The horse snorted and tossed his nosebag, trying to get the last of the grains as the driver sat hunched against the cold, with a blanket around him and a pipe, upside down, in his mouth. The back flap of the wagon opened and Ruth jumped down. 'I'll just lock the trapdoor from the inside and then we can be off. You get in.'

Phillip climbed up into the wagon. It was almost as cold inside as outside, but the canvas kept out the wind and hid him from sight. He was glad to be leaving Bayreuth, the images of the fight in the beer hall and the Brownshirts attacking the man in the street had never left his mind.

Ruth clambered into the wagon, pulled the flap down and shouted for the driver to go. There was a jolt and jangling of harnesses as the horse snorted and clumped forwards. Phillip peered through the gap in the flap and gazed at the two lines in the snow traced by the cartwheels, measuring the growing distance from Bayreuth.

Was he really going to a safer place?

Chapter 13

The wagon shuddered to a halt.

Ruth jerked open the flap. Phillip gazed out at the snow-covered fields, at the expanse of white-topped trees, at the grey hills that moulded the horizon and felt reassured by the remoteness.

Ruth clambered out and stood while Phillip handed her the canvases which she stacked against the side of the wagon. When all were unloaded, Phillip climbed down. A sudden gust scattered the canvases like large leaves, causing the horse to snort and stamp its hooves as Phillip and Ruth ran around gathering them up. Phillip then held the canvases while Ruth grabbed a rope from inside the wagon and tied the canvases together.

'Thank you,' Ruth shouted to the driver.

The driver didn't reply. He loosened the reins and flicked the horse forwards.

Ruth shrugged. 'He's not happy. It was his day off but Gunter said he had to help us. Not that he helped much. Still, I'll give him some money when I next see him.' She lifted one side of the bound canvases and Phillip held the other. 'Follow me.'

As they made their way towards a gate that had been wedged open, Phillip thought Gunter must be the owner of the farm and wondered what he was like. Could he be trusted not to talk about the Englishman who had arrived on his land? Did he still hold a grudge about the war?

Holding the canvases steady, they passed through the gate and followed the track towards a snow-covered barn. In the wood behind the barn, unsettled crows fluttered and circled above the trees, their calls echoing in the chill air as if proclaiming the arrival of a stranger.

They reached the barn. Ruth yanked a wooden peg from the lock and pulled open the door. Inside it was dark and the smell of rotting hay hung in the air along with another scent Phillip knew but couldn't identify. Ruth guided the way to the side wall. 'You don't have a lighter or matches, do you?'

'Sorry, no.'

'OK. Put them down. I'll be back in a minute.'

Light from the open door fell across the flagstone floor, and the barn's interior gradually emerged from the gloom, its whitewashed walls, its earthen floor and its roof of wooden beams with thin struts supporting the thatch. Phillip traced the scent he couldn't identify to the end of the barn, where a gluepot stood on top of a wood-burning stove – it was animal glue, the kind he had used in woodwork at school and when making frames for the art students at university. Nearby was a bench with a vice. A timber frame, without canvas, was propped against the wall, along with thin slats of wood.

The barn door scraped open and a pool of light floated in through the doorway as Ruth glided towards Phillip holding a hurricane lamp and carrying a gleaming oilcloth, reminding him of paintings by Caravaggio. Ruth set the lamp on the floor and Phillip helped her bind the oilcloth around the canvases. 'That will keep them safe till tomorrow,' Ruth said, and then picked up the lamp. 'Come on, let's get something to eat and drink.'

Ruth held the hurricane lamp like a traveller in a strange land as Phillip followed her into the black night. He had forgotten how dark it was in the countryside. She led him into a field with wooden cabins, their windows spilling welcoming light onto the snow like an Alpine village. In the middle of the huts blazed an open fire with a pot suspended above it. The man standing by the cauldron waved a long, wooden ladle and Ruth waved back. 'That's Gunter. He owns the farm and organises the artists' colony. He cooks an evening meal for anyone who wants to share it.'

Ruth guided him towards one of the cabins. 'Soon be in the warmth.' She thrust the door open.

'Sorry. Sorry,' Phillip said, spinning round to face away from Anna who was posing naked on a table covered in cushions.

Christoph was painting brushstrokes on a canvas perched on an easel. He smiled at Phillip. 'It's OK. Don't worry. In fact, Phillip, why don't you take your clothes off and I'll paint you. I've been looking for a blond-haired, blue-eyed Adonis.'

'Er, no. Sorry. No ... I ...'

Anna sat up. 'Don't be cruel to him. Anyway, that's enough for now. I'm hungry.' She rolled off the cushions and slipped into a woollen dressing gown.

Phillip remained facing the wall.

Christoph threw his palette on the table and plonked his brush in a jar of cloudy liquid. 'It's OK. She's decent. Have a drink.' He poured beer from a pitcher into an earthenware mug, froth foaming over the side. 'Here.' Phillip turned round and took the mug. Ruth then filled two mugs from the pitcher and gave one to Anna. Christoph raised his mug in front of Phillip. 'Welcome to camp freedom.' They chinked their mugs with each other and drank the toast.

'Now you've arrived,' Anna said, 'time for food.' She cleared the cushions from the table and laid wooden plates and spoons, while Ruth disentangled a large saucepan from a cupboard full of pots and pans. 'Come on, Phillip,' Ruth said. 'I'll introduce you.'

They crunched across the snow towards the fire. 'Christoph's cabin is rather small; that's why they use mine as a studio. Theirs is over there.' Ruth pointed towards three small cabins on the edge of the wood.

They reached the open fire, now a glowing bed of embers, and joined those gathered round the fire, their backs a wall of dark, their faces bright with fire-glow, talking and laughing as they handed bowls to Gunter who filled them with stew from the cauldron.

Phillip thought Gunter to be in his early thirties. He was tall and well built with a red scarf tied pirate style around his head and a gold earring in his left ear that flashed red from the fire. He wore a sheepskin coat tied with string to keep out the cold. He had a relaxed smile but his eyes danced around, absorbing every movement and gesture.

'This is Phillip,' Ruth said. 'He's a student from England. Here to study out poets.'

There was a murmur of welcome.

'Ah, and here is Lena,' Ruth said.

A small woman with a knitted coat stepped up to the fire. She had dark, sharp eyes that stared hard at Phillip. 'Lena, this is Phillip the student I was telling you about who is studying our poets. Phillip, Lena.' Lena nodded and Phillip smiled back. There was an awkward silence.

Ruth handed her metal pot to Gunter.

Gunter held up the ladle. 'Four?'

Ruth nodded. 'Please.'

Gunter nodded at Phillip. 'Aren't you cold in just a jacket.'

'Yes,' Ruth said. 'Where is your coat?'

'Oh, I lost it.'

'Lost it?'

'Well, I took it off. In the library, and it disappeared. Not to worry. I didn't like it anyway. I'll get another one.'

'I liked it,' Ruth said. 'You really stood out; made you look different.' She turned to Gunter. 'He had a lovely red duffle coat.'

'With a hood?' Lena said.

'Yes,' Ruth said. 'Like Little Red Riding Hood.'

They all laugh.

'Perhaps somebody found it,' Gunter said. 'We could put an ad in the papers for an English red duffle coat.'

'No. No,' Phillip said.

There was a long silence.

'You need a coat,' Lena said. 'Actually, I've got something that would fit you. Come over tomorrow and we'll talk about the poems and I can give you the coat. I have no use for it.'

'Thank you. But ...'

Lena waved her hand. 'You must have a coat and I have a really nice one that isn't being used. Ruth, make sure you bring him over first thing tomorrow.'

'Of course,' Ruth said. She gave Phillip a hug.

A man with a red handlebar moustache, smoking a pipe whose bowl was a carved head, turned to Phillip. 'If you are searching for the German soul, much better to study our music and painters.'

Gunter laughed. 'Like you. With your Expressionism, your dark shapes voicing the pain and angst of life. All you do is plant a flag on every wound felt by our people. Self-indulgent brooding.'

'Better my kind of painting than your distorted figures and mad landscapes where the grass is blue.'

'Kandinsky and the Bauhaus are the future,' Ruth said. 'You're stuck bemoaning the past.'

'Here.' Gunter handed the steaming saucepan to Ruth. 'Instead of the soul, you should be feeding the body.' He turned to Phillip. 'Have you ever had hare cooked in beer?'

'No. No I haven't, actually.'

'Then you're in for a treat. Now off you both go before the food gets cold.'

As they walked back, the lighted cabins cast an aura of peace, like a nestling village. Phillip felt less anxious. Maybe this was a place of safety.

A gust of warmth enveloped them as they entered the cabin. The doors of the stove had been opened and the logs blazed. Anna laid a large triangle of fresh bread beside each plate, while Ruth ladled the stew into wooden bowls.

Phillip took his first mouthful.

Christoph looked at him. 'Well?'

Phillip put his hand to his mouth and finished chewing. 'Delicious.'

Christoph tore a chunk of bread and dipped it in his bowl. 'You don't have to be polite. But this is the best we can offer since we Germans are so poor we have to hunt in the woods for food.'

'No. No, really. I mean it. It is delicious. Honestly.'

Anna tapped Christoph's hand with her spoon. 'Stop teasing him. You mustn't take any notice of Christoph. It's his upbringing.'

Christoph grunted. 'If only it were. More beer.' He jumped up, lifted a stone flagon from the floor and poured beer into all the mugs. He tilted the flagon and drank directly from it, then tipped it up to show it was empty. 'We must replenish our supplies.'

Anna and Ruth exchanged glances and they continued the meal in silence.

'Come on, Phillip,' Christoph said, as they finished their meal. 'We need more beer. I will show you a real Bavarian inn. Much better than your English pubs.'

Ruth kissed Phillip's cheek. 'See you later.'

As they stepped out into the dark, Phillip wasn't sure he wanted to go to a pub, especially after his last experience in one. 'Isn't it a bit late?'

'Late? Don't be silly. Come on.' Christoph put his arm round Phillip's shoulders and marched him across the field.

'That's our cabin, over there.' Christoph pointed towards a small cabin on the edge of the wood with a door painted bright red. 'Not only is our cabin small, but the bloody gypsies keep us awake when they are celebrating.'

'Gypsies?'

'Yeah, there's a group of them in the wood. Gunter lets them stay during the winter.'

Gunter waved to them as they passed the fire. 'So, how did you like my stew?'

'Oh, it was excellent,' Phillip said. 'Thank you very much.'

'Do come and see me some time. I would like to practise my English. We can talk about poetry.'

'Yes, I will. Good night.'

Christoph saluted Gunter. 'Good bloke, Gunter. He started it all after his father died and he inherited the farm with his brother. Gunter didn't want to farm. He wanted to paint and write poetry and create an artist's colony, but his brother was against it and so they split the farm in half. His brother hasn't spoken to him since.'

'Is this a commune?'

'Not exactly a commune because we don't share everything, but nobody pays rent, Gunter provides the evening meal so nobody starves and everyone can pursue their dream of being an artist. Most people here are painters, but we do have a few poets and writers.'

They reached the main road and began walking towards lights in the distance. Christoph stumbled in the dark and fell.

Phillip helped him to his feet. 'Perhaps you've had enough to drink for tonight.' Phillip was also feeling the effects of the alcohol, which seemed a lot stronger than English beer.

'Don't be ridiculous! You can never have too much.' He put his arm round Phillip. 'Thank you, comrade. We should never have gone to war, us Germans and you English. We are from the same roots and so we should stick together. Good thing you are studying Stefan George's poetry. You'll learn about the soul of Germany. England is becoming a race of mongrels. You mustn't lose Englishness. We mustn't lose Germanness. The French mustn't lose Frenchness.'

Christoph was slurring his words. They passed a ditch running along the side of the road, the ice on the surface a line of frozen moonlight. Christoph stopped, reached inside his pocket and took out a flask. He unscrewed the top and handed it to Phillip. Phillip took a sip. It burned his mouth but had a soft, peaty taste. 'What's this called?'

'Vodka. Better than your whisky. Have some more.'

Phillip took another sip and felt the liquid warm his insides. He handed the flask back to Christoph.

Christoph drank. 'Poetry will show the way. Poets will be the new leaders. That's why Stefan George is so important. As Heine said: "the poet's heart is the centre of the world". What we need is a new order, based on what it means to be German.' He waved his hand towards the open field. 'The soul of a nation is known through its blood. Blood is race, race is soul and soul is blood. Only then can all Germans unite and become whole again.' He raised the flask. 'Here's to the poet Fhurer, Stefan George.'

Phillip felt a jolt inside him as he listened to the words 'a nation is known through its blood. Blood is race, race is soul and soul is blood.' It was what was written in Doctor Schmelter's proposal for a Race Hygiene Centre.

Christoph drained the flask, and then threw it across the ditch into the field. He stared across the open ground at the encampment, an oasis of soft lights in the snowy landscape. 'Be careful, Phillip. Don't get drawn in. You are in danger. You must get away from here, while you still can.'

Christoph jumped over the ditch and ran into the field. He stripped his clothes off and danced naked, his arms stretched wide.

'Get away while you still can,' Christoph called, and then ran across the field towards the wood and disappeared.

Phillip stood peering into the night. What danger was in?

Chapter 14

Frost patterns adorned the bedroom window of Ruth's cabin.

Phillip could hear clanking from the main room which meant Ruth must be lighting the stove. He pulled the bed covers up to his eyes; he'd wait till the fire had warmed the front room. He'd promised to help Ruth with the Parsifal sets, which he could do this morning, but then he needed to go back to Bayreuth. Tonight, *Evil Flowers* opened at the Cockatoo Club.

By the time he'd returned to Ruth's cabin the previous evening, Christoph's vodka, on top of the beer, had wrapped him in a gentle haze of well-being, so that when Ruth led him into the bedroom and took his clothes off, it all seemed natural.

They had had sex twice in the night. At first, he'd held back when she explored his body, but Ruth gently assured him that anything consensual was permissible. The smell of rosemary and vinegar from her hair was still in the bed, invoking the image of her naked body floating above him, soft as a cloud, taking him into her. The warmth of the bed and the scent from her hair made him feel safe and secure, just as he had in India when his mother was alive and before he went to school.

But he wasn't safe. The police must be looking for the murderers of the tramp who'd been wearing his red coat. Also, the killers, no doubt communists, were after him because they knew he was involved in trying to get the document. What was the document? Why was it so important?

He should have told SIS what had happened at the church, but he just wanted to get home without too many questions being asked. But it hadn't worked and now he was forced to stay in Germany without the proper papers, and SIS had made it clear that he was expendable. Was it because he wasn't one hundred percent British? Half Indian. Was the British establishment as racist as America?

Ruth padded in, clasping a steaming mug of tea. 'Here you are sleepy head.'

Phillip sat up. 'Did Christoph come back last night?'

'Must have.' Ruth carefully handed Phillip the hot mug. 'If not, Anna would have sent out a search party. It's not the first time he's done it.'

Christoph's words of warning rang in his mind. What danger? What did he mean? Germany had changed so much since he was last here, with everyone taking sides and seeing those who didn't agree with them as the enemy. There was no middle ground.

Ruth did a little curtsy. 'What would sir like for breakfast? Gunter has brought some sliced bacon. He said bacon and eggs was a typical English breakfast.'

'Oh, thank you.' He loved bacon and eggs. How kind of Ruth and Gunter to go to the trouble of providing them for him.

Ruth kissed him and smiled. 'Lena has asked us to go over after breakfast.'

As they passed the wood on the way to Lena's cabin, Phillip heard music. In a clearing in the trees, he saw people sitting on chairs round a fire, while a woman danced to the vivacious strokes of a violin and the vibrant strumming of a guitar. Around them were wooden caravans and grazing horses. 'I think this is the first time I have seen a gypsy camp. Are there many in Germany?'

'Actually, they are not gypsies; they are Roma, an Indo-European tribe who migrated to Europe, like the rest of us. People only call them gypsies because when the Roma first came to Europe people thought they were from Egypt, and so they called them Gyptians and then Gypsies, which is derogatory.'

'Oh. Sorry. So I shouldn't call them gypsies?'

She hugged his arm. 'Hey, don't look so serious. Everybody makes that mistake.'

Ruth stopped at a cabin with a picket fence round a front garden, and a coach lamp next to the front door.

She knocked gently. Moments later the door opened and Lena beckoned them inside. Phillip now saw she was in her thirties, small and thin, with long bony fingers, a sharp nose and iron-grey hair tied back. She reminded Phillip of a bird of prey.

The interior surprised Phillip. It was riot of colour, with floral shaded lamps, a sofa and chairs draped in rich fabrics and a multi-coloured tablecloth.

'And this is Kharos,' Ruth said, 'her daughter.'

A young girl seated at the table turned and Phillip was shocked when he saw she had dark skin and tight, curly brown hair.

She looked to be eleven or twelve. It was the first person of colour he had seen in Germany. She held up a sheet of paper with a watercolour of the camp.

'Wow,' Ruth said. 'That's really good.' She turned to Phillip.

'Yes, yes it is,' Phillip said. 'I love the way you paint the trees; you can feel them moving in the wind. And your use of perspective is spot on.'

Ruth looked at him.

Phillip shrugged. 'I did Art History as part of my degree.'

'Would you like some tea or coffee and cake?' Lena said.

'No thank you, Lena. We've just had breakfast.'

'Well, take some with you. It's apple and blueberry.'

'That's why the farm is called Blue Ridge Farm,' Ruth said. 'There are hundreds of blueberry bushes running up the side of the hill. It looks glorious in late summer.'

'This is the coat,' Lena said, holding a pale fawn coat with a black sable collar. 'Come, try it on.'

Phillip put the coat on.

'Wow, you look good,' Ruth said. 'Very elegant and distinctive. People will think you are a Prussian gentleman with such a nice coat.'

'It's because you're tall,' Lena said. 'You can carry it off.'

'But I must pay you something for …'

'Nonsense,' Lena said. 'Just make sure you wear it all the time. Make use of it.'

'Kharos's father?' Phillip said, as they walked back to Ruth's cabin

'Dead. Killed by Nazi thugs. Beaten up and his body thrown in the river.'

'My god.'

'It happened three years ago in Hamburg. Lena fled south, hoping to protect Kharos. Lena is Bavarian, born in Munich. Her mother still lives in Munich but has rejected both Lena and Kharos because Lena married an African. Lena and Gunter were at university together so he invited her here. Gunter fancies himself not only as a painter, but also as a poet. But to be honest, he's a bit …'

Phillip smiled. He wondered what Ruth would make of his poems.

Ruth guided him towards the barn.

'I'll just pop home and change my coat,' Phillip said, knowing how easily animal glue stuck to clothes and he didn't want to damage such a nice coat. 'Do you have a smock or overall?'

'Sure.'

The sordid smell of animal glue greeted him as he entered the barn. The glue pot was bubbling on the stove while Ruth was trying to chisel a hole in a wooden slat clenched in the vice. When the mallet struck the chisel, the slat jerked downwards. Phillip eyed the finished frame, propped against the wall.

Ruth rested the mallet on the bench. 'Yes, the frame's not straight, but it took me three days to make, so it will have to do. The person who usually makes them has left.' Ruth sighed, and flung the chisel on the bench. 'I don't blame him; his father is a Nazi.'

'Why are they called Nazi?'

'It's an abbreviation for National Socialist, Nationalsozialisten. Na for national, then the zi for socialist. They don't like being called Nazis because in Bavarian dialect it sounds like 'country bumpkins'. Which is why we all use it.'

'Do you think Parsifal will be staged?'

'Of course. We're not going to let a bunch of Nazis stops us and, as you know, the police have promised to protect the theatre when *Parsifal* is on.' She sighed and jerked the slat upright. 'Somehow I've got to get this set finished. Anna said she will help with the painting, but …'

Phillip hugged her from behind. 'Don't worry. I'll make the frames.'

Ruth released herself. 'You know how to make frames?'

'Yes. I learned at school. And at college I earned extra money making canvases for the fine art students. But if these frames are to hold up on a stage, I'd suggest a haunched mortise and tenon joint with a full length brace.'

Ruth threw her arms round him and kissed him full on the lips.

Phillip untangled himself. 'Why don't you get on with painting those,' he said, nodding towards the canvases covered in the oilcloth, 'and I'll get on with the frames.'

The policeman on the other side of the road was watching the Cockatoo Club.

Phillip pulled the collar of his coat up around his face, the soft sable caressing his cheeks, and strode towards the club, his heart pounding. All the premises along Woolfstreet were dark, except for the Cockatoo Club whose illuminated bird above the entrance pulsated like a beacon. As he passed the club, Phillip saw a man in tails loitering in the foyer next to an A frame with a poster for *Evil Flowers*, 'Opening Night'.

His map of Bayreuth showed an alleyway ran along the back of Woolfstreet, and so Phillip turned down the next street and then left into a narrow passageway with cobbled stones. Dustbins and bags of rubbish were stacked at the back of the buildings, and only one building had lights inside. He strode carefully to the back of the building with lights and saw a red door with a sign, Cockatoo Club. Stage Door. Keep Clear. If the actors exited from here, he could wait till the show ended and then ask for Max as people came out.

Two o'clock in the morning the club went dark, except for a light in the window next to the back door.

A red bulb above the back door came on and two men emerged. As they reached the alleyway, Phillip stepped forwards and asked for Max Schneider. Both men turned their heads away and dashed down the alleyway. Perhaps he should ask for Antonio Martini, Max's stage name. Four more people emerged and Phillip asked for Antonio Martini, but they all pushed past him and hurried down the alley.

Five minutes later a man came out and put rubbish next to the bin. Phillip went up to him. 'Excuse me?'

The man jumped and spun round. He put his hand on his chest. 'My god, you frightened me.' The man was small and dumpy and seemed to be covered from head to foot in a black coat and a broad hat that shadowed his features.

'Sorry, but I'm looking for Max Schneider, Antonio Martini.'

The man was silent, the brim of his hat shielding his eyes. Then, without looking up, 'And who are you? If you are the police you must come in the front door and have a warrant.'

'No. No. I'm not the police. I just need to talk to Max.'

The man raised his head, his blue-black eyes gleaming. 'Max is still inside. On his own. I'll take you in.'

'Thank you. Thank you.'

As Phillip stepped into the club the man flicked off a light, leaving only a dull glow from what Phillip thought was the auditorium. It was hard to see, but they appeared to be in a dressing room that had mirrors surrounded by light bulbs, racks of costumes and shelves of hatboxes. It smelled of sweat and make-up.

The man slipped to one side, his back to Phillip. 'Go straight ahead to the auditorium. Through that green door.'

Phillip went through the door covered in green felt and for a moment he didn't recognise where he was. In the low light from a red bulb he made out the tables stacked with chairs and the bar, which looked much smaller than he remembered. The lights went out. He was in complete darkness. Panic rose inside him. 'Hello!' he said. There was no response. His arms were pulled behind him and tied, and then a cloth stuck over his head. A click, then hazy light seeped through the cloth covering his face.

Hands grabbed his shoulders and he was pushed down onto a seat. Someone unbuttoned his coat and searched his pockets. From his inside pocket, they took out the silver cigarette case, and then, as he heard it click open his heart beat faster and his mouth went dry. They then took out his passport. They moved away from him and he could hear whispered words. He caught the names Antonio and Max. He calculated that there were three of them.

Steps came up to him and something was thrust into his inside pocket. Then a deep voice said, 'You stay here for thirty minutes. Understood?'

Phillip could hardly speak. 'Yes.'

'And for your own good, stop looking for Max Schneider.'

His hands were released and then he heard receding footsteps. The lights went out and a door banged shut. Silence.

Phillip counted till he felt he'd reached thirty minutes, then took off the hood. It was a large piece of cloth. His eyes gradually discerned the outline of forms. He stood up and fumbled his way to the green door and into the dressing room. The back door was locked.

He felt round the window next to the back door and found the catch. The window shifted a couple of inches, then stopped. An iron peg prevented it being fully opened. His heart pounded. Why had they locked all the doors? Was he trapped till morning?

He fumbled his way back to the green door and into the auditorium. Gradually his eyes grew accustomed to the dark. Maybe he could get out the front door. He started opening the door to the lobby and then banged it shut. A figure was outside the club looking in through the glass doors. It was a policeman. Phillip legs wobbled and he nearly peed himself.

He stumbled back through the auditorium and into the dressing room. Standing on a chair, he pressed his hand on the window frame, and then pushed with all his might. The window frame splintered open and he climbed out.

The alleyway was deserted. Half walking, half running he made it to the main road and then turned left, opposite to the way he had come.

The front door to his lodgings would be bolted, but Ruth had told him where she hid a key to the back door. Phillip slipped through the side gate, and avoiding the rubbish bins, felt his way round to the back garden. He found the birdbath, and then took the key from beneath it.

In his room he lay on the bed, his throat dry and his heart pounding. The man who let him into the club had led him into a trap.

Why did they warn him off? 'For your own good, don't try to find Max Schneider.' How serious was the threat? It didn't matter. He had to chance it and go back to the Cockatoo Club; it was the only place he knew where Max Schneider would be. But next time he would go in the front entrance as a customer, identify who on the stage was Max Schneider, and, when the show was over, immediately go backstage.

The layout of the club was straightforward, and he knew how to get from the auditorium to the dressing room. They could talk in the backyard.

They surely wouldn't call the police.

Chapter 15

Ten thirty next morning, Phillip settled himself in the university library and got out George's book of poems.

He needed to fill the hours before going back to the Cockatoo Club that evening. What if the police raided the club while he was there? Was the policeman last night inspecting the club before they raided it? He planned to stand at the bar with his coat on, and once he had identified Max, slip backstage and tell him SIS agreed his terms.

Schneider seemed perfectly reasonable in the church and should be pleased he was getting what he wanted, but those who locked him in the club last night had told him to stop looking for Max Schneider. Who were they?

Michael and Alex were sitting on the other side of the room with Wolfgang. They must all be in the same English class. Michael and Alex gave him a wave, but Wolfgang pretended not to have seen him, no doubt still angry he lost the job of translating the eugenics' papers. Phillip felt his stomach turn when he thought of the skulls in the glass case in Doctor Schmelter's room. He would try to avoid her, but if she pressed him, he would have to make a start translating the proposal for the Race Hygiene Centre.

He had no intention of completing the translations and was thinking about how he could destroy the folder. But that would have to be after he completed his mission.

He opened George's *Secret Germany*, the light from the window highlighting the black text. Again, the idea of Stefan George on the streets with a banner made him smile, but plenty of educated people throughout Europe revered George and saw him as an oracle, destined to lead Germany into a new era. The conductor Conti thought Mussolini was doing a good job in Italy. But was '*The true symbol onto the people's banner*' really the swastika as Professor Muller thought? George didn't appear a typical Nazi.

'Glad to see you are studying the Fhurer.'

Phillip looked up and met twinkling eyes, a handsome face, strong nose, full lips, and brown hair parted on the left side. The man was dressed in a bow tie and wore a double-breasted suit, with the jacket undone and no waistcoat. He sat down opposite Phillip, leaned back and crossed his legs, giving the air of someone at complete ease with himself and the world. 'I saw you at Madam Bernstein's party. You were with Christoph and his muse.' He leaned over and shook Phillip's hand. 'Professor Ernst Kantorowicz.' He smiled. 'I see it means nothing to you. I'm here to give a lecture. I have an academic chair at Frankfurt University.'

'Oh … I'm very new here. I'm studying …'

'T.S. Eliot and Stefan George, the master.' Kantorowicz rocked gently on his chair. 'The academic world of the arts is very small, and you are something of a talking point in our circle.'

Phillip stared at him.

Kantorowicz gave an easy laugh. 'Don't worry. All good. In fact, I read your poems. A colleague at Tübingen University sent me a copy. Like I said, small world.'

Phillip lowered his head.

Kantorowicz laughed. 'Don't look so embarrassed. Your poems are good. OK, highly derivate of Holderlin and Keats, but that's how all the good poets start, borrowing from the masters they admire.' He leaned forwards and patted Phillip's arm. 'I'm pleased I ran into you. There is a gathering of the George Circle, of which you are now an honorary member, in a couple of days' time. Christoph was meant to bring you but he seems to have disappeared, probably at the artist's colony in Blue Ridge Farm, painting abstract images of his muse, Anna. He should take himself off to Dessau and join the Bauhause, where people like Kandinsky are exploring abstract art.'

Phillip didn't understand abstract art. He found it unsettling the way it paid no heed to the logic of perspective, and used colour, form and shape to invoke feeling in the viewer, rather than depicting the normal world. And Christoph's paintings of Anna were really strange. He separated her image into different parts and then reassembled them in the wrong places. Ruth said it was Cubism.

Kantorowicz took out a card, wrote on the back and handed it to Phillip. 'This is where the reading will take place.' It was at Madam Bernstein's, the same place he had first met George. If it were just the George Circle, he couldn't imagine Drexler, the German Secret Service officer, being there. Then again, perhaps he shouldn't expose himself unnecessarily.

'Do come to the gathering. It will help you with your dissertation. I don't know how Professor Muller can judge your work since he doesn't really believe in George, and is much more devoted to the Nazis and their notions of a political strongman leading the country out of this mess that is this republic. Also, the Nazis have adopted your Holderlin for inspiration, the poet who is supposed to be the most German of Germans'. He shook his head. 'OK, Holderlin is good, but the Nazis have only adopted him because the Holderlin Society support the National Socialists.'

So it was true. The Holderlin Society was supporting the Nazis. How could they? It was a perversion of all that Holderlin stood for.

'You should move to Heidelberg,' Kantorowicz said, 'where the arts are really explored.'

'Well, I'm signed up to this, and so …'

'Indeed, indeed. So, have you grasped *Das Geheime Deutschland, Secret Germany?*'

'Well …'

'That's the key to understanding the master, Stefan George. Secret Germany exists not in the physical world, but in the metaphysical sphere – in a union of past poets and sages, the heroes and the saints, the sacrificers and the martyrs, who brought Germany into being. They devoted themselves to Ideal Germany, just as George is doing. This secret union may seem alien in the world we live in, but it still exists in the metaphysical world, the true world, and it alone forms the true Germany.'

Kantorowicz's eyes were shining. Phillip wasn't sure what Kantorowicz was saying. 'Like heaven?'

Kantorowicz laughed deeply. Heads turned.

Kantorowicz sat upright in his chair. 'Sorry. That was rude of me. But on reflection, there is something in what you say. I published a book last year, *Kaiser Friedrich der Zweite*. It might help if you read it. In the twelfth and thirteen century, Frederick the Great created Germany and the Holy Roman Empire. His empire, or reich as we would say, brought forth the German Spirit and gave it the means to express itself and realise its divine mission to lead the world. That divine mission has been there ever since, made flesh by saints such as Beethoven, Goethe and even your Shakespeare. True Germanness can often be expressed by uber-Germans.'

Kantorowicz stopped and gazed out the window, as if seeking inspiration. 'There is a living spirit that gathers to itself the vital forces of a nation's past. They are the great men, poets, kings, sages – Plato, Caesar, Frederick The Great, King Arthur, Dante, Shakespeare, Goethe, Nietzsche and now George, all filled with a spark of the divine spirit, which turned them into demi-gods, so they act as mediators between the Volk, the people, and the Secret World of the nation's spirit. George is now that Poet Fhurer, the leader, the guide, of this spiritual movement, and we must be ready for when the time comes to impose Germany's Secret World onto politics, so it can guide the nation to its true destiny.'

Kantorowicz sat in silence, gazing out at the bright sky. He stood up and shook himself. 'Don't forget. Madam Bernstein's for the George reading.' He bowed and left.

Students watched Kantorowicz leave, clearly in awe of him, and then looked at Phillip. Phillip gazed down at the pages of his book with a feeling of superiority. Perhaps he should go to George's reading, since mixing with the George Circle gave him extra cover as a student of poetry, and possibly the protection of mixing with the elite.

'So,' Alex said, as he and Michael and Wolfgang occupied the table next to him, 'we are becoming the toast of Bayreuth.'

'And he's only been here five minutes,' Wolfgang said.

Michael shook his head.

'OK. Spill,' Alex said. 'Did I hear you being invited to a George reading?'

Phillip shrugged. 'Seems so.'

'My god,' Michael said. 'The inner sanctum.'

'I wouldn't go,' Wolfgang said. 'Kantorowicz is a bloody Jew, just like half of George's circle. When we come to power, they will not be allowed into our universities or anywhere else.'

'In that case we will all be the poorer,' Michel said.

Alex nudged Wolfgang. 'You're just jealous you haven't been invited to a George gathering.'

'Holderlin is the true German poet,' Wolfgang said. 'He was a Romantic who fostered the unity of the Volk as one soul.'

'Actually,' Phillip said, 'as I understand it, Romanticism is all about the freedom of the individual to find the soul of the universe through nature and the imagination.'

'Too soft,' said Wolfgang. 'Our National Socialist Romanticism is a new type. The Volk, the true German people, is understood not only from an historical framework, but equally it has a foundation in science and biology.'

'God,' Michael said, 'you sound like a stuck record for Goebbels.' He went into his case and took out a newspaper. 'Goebbels said Nazi Romanticism is Steel Romanticism, harder and crueller than previous versions but just as Romantic. And I quote, 'it manifests itself in intoxicating actions and restless deeds in service of a great national goal'.'

'Exactly,' Wolfgang said. 'We must be ready to shed our blood in service of the Nazi Ideal. The New Germany.'

'Bollocks,' Michael said. 'We don't need blood shedding or more wars, we need democratic ideas so that we can all realise our full potential. Not your Nazi clap-trap of 'blood and soil'.'

Wolfgang clenched his fists.

Michael drew himself up. He was bigger than Wolfgang.

Wolfgang stood up and scrambled his papers together.

'Not so brave when you're not in a gang,' Michael said.

'Wait,' Wolfgang said. 'We will settle our scores.' He pushed the chair back and stomped out the library.

'Actually,' Phillip said. 'Byron went off to fight the Turks to try to free Greece and died from his wounds.'

'Wow,' Alex said. 'What a career move.'

'Who knows,' Michael said, turning to Alex, 'when you're out tree hugging and listening to your ancestors through the rising sap, a branch might fall on your head and kill you and you will be immortalised by the Volkish Community as a martyr now living in mythos land.'

Alex stared at him. He then sighed. 'I'm hungry. Let's have lunch.'

Phillip strode along Woolfstreet Street.

It was nearly nine o'clock. He calculated that *Evil Flowers* must have started by now. He reached the Cockatoo Club and saw all the lights were out.

'Closed till further notice,' said a voice. 'But I doubt if it will open again any time soon. The times are too dangerous.'

Phillip turned and faced a tall man dressed in a long black coat, white silk scarf and top hat. 'Where have they gone?'

'Who knows,' the man smiled. 'Back to their hidey-holes, but I know where you can get a drink. Or, back to my hotel if you wish for something more private.'

'No thank you,' Phillip said, and walked off.

Back home he lit the gas ring and made tea. What was he to do? Tell SIS he had failed and there was no way to trace Max Schneider. What then? Would they let him return to England? But they wouldn't give him the job in the Foreign Office. He poured the boiled water into the teapot. If Ruth were willing to come to England he would try to become a teacher or find some other job. He would need a new passport. Also, did Ruth have a passport? But would SIS let him leave Germany?

There was a knock on the door. His stomach tightened. It was nearly ten o'clock. Who would call on him at this hour?

Frau Weiser stood in the hall, scowling. She wore a woollen dressing gown pulled tightly around her, and a crocheted nightcap. 'There is a drunken man outside who wants to see you. He says he is Captain Christoph von Allenbach. If that is so, he is a disgrace to his family and his regiment.'

Phillip closed the door behind him and followed Frau Weiser down the stairs.

Frau Weiser opened the front door. 'You have your key?'

'Yes, thank you.'

'Bolt the door when you return.' She then slammed the door shut.

A figure in a long officer's coat was sitting in the snow beneath the streetlamp. The person turned as Phillip approached. It was Christoph, holding a bottle of Schnapps. Phillip didn't know what to say. He felt deeply embarrassed seeing him in such a state, like a common drunk on the street.

Christoph raised his head. 'What am I going to do?'

Phillip crouched beside him. The curtain moved in the house opposite. Phillip stood up. 'Shall we go for a walk?'

Christoph struggled to his feet. 'Why not.'

They came to the top of the alleyway and then headed towards Prince William Square. As they crossed the square, Christoph stumbled. Phillip's heart jumped when he saw a policeman walking towards them. As the policeman came up to them, he saluted Christoph and then carried on by. Phillip guided Christoph down a side street to the Red River. The officers from Christoph's regiment were billeted in a small, Baroque palace on the eastern outskirts of Bayreuth, and Phillip knew the river ran past it.

Christoph stopped and peered at the dark river. He stood motionless for several minutes and then said, 'I have been called back to Prussia. I have been given a promotion and will head a cavalry unit.'

'Congratulations.'

Christoph snorted. He shuffled round unsteadily and stared at Phillip. 'This damned republic. Mixing everything up. Destroying all the old ways, all the old certainties.' He took a swig of Schnapps and then turned and staggered along the riverbank. 'I don't know what to do. We are the class that united Germany and built it into the third largest economy in the world. We could take it even further, we are already overtaking Britain, but this bloody Republic is scattering the soul of the people, confusing them.'

They stopped next to a stone bridge. On the other side of the river Phillip could see the Baroque palace. A sentry box stood by the iron gates. An owl screeched in the night, and bells pealed across the fields from some unseen tower, marking the hour.

Christoph sighed and took a long drink of Schnapps. 'I love being at the farm, at the artist's colony. I'm told I have real talent. But what can I do? I must do my duty. I have sworn an oath with my fellow officers. Look.' He took a pouch from inside his jacket and handed it to Phillip. It had the Royal Crest of the Swabian Hohenzollern Dynasty on the cover. 'That's the family I belong to. Read it.'

Phillip opened the pouch and drew out a folded piece of parchment. He carefully opened the document and read: 'That we believe in the divine mission of Germany. That if we Germans can cultivate our true essence, a mixture of Hellenic and Christian traditions, then it is our mission to lead the community of the Western peoples to a more beautiful life. This new order would guarantee rights and justice. We also despise the lie of equality and bow before the ranks assigned by nature. We commit to join an inseparable community that through its attitudes and actions serves the New Order and forms the fighters the future leader will need.'

Christoph shook his head. 'You see. The ranks assigned by nature. The Hohenzollern's have ruled Germany, the Principalities, before unification, for over a thousand years. I can't go against my history and nature.' He took a swig of from the bottle. 'Anna is pregnant.'

Phillip didn't know what to say.

'I can't go back to Prussia with her,' Christoph said.

'Then stay here.'

'I can't. This Republic won't last and then a new leader will emerge. He will be born from Secret Germany. The George Circle. That's why George dedicated the book to Von Stauffenberg. We Germans only reach our full potential when we are united under one leader with a clear mission, as in the Empire, the First Reich. We now need a Third Reich.' He lifted the bottle to his lips, then withdrew it and turned it upside down. It was empty. He threw it into the river and started to walk across the bridge.

Christoph stopped and turned. 'You must get out of Germany while you still can. You are in real danger.' He turned and walked past the sentry who saluted, and into the courtyard of the house.

All the way home Phillip kept thinking about what Christoph had said. It was the second time Christoph had told him he was in danger. How did he know? Did he know what happened at the church when the tramp was killed while wearing his red coat? Christoph knew Drexler who was an agent in the German Army's Secret Service.

Had Christoph learned something about him from Drexler?

Chapter 16

The morning bus was at the terminus ready to go.

Phillip jumped on. He would get the *Volkischer Beobachter* newspaper when he got to the camp and see if SIS had sent a message. Perhaps when it got back to London what had happened with his certificates, Smythe would help. Smythe had appeared to like him. But what if he was overruled? That Phillip Kumar was just another expendable commodity that was not important enough. So much for his loyalty to king and country.

As he alighted from the bus an icy wind ruffled the fur collar of his coat. At first, he had had reservations about wearing the coat when he learned it had belonged to Lena's dead husband, but the change in the weather made him grateful to have it.

He trudged across the field to Ruth's cabin, the frost-glazed grass crunching beneath his steps, the compound like a Bruegel winter-scape with people silhouetted against the snow, while from the woods came the harsh croak of the crows, fluttering up and the resettling as if the branches were too cold for permanent resting.

Sobbing greeted him as he stepped into Ruth's cabin. Ruth was standing beside Anna who was sitting at the table with tears streaming down her face.

'Anna's pregnant,' Ruth said. 'But Christoph doesn't want the baby.'

Anna sobbed, then turned her tear-stained face to Phillip. 'Have you seen him?'

'No,' he lied. 'No, I haven't.'

'Please, if you see him tell him we must talk. Things can be fixed. I'll get rid of the baby. Please look for him and tell him.'

Phillip knew that getting rid of the baby meant an abortion. 'Well, I … I've been invited to a George gathering in a few days' time and if he's …'

'Yes, yes,' Anna said, standing up. 'He worships George and if Christoph's not there, some of his friends will be. You can tell them to contact Christoph and tell him we must meet, talk about things.'

'Well, yes. OK.'

'I'll go to Bayreuth now,' Anna said. 'I know where he sometimes goes with his army friends.'

As Anna left, Ruth came up to Phillip and slipped her arms round him. 'You really will look for Christoph?'

'Yes, of course.'

'It's just that Christoph is in a bit of an emotional state. He can't make up his mind what he really wants.' She released him. 'Now, have you eaten?'

'Well, actually I could do with …'

After breakfast they trudged through the snow to the barn. Phillip inspected the frames he had made and then undid the string tourniquets. The joints were solid and the frames square. He stacked them against the wall. Ruth examined the frames and then flung her arms round him and kissed him. 'My hero.'

Ruth picked up one of the frames, carried it to the other end of the barn and placed it against the wall next to a table with a roll of canvas.

There was a noise near the door. It was Kharos. 'Mummy said to come and see her any time to talk about the poetry and do you like the coat?'

'Oh, OK. Thanks,' Phillip said. 'Yes, tell Mummy the coat is great.'

'Do you need any help?' Kharos asked, looking at Ruth.

'Not really, thank you, Kharos. I have to cut this cloth.'

'Kharos,' Phillip said. 'That's a pretty name.'

'It is the name of a flower in my daddy's country.'

'Oh, that's nice. What country is that?'

'Namibia.'

Phillip wasn't sure where Namibia was and thought it must be near Egypt. He sawed the top of the slat. Wood dust cascaded to the floor and Kharos put out her hand and let the fine grain trickle through her fingers. 'Wood snow.'

Phillip laughed. 'You would make a good poet.'

'My daddy was a poet.'

Phillip avoided her eyes.

'Can I help you?' Kharos said.

'Well,' Phillip said. 'OK. Perhaps you could stir the glue. Here, I'll show you.'

Phillip took Kharos to the woodstove, where the glue pot bubbled and popped like a volcano. 'Now you must be careful not to burn yourself. Just stir it gently. Like this.'

'That's how I help Mummy make stews.'

'Exactly. The thing is the glue must be at the right temperature, not too hot and not too cold. Yes, that's it, you are stirring it just right. Clever girl.'

'You would make a good teacher,' Ruth said.

'I was thinking about it,' Phillip said, returning to the bench. 'But jobs are scarce. In fact, that's why I'm here studying German poets.' He thought he would reinforce his cover. 'I hope to teach German when I get back to England.'

'My cousin runs a school for young children in England,' Ruth said, coming across to Phillip's bench. 'I think she calls it a prep school and she needs someone fluent in German and or French. She asked me to go over and teach with her.'

Phillip stopped sawing. 'Why don't you go?' It was a way for Ruth to come to England and they could be together.

Ruth gazed at Phillip who blushed slightly, smiled and shrugged.

'Would you like me to?' Ruth said, holding his gaze.

'Yes, yes. Very much.'

Ruth turned and went back to the table. 'The problem is I don't have a passport. Perhaps you could stay here? You could ...'

The barn door creaked open and Gunter stood in the doorway. He stared at Ruth. 'There's someone who wants a word with you before he goes.'

'Bluum? Tell him I'm not here.'

Gunter spread his arms. 'He just wants to give you some Zionist leaflets and then he'll go. Do us all a favour and just take the leaflets and promise to read them. That's what I do.'

Ruth sighed and strode out the door.

Gunter winked at Phillip. 'How do you like my glue?'

'It's good. Very good.'

'I see Kharos is learning how to stir it.' He ruffled Kharos's hair. 'I make it myself, very easy.' He lit a cigarette, strolled over and inspected the wooden frames. 'Mmm. We have a craftsman in our midst. You, young Phillip, are going to be much in demand round here. There are never enough canvases for this lot of painters.' He patted Phillip on the shoulder. 'Don't worry about Ruth, she's not going anywhere. However, I will say our Mister Bluum is committed. He's not only after Ruth and Anna, he wants me and my brother to go to Palestine.'

'But you are far ...'

'Farmers. Yes, they need farmers in their new world. Some of the Jewish groups who went there starved to death because they didn't know how to grow food and didn't want to mix with the local Arab population.' He laughed. 'So, you're surprised a Jew is a farmer.'

'Well ... actually ...'

'You thought all Jews were money lenders or lawyers or doctors.' He winked. 'Like I say, don't worry, Ruth is not going anywhere. Like me, she thinks Judaism is just a religion, not a nationality. What are you?'

'Catholic.'

'Observant?'

'No.'

'Yeah, all religions are rubbish. I've seen enough bodies ripped open to know we are all the same inside – white men in our army, black men in the French army, brown men in the British army – all men without their skins look the same.'

'Who do you support?'

'In the elections?'

'Yes.'

'None of them. I hate ideologies. Ideas are like dangerous toys; too powerful for humans to cope with, too potent, they create illusions and make us irrational. In the last war our soldiers went off to war with a copy of Holderlin's poems and Hagel's philosophy, neither of which they understood. The next war, their knapsacks will hold a copy of Heidegger's *Being and Time* and George's *Secret Germany*. Again, they won't have a clue what they're about.' He shook his head. 'OK. I'll let you and Kharos get on with the good work. See you later for diner.'

Phillip remembered he needed to get the *Volkischer Beobachter* and see if there was a new message from SIS. Perhaps things had changed. 'Kharos, do you know where the village shop is?'

'Yes, it's over the other side of the fields.'

'Could you show me?'

'If you want me to.'

'Good girl.'

Phillip donned his coat and checked his pockets. He had his wallet and the codebook. The codebook needed to be hidden, but he hadn't found a safe place in Ruth's cabin. He would just have to be careful. 'OK. Let's go.'

Gunter was building the fire in the middle of the open ground, while nearby Bluum was talking to Ruth. It worried Phillip the way Ruth stood listening to Bluum. What if Bluum persuaded her to go to Palestine? He realised how deeply he felt about her. Kharos gripped Phillip's hand. 'This way.'

Kharos led him round the back of the cabins and along the side of the wood where the Roma were camped. Panic shot through him. A Roma man was kneeling on the ground in the snow while Doctor Krystal Schmelter, dressed in a white fur coat and sable hat and looking to be from another world, measured his head.

Phillip realised he was holding the hand of someone Krystal despised, a Rehoboth Baster. He tried to release his hand, but Kharos clung to it. Phillip pulled his coat collar up around his head and hurried past the woods.

As they trekked across a barren field Phillip felt shame rise within him. Why had he tried to release himself from Kharos's grip?

She was a lovely, sweet girl. How dare the likes of Muller and Schmelter and the American eugenicists see her as something to be eliminated? He had acted like a coward because, as always, he feared how others saw and judged him.

They reached the far end of the field, passed through a gate and joined a narrow road. They trudged along the road and arrived at a cluster of houses nestled in a dip. Just before the village, a sign for Saint Boniface's pointed up a stony path bristling with flint like a pilgrim's penance, to a commanding church set on high ground. Kharos led him past an inn called The Black Boar, then a flourmill and stopped outside what looked to Phillip like a grocers.

A bell tinkled as they stepped into the shop and multiple aromas greeted them. There were glass shelves full of sweets, marble slabs leaden with meats and wooden counters covered with cheeses. The man behind the counter smiled at Phillip. He was fat with a white baker's hat, and was wrapped in a copious white apron that made him look like a lump of dough.

A rack with newspapers and magazines stood on one side. A man in a beige raincoat and trilby hat stood holding a magazine while he stared at Kharos.

Phillip looked at the array of foods. 'What do your mum and Ruth like to eat?'

Kharos shrugged. 'I'm not sure. Whatever Gunter cooks. Mum says Gunter is a very good cook.'

'Yes, he is.' Phillip let go of Kharos's hand. 'Well, you look around and see if there is anything you like.' Phillip went up to the rack and pulled out the *Volkischer Beobachter*.

'Now Kharos, you've been very good helping me make the frames, so what sweets would you like?'

Kharos shook her head.

The shopkeeper winked at Kharos and then nodded towards a counter facing the window. Then he looked at Phillip. 'My wife makes excellent Schwarzwalder Kirschtorte.'

Phillip thought for a moment, and then realised the man meant Black Forest Gateau. Phillip bent down to Kharos. 'Do you like Schwarzwalder Kirschtorte?'

Kharos squeezed her lips together and looked at the floor.

Phillip stood up and smiled at the shopkeeper. 'I think that is a yes. Yes, we'll have one, please.'

The shopkeeper carefully took the cake from the window and wrapped it in a cardboard box. He handed the box to Phillip with both hands, as if it might spill. 'You are English?'

'Err, yes.'

'Your German is very good, but I caught the slight accent. I used to be a prisoner of war in an English camp.'

'Did you bring the half-breed over from England with you?' the man in the raincoat said.

Phillip stared at the man. Who was he? How dare he? 'She lives at Blue Ridge Farm. She's German.'

'No she's not German. She is a Rhineland Bastard. No doubt her mother was fucked by a nigger in the French Army.'

Phillip squared his shoulders.

The shopkeeper stepped out from behind the counter. 'Be quiet Sigmund. Are you buying that magazine? If not, out.'

Kharos slipped her hand into Phillip's. Phillip squeezed it gently and stood facing the man in the raincoat.

The man in the raincoat rammed the magazine into the rack. 'I wouldn't buy anything in a place that serves the likes of her.' He then banged out of the shop.

The shopkeeper let out a long sigh and slipped back behind the counter. 'Don't worry. He's all talk. He never buys anything. He just comes in, reads the magazine, and then tells me there is nothing in it.'

Phillip fumbled in his pocket for money and paid. Deep anger stirred inside him. What had happened to Germany? When he was last here, he hadn't witnessed such vile racism. Yes, some in England were racist, but this felt different. Doctor Schmelter's proposal for a Race Hygiene Centre based on American ideas for eliminating people they thought unfit to live was frightening. He wanted to get back to the farm as quickly as possible, to the safety, warmth and camaraderie at the artists' colony.

Phillip paid and as they left he slipped Kharos's hand in his. 'Let's go back by the main road,' said Phillip. He wanted to protect Kharos from the gaze of Doctor Schmelter.

'It's quicker through the wood.'

Phillip thought for a moment. 'Yes, but I want to see where the bus stop is for the bus to Bayreuth.'

'Oh, I'll show you. I know where it is.'

'Good girl.'

'Where have you been?' Ruth shouted as they entered the compound.

She came running up to them and grabbed Kharos.

Phillip held up the cake box. 'Just to the shop. I bought a ...'

'You must never take her out of the encampment.' Ruth dragged Kharos by the hand. 'Your mother is up at the farmhouse. Everyone has been out looking for you.'

'Oh, I'm really sorry,' Phillip said. 'I really ...'

Ruth pulled Kharos across the field towards the farmhouse. Phillip's mind was racing as he made his way to Ruth's cabin. What had he done? Why must Kharos never leave the encampment? A figure rose from a chair as Phillip stepped into Ruth's cabin. It was Bluum. 'You should mix with your own kind.'

Phillip felt nervous. Bluum was shorter than he was, but he was stocky and muscular, and his eyes seethed with anger. 'Ruth is a Jew and belongs amongst Jews, her own people. Just like you belong with your own people.' He pushed past Phillip. Through the open door, Phillip watched Bluum march across the field with resolute steps, as if the world were mapped out for him and there was only one path.

Phillip sat at the table and got out the *Volkischer Beobachter*. Ruth walked in and stamped the snow from her boots. Phillip closed the newspaper and slipped it into his inside pocket.

'Sorry,' Ruth said, as she hung her coat on the peg behind the door. 'I shouldn't have been cross with you. You didn't know, but Lena and Kharos are in hiding here. Lena's mother has applied for a court order to commit Lena to a mental institution and have Kharos taken into care. The Bavarian judges grant committal orders for unmarried women who have children, especially whose partners are black. They call all children like Kharos Rhineland Bastards, half-breeds, and want to eliminate them from Germany. Some want to expel them to Africa, others want them sterilised, or worse.'

Phillip thought of Krystal's Eugenics Programme. It wasn't an academic exercise; they were applying it, just like the Americans and they were hunting down Kharos and her mother. 'But what does the law say? Surely they just can't …'

'This is Bavaria. The judges here are right wing, often Nazis, and hate the Republic. Seven years ago in Munich, Hitler staged a rebellion and murdered four police officers, and all he served was nine months in prison. In any other country he would have been hanged. Not in Bavaria.' Ruth gave him a hug. 'Still, no harm done. You only went to the shop.'

Should he tell Ruth what happened in the shop, about the man in the raincoat? When he had defended Kharos he had said she was German and lived at Blue Ridge Farm. The man also knew Phillip was English. What if he told people? Told the police? What if the police raid the camp and the man identifies him as the Englishman and the police demand his papers?

'Tea or coffee?' Ruth said.

'Oh, tea, please.'

'In that case, I need to get some from Gunter.'

He was about to say don't bother, but Ruth leaving would give him a chance to look at the ads in the paper. Nowhere was safe. He just wanted to get back to England with Ruth.

There was a message from SIS. When he'd deciphered it, his heart jumped. They wanted to meet urgently, next day at noon. Were they sending him home? He read the ad again. *'Urgent. Change of plan. Meet in Bayreuth Park tomorrow at noon. Carry a copy of this newspaper. Your new contact will be wearing a red fedora hat and will be seated on a park bench next to the pond.'*

Perhaps the whole mission had been called off. That meant he would be sent back to England. But before he went, he could make plans with Ruth. She had said her cousin was looking for someone fluent in German and or French and he was fluent in both. Then, if he got the job, he could write to Ruth and ask her to join him.

Chapter 17

The usual travellers were on the morning bus to Bayreuth.

Phillip gazed out at the frozen fields as the bus ploughed through the slush towards Bayreuth. He should have told Ruth about the man in the shop. What if he tips off the police and they come to the colony looking for Lena and Kharos? He would tell her and Lena as soon as he got back.

Ruth had said nothing about Bluum's latest visit, but he'd found a Zionist pamphlet in her waste bin, which he'd retrieved. He took the pamphlet from his pocket and began reading. The cover page had a photo of a man called Theodor Herzl (1860-1904), and underneath the caption: *The Founder of Modern Zionism*. Below the photo were quotes from his diaries and a running commentary that Zionism offered the world a welcome *Final solution of the Jewish Question*. It said that in his diaries, Herzl stated: *Anti-Semites will become our surest friends, anti-Semitic countries our allies.*

It went on, *The Jews who will it shall achieve their State. We shall live at last as free men on our own soil, and in our own homes peacefully die. The world will be liberated by our freedom, enriched by our wealth, magnified by our greatness. And whatever we attempt there for our own benefit will redound mightily and beneficially to the good of all mankind.*

Phillip thought a country filled with people like Ruth and Gunter and Kantorowicz and Conti, would be a very special place. What if she left him and went to Palestine?

The bus was delayed because of a broken cart blocking the road, and it was just after noon when Phillip arrived in Bayreuth.

He took out his copy of the *Volkischer Beobachter*, placed it under his arm and sped towards the park.

The park was full of people gathered around the pond, most with young children, trying to manoeuvre model boats across the surface of the pond. Most were sailing boats but there were a few model steamships with smoke trailing from their funnels.

Across the pond, Phillip spied a man on a bench wearing a red fedora hat.

Phillip began making his way round the pond but was impeded by a group who were arguing about who had the right of way. A model sailing boat was upside down in the water and the owner was shouting that steam must give way as in maritime law. Phillip was forced to walk on the grass next to the flowerbeds.

He stopped. Wolfgang Drexler was standing near the main gate and looking at the man wearing the red fedora. The man on the bench was Major Drexler. Phillip turned, put his head down and barged his way through the crowd to the side gate.

Once outside, he ran for the bus stop.

As Phillip stepped off the bus outside the farm, his arm was grabbed.

He spun to shove the man away and run, but then saw it was the SIS agent he'd met in the library. 'It's OK. It's me,' said the agent. 'You're a hard man to find. You should have told us you had moved. This way.'

The agent led Phillip along the road and then onto a dirt track. They trudged along the track and into a field surrounded by poplars. Just inside the field was a parked Mercedes-Benz. The agent got in the drivers seat and motioned to Phillip to sit in the passenger seat. He then adjusted the rear-view-mirror to reflect the entrance to the field.

'The mission has been compromised,' the man said. 'But they don't know who our agent is, i.e. you.'

'But surely I can't …'

'Yes, you can.'

'But they know I'm in Bayreuth.'

'No, they don't. Today they were just fishing. They know you placed the ads in the postbox of the Bayreuth printers, but they probably think you did it to throw them off the scent and you are really in Munich, or somewhere else.'

'Or perhaps they don't. Look …'

'It's all cat and mouse. Get used to it.'

Phillip felt angry. It was as if he didn't matter. Expendable. He stared straight ahead at the open field and the overcast sky. The wind blew the poplars like dark candle flames. 'I want to know what has happened. I have a right.'

The agent lit up a cigarette and then offered one to Phillip. Phillip shook his head.

'Still haven't learned to smoke?'

'No.'

The agent blew smoke against the windscreen and watched it as it curled in the air. He opened his window. 'Berlin. One of our agents was in a nightclub there, the kind that puts on reviews that take the piss out of everybody, especially the Nazis. Well, the Brownshirts stormed it and our man legged it, but he was chased and caught and then beaten up and thrown in the river. He drowned. The local police fished him out next morning and found the codebook and a few other things and handed them over to the Abwehr, the German Army's Secret Service.' He threw his cigarette out the window.

'So you see,' he said, as he wound up the window, 'they know nothing. Only fishing. If they knew who you were they would have picked you up by now.'

Phillip looked out at the darkening sky. But the Abwehr knew he existed.

'I see you have a new coat,' the agent said.

Phillip was about to speak but stopped. How did he know he had a new coat? He had never seen the original one. When they first met in the library he was wearing just a jacket. SIS must know it was stolen at the church when someone tried to kill him. They knew, and they didn't care.

'Next time we will meet in the church in the village,' the agent said, nodding towards the farm. He took out a package and handed it to Phillip. 'This is the visa for Maximilian Schneider and two hundred American dollars. Only make contact when you have the document.'

He handed Phillip a slip of paper. 'Send a telegram to this address in Berlin for Herr Strauss, with arrangements for a funeral of Mister Joseph Albert Marks. Aged 70. Saint Marys. Then date and time.'

'That's not what the church in the village is called. It's called Saint Boniface's.'

The SIS agent sighed. 'I know. But I'll know it's you and we are to meet in this church.'

'What about my new passport?'

'Get the document, and you can have it within twenty-four hours.' He turned the key and the car jumped into life. 'OK. Go. And remember, no contact till you have the document.'

'It seems this document is extremely important.'

'You have no idea.'

Phillip watched the lights of the car turn onto the main road and drive in the direction away from Bayreuth. He was alone. The British Government didn't care a fig about him. He was totally expendable. They were probably prepared to see him killed rather than be compromised. If his father were white and belonged to the British establishment, then they would care. OK. Once he had the document he would play by his rules.

Gunter stood over a steaming cauldron and gave Phillip a big wave and a smile. Phillip reached Ruth's cabin and hurried inside.

Ruth rushed up to him. 'Have you seen Christoph?'

'Actually, yes. He came round to my lodgings, drunk. He said he was going back to Berlin with his regiment.'

Ruth's face clouded. 'Strange. Anna says nobody's seen him for the past few days, even his closest friends.'

'Perhaps he's with his regiment.'

Ruth shook her head. She peered at Phillip. 'You look worried. What's wrong?'

'Oh, nothing. Just the dissertation.'

'Lena says to pop in anytime. In fact, she said to tell you she has some notes for you on George and … what's his name?'

'T.S. Eliot.'

'That's the man.'

'Look, when I took Kharos to the shop there was a man …'

'Yes, Kharos told us.' Ruth took him in her arms. 'Gunter was told you stood up to the man and the shopkeeper thought the war was starting again.'

Phillip shook his head. 'Would you mind if I went for a walk on my own.'

Ruth touched his arm. 'Are you OK?'

'Yes. I just need some fresh air.'

'OK. But be careful, it's getting dark.'

Phillip grabbed Ruth and kissed her deeply, holding her tight for some minutes before releasing her slowly. Ruth cradled his head in her hands, kissing his face and his closed eyes. Phillip fought to hold back the emotion rising within him. He hurried out of the cabin.

Before he knew it, he had passed the woods and reached the river. He watched the black water slide between the snowy banks, then gazed at the bleak landscape dotted with dark trees, standing like mourners beneath the gloomy sky.

Was it worth it, all this for a job in the Foreign Office? And is that what he really wanted? He had enjoyed painting and making the sets for *Parsifal*, being creative. And he was beginning to relish writing the critique of George and Eliot's poems and to argue for what he thought was the right interpretation and meaning of their works.

Perhaps he really was meant to be a teacher. Both of them could be employed in her cousin's school. Ruth didn't have a passport and his was dangerous to use. A chill wind swept up from the river. But if he had the document, there was another way for both of them to get out of Germany. He would have to think carefully. He headed back.

The fire in the middle of the compound blazed. Gunter was on his own, stirring the pot. Phillip wandered over to the fire and warmed himself. Gunter sprinkled powder into the cauldron and stirred. Phillip smelled chilli powder. 'Were you in the war?' Phillip heard himself ask, as if he'd spoken involuntarily.

'Of course. All men my age were conscripted.'

'Did you see many men die?'

Gunter stopped stirring and gazed into the fire. 'The most upsetting thing was seeing your friends blown to pieces, or, so badly hurt, you watched them die. Also, trenches full of enemy corpses.'

'How did you cope?'

'You have to settle yourself inside, deep inside. What are you prepared to do? What you will not do? Be totally honest with yourself. Then, live by that creed and that way you keep the demons at bay, so they don't seep up from the swamp of your hidden psyche, as those Vienna psychoanalysts would have it, and cripple you.' Gunter stirred the pot and sprinkled in more chilli powder.

Phillip gazed at the glowing embers, pulsing deep red as the wind passed over them. But how could he, as Gunter suggested, be totally honest with himself? Where could he find the strength to be his own self, become who he was? A poem he had written expressed his inner being as a seed. But he knew for the seed to grow he must change; he must cultivate inner strength. He took a deep breath. He had to find the courage to become himself.

'There were plenty of non-firers,' Gunter said. 'Or soldiers who fired over the enemy's heads. Especially amongst the conscripts, of which I was one. I imagine the allies were the same, which is why the war went on for so long. But, if you were faced with killing or being killed, you killed.'

Phillip wanted to ask if Gunter had killed, but stayed silent.

Gunter stared across the fire at Phillip. 'Like I said, you settle yourself inside, have a clear moral and ethical framework, decide what is right, what you know is right, and act accordingly.' He stopped stirring the pot. 'Forget what the world thinks, Phillip, even what those closest to you think. Keep focused on what you, in your heart-of-hearts, know is right, and therefore how you would have all others act.'

'Well, well. The Sermon on the Mount,' said a man, emerging out of the dark.

'Go stick your religion up your arse,' Gunter said. 'It's Kant's categorical imperative: *Act only according to that maxim by which you can at the same time will that it should become a universal law.*'

Phillip turned from the fire. 'Well. I'd better be getting back. Ruth will want to eat.'

Gunter pointed the ladle. 'Too late, here she comes.'

Ruth, carrying two bowls, stepped into the circle of light cast by the fire. 'I hear we have venison tonight. You shot a deer in the forest.'

Gunter smiled.

Ruth huddled up to Phillip. 'Have a nice walk?'

'Yes. Just needed to clear my head a bit.'

Lena and Kharos joined them at the fire.

'I hear you're mixing with the Literati in Bayreuth,' Lena said.

Ruth laughed. 'I told you Bayreuth is a village and full of gossip. And, of course, because you are so good looking.' She squeezed him. 'My little Barchen.'

Phillip translated Barchen as little bear but had no idea what kind of endearment it was. But how did Lena know he'd met Kantorowicz and been invited to a George reading?

Gunter ladled stew into Ruth's bowls. 'That's why Kharos wants to marry Phillip when she grows up.'

Kharos retreated into the folds of her mother's coat. Ruth put one arm around Phillip and the other around Kharos. 'We can share him.' Ruth let go of Phillip and Kharos and took the two steaming bowls from Gunter. 'Thank you, Gunter. I do hope you put in lots of that spicy powder.'

Gunter smiled. 'Of course, my dear. Just for you.'

Ruth turned to Phillip. 'Come on. We need to eat these before they get cold. This is my favourite stew.'

As they walked back Phillip made up his mind. He had to find Max Schneider as quickly as possible, and once he had the document, ask Ruth about their future. If she were willing to come to England with him, then he would bargain with SIS and get Ruth on his passport.

The way to contact Max Schneider was to find the man in the tin mask.

He shouldn't be too hard to find since there can't be many men with a tin mask for a face in Bayreuth. The church where he had met Schneider was the best bet since the man in the tin mask was clearly religious. But would someone recognise him as being at the church when the beggar was murdered and call the police? What about the Blue Lagoon? But what if it was raided like the club in Berlin? Then there was the beggar in the square with the medals. The man with the tin mask had been talking to him. They had both been wounded in the war. They must know each other.

Perhaps the beggar knew where the man in the mask lived.

Chapter 18

The medals glittered in the morning sunlight.

Phillip made his way across Prince William Square and stood in front of the beggar. 'Ah. Good day, young gentleman,' the man said, saluting Phillip. 'I hope you are well.'

'I'm going to have some coffee,' Phillip said, bending down to make eye contact. 'Please join me.'

'I'd prefer money, sir.' He raised the arm without a hand. 'You see I need to get one of them false hands so I can go back to work.'

'OK. But first coffee and then I'll give you some money.'

The beggar stared at Phillip.

'An American dollar,' Phillip said.

The man scrambled to his feet, his bright blue eyes sparkling in his grimy, unshaven face. As they headed to the café, the beggar strode with the bearing of a soldier, and Phillip wondered how much begging had hurt the man's pride.

The café was crowded. Phillip ordered two coffees and a plate of small kermesse cakes, which Ruth had introduced him to and which he found very tasty. Chairs scraped the floor and the beggar nodded to the vacating table. Phillip nodded back.

'My name is Karl,' the beggar said, as Phillip put the tray on the table. Karl extended his left hand and Phillip, using his left hand, shook it awkwardly. 'Phillip.'

'You are English?'

'Yes.'

'You speak good German.'

'But with an Austrian accent, which I'm trying to lose.'

'Why? It is a good accent. My mother was Austrian.'

'Sorry, I didn't mean …' He took a sip of coffee.

'You were in the war?' Phillip said, after a long silence. He then realised it was a stupid statement.

Karl sighed, picked up a cake and took a big bite. He finished chewing and said, 'We were all in the war, even those not at the front.'

'What work do you want to get back to?'

'I was a shoemaker.'

'Ah. I need to buy a pair of boots. What do you recommend?'

Karl gave a broad smile and drained his coffee. 'I know where you can buy ex-army boots. Just the thing for this snow. And they're cheap. But you must get the ones made before 1916. After that, they used inferior materials.'

Karl placed his empty cup in the saucer.

'Another one?' Phillip said.

Karl shook his head. Phillip couldn't think of anything to say. Karl placed his good hand on the table and levered himself up. Phillip stood. He still hadn't asked Karl about the man with the tin mask.

Karl nodded to the two cakes on the plate. 'Are you going to take them?'

'No. I'm full. Please take them; no point in wasting them.'

With one hand, Karl deftly wrapped the cakes in a paper napkin. 'I know someone who will be pleased to have such a treat.'

'The man in the tin mask?'

'No.'

'Actually, I met him at a club and would like to talk to him, but I haven't seen him lately.'

Karl stared at Phillip and then headed for the door. Phillip rushed after him.

'What do you want with him?' asked Karl, standing on the pavement and pulling his coat around him.

'Oh, err. We have a mutual acquaintance. I need to pass on a message.'

Karl shook his shoulders. 'You'll find him sometimes at the Salvation Army's "Old Soldiers Rest".'

Phillip didn't ask for the address. He could find it out in the post office.

Karl pulled on his woollen hat. 'Come on. I'll show you where to buy the boots.'

In the main square, four Nazis Brownshirts were standing under a swastika flag giving out leaflets, while two policemen, with Munich insignia on their helmets, stood to one side. One of the policemen was watching the Blue Lagoon club. Phillip avoided eye contact and was thankful he was with someone wearing an army coat with medals. They left the square and headed for the east side of town.

They arrived at a small parade of run-down shops selling second-hand goods, such a tin baths and clothes wringers. Karl stopped outside a shop, in front of which stood a battered mannequin, dressed in a German Army uniform and metal helmet. 'This is the place. And remember, ask for boots made before 1916.' He turned to walk away.

'Wait.' Phillip took out five dollars from his wallet. 'Here.'

Karl stared at the money.

'Come on. It's for your new hand.'

Karl smiled and pocketed the money.

The shop smelled of dried sacks, reminding Phillip of jumble sales. Most of the floor space was occupied with tables stacked with piles of clothes. A man who looked to be in his fifties was behind the counter, folding beige trousers into a neat pile.

Phillip smiled and went up to the counter. 'I would like a pair of army boots made before 1916, please.'

The man continued folding the trousers. He laid the last pair on the pile and gave Phillip a long look. 'Size?'

'Nine.'

The man stared at Phillip. 'Give me your shoe.'

Phillip took off his shoe and handed it to the man. The man disappeared into the back of the shop. Phillip realised Germans measured shoes sizes in centimetres. What if the man was phoning to say an Englishman was in his shop asking for German army boots? He thought of running out of the shop but he only had one shoe.

The man came back with a pair of brown boots. He handed Phillip his shoe and began wrapping the boots in newspaper. Phillip had no idea if they were real army boots and made before nineteen sixteen, but he didn't dare ask. He paid and left.

Back at his lodgings, Phillip changed into the boots. They fitted perfectly. He would need to buy some thick socks.

The Salvation Army centre was in a large, single-storey building next to the river.

Inside it reeked of damp. Its whitewashed walls were covered in patches of curled plaster and just below the ceiling ran a row of small, mean windows with bars. Phillip thought it must have been built as a warehouse. Long wooden tables stacked with clothes ran along each side of the room. On the table near the door was an honesty box along with a notice to pay what you could afford. Men and women in Salvation Army uniform, along with civilian helpers, were busy tidying the piles of clothes, helping customers and dispensing tea from a large urn. Phillip was surprised the Salvation Army uniforms were the same as in England.

There was no sign of the man with the tin mask.

In an area set out with tables and chairs, men with disfigured faces and missing limbs sat drinking from mugs. Some of the men were dressed in full army uniforms, while others had military jackets with civilian trousers. They stopped talking and turned to look at Phillip. He clearly didn't belong and felt they were reproaching him for his unblemished body and fine coat with a sable collar. A beaming woman in a Salvation Army uniform came up to him. 'Can I help you?'

'Well, actually, I'm looking for someone.'

'Was he once a soldier?'

'Yes.'

'Well, maybe we can help. Do you know his name?'

'No. Sorry, no I don't.' He heisted. 'Actually, he … he wears a tin mask. His face …'

'Oh, yes. I know who you mean.' She looked round the room. 'He's not here at the moment.

'I really need to talk to him. Do you know where he lives?'

'I'm sorry, no.' She smiled at Phillip. 'Why don't you have a cup of tea; perhaps he'll pop in.'

Phillip crossed to the canteen area and sat at a vacant table. He then realised he had to go to a table with the urn to get a cup of tea.

Dropping the equivalent of a shilling into the cut-glass bowl, Phillip carried his tea back to his table, which was now occupied by a man in an army coat many sizes too big for him. As Phillip sat down he caught an aroma of sweat and stale beer. The man wore a handlebar moustache plastered with wax and had sleek black hair. The tips of his fingernails were lines of black. The man smiled at Phillip, exposing cracked, discoloured teeth. 'What regiment were you in?'

'Oh, I wasn't in the war.'

The man laughed, displaying dark holes behind the cracked teeth. 'No, my little Austrian, you were too young. So, you're looking for someone?'

'Yes.'

'Who?'

'I don't know his name.'

'What does he look like?'

Phillip hesitated. 'Well, he has a tin mask on his face.'

The man looked at him. There was a long silence. Phillip thought maybe he shouldn't have mentioned the mask. The man studied his fingernails. 'Yes. I know him.'

Phillip desperately tried to think of a plausible reason for wanting to find the man in the mask. 'I need to have a word with him. We know each other.'

'And you would like me to help you find him.'

'Err, yes. Yes, please.'

The man leaned forwards and spoke quietly. 'Of course, information costs.' He leaned back and rubbed his thumb and index finger together.

'OK,' Phillip said.

The man stood up and cocked his head sideways. Phillip followed him out. The man gathered his oversized coat around him and walked with his head down, the wind flapping the folds of his coat, which almost reached the ground. The man was hatless and his sleeked black hair glistened in the wintry light.

The man led Phillip to a tall building near the university, which had glass-panelled doors and a sign that said Bibliothek House. The man looked at Phillip. 'Do you have American dollars?'

'Yes.'

'How many?'

Phillip wasn't sure what to say. 'I have a couple.'

'I want five.'

'Five.' That seemed a lot to Phillip. It was what the taxi driver had charged. But then again, he had given five dollars to the tramp and this man looked like he needed money.

The man shrugged and started to walk away.

'Wait.' Phillip got out his wallet. There were only six dollars in it. He had no choice; he had to exchange the visas and money for the document as soon as possible, and then get out of Germany. He gave the man five dollars.

The man thrust the money into his coat pocket. 'Top floor. Ask for Mister Engels.' The man turned and hurried away.

Phillip pushed open the glass doors and began climbing the ornate Art Nouveau staircase. On the top-floor landing he found a glass door with the word Reception. He went through the door and up to a counter, behind which was a screen that blocked the view into the room. Phillip rang the small bell under the sign Service. A middle-aged man with rimless glasses and sweptback hair emerged from behind the screen and smiled at Phillip.

'I'd like to speak to Mister Engels, please,' Phillip said.

The man's smile broadened. 'So would I.'

Phillip stared at the man. 'I was told I could find him here. He wears a tin mask.'

The man took a deep breath. 'I assume you are referring to Friedrich Engels, collaborator of Karl Marx. We publish their work. We can sell you a copy of the Communist Manifesto, but we cannot introduce you to Friedrich Engels, since he died thirty-three years ago in England and was cremated and, we believe, since it was his dying wish, his ashes scattered off Beachy Head cliffs in the south of England.'

Phillip blushed. 'Thank you.'

Phillip ran down the stairs and out of the building. The man who had taken his money was nowhere to be seen.

But what would he do if he did find him? He couldn't go to the police. A woman on a bicycle rattled past over the cobblestones. A policeman with Munich insignia on his lapels strolled past. The Munich police were everywhere.

What should he do? The church must know who the man in the mask was. He had been saying the rosary when they met and so was clearly religious. But what if someone at the church recognised him as being there when the tramp was killed? What if they then called the police?

He had no choice – he would have to take the chance.

The church was locked. Knocking would attract attention and he didn't know if the priest was at home. Tomorrow was Sunday so the church would be packed. Best time would be Monday after the morning mass.

He headed for the bus station. It was safer at the farm.

Chapter 19

Church bells rang across the frozen ground as Phillip made his way to the colony's communal washroom.

Bright, sparkling sunlight reflected off the frozen snow, while the pure blue sky was filled with small white clouds, like girls at a first communion. A dog trotted across the virgin snow towards the wood, leaving a trail of paw-shadows. Smoke curled up from the cabin's chimneys and Phillip imagined he would be happy living with Ruth in such a peaceful place, away from the world.

The washroom, that included toilets and showers, was housed in a concrete block with hot and cold water pipes that ran from the farmhouse. Phillip was uncomfortable that both men and women used the same toilet cubicles and that the male and female showers were divided by a flimsy piece of tarpaulin. After using the toilet, he washed his face and hands and decided to bath at home in Bayreuth.

Kharos was standing by the barn. He waved at her. She waved back and then ran to her cabin. The mist was beginning to retreat before the sun, exposing the tops of the hills which were dappled with snow like a piebald horse, while the slopes were wreathed in layers of vapour. Birds, black in the winter sky, sailed silently in the air.

The sound of a car door bounced across the frozen ground. Doctor Schmelter was standing beside a black Mercedes parked near the bus stop, taking a notebook from her bag. She was dressed in an ivory coloured coat, trimmed with auburn fur, and a white fur hat.

Her blond hair hung down to her shoulders. Phillip thought she looked radiant as she walked up the track towards the cabins. He dashed into the barn.

At the back of the barn, he stood in the shadows next to the stove. Had Krystal seen him? The barn door was half-open. It needed to be shut. He began making his way towards the door but stopped when he heard Krystal's voice. 'What's your name?'

'Kharos.'

Phillip froze. His stomach tightened.

'And where's your mummy and daddy?'

'My mummy's at home. My daddy is in heaven.'

There was a long silence.

'And where do you live?'

Silence.

'The one with the red door,' Krystal said.

'Yes.'

'What is your mother's name?'

'Lena.'

'Really. That's a nice name. Does she have a second name?'

'Maharero.'

'Maharero? So you are Kharos Maharero?'

'Yes.'

'You're a clever girl. Would you write your full name on this paper?'

Phillip clenched his fists. What should he do? What was Doctor Schmelter up to? She had been measuring the Roma. Was she going to do the same with Kharos? Why? Did it have anything to do with the Eugenics Programme? His blood ran cold.

'Thank you, Kharos. Your writing is very beautiful.'

'My daddy taught me.'

'Really? And where did you live before you came here?'

'In Hamburg.'

'Oh, that's a nice city. Do you remember your address in Hamburg?'

'Yes.'

'Can you write it down for me?'

There was a long pause.

'Well, you are a very clever girl, Kharos, and very pretty. I hope to see you again. Goodbye.'

Kharos shuffled into the barn, carefully carrying a mug of coffee with both hands. 'Mummy said you might like some coffee.'

Phillip grabbed the coffee from Kharos and plonked it on the bench. He crept to the door and slowly closed it till there was just a crack for him to peek through. He waited till he heard the sound of a car starting, and then driving off. He peered out and saw the Mercedes had gone.

He must tell Lena.

'Mummy said she has some notes for you for the poetry,' Kharos said. 'She said you should come over this afternoon.'

'Oh, well, I shall do that.' He didn't want to alarm Kharos. He would have a quiet word with Lena this afternoon.

Phillip selected four slats, laid them on the bench, marked them out and began to saw and chisel the mortice and tenon joints. Gunter staggered into the barn holding a gramophone, followed by Ruth holding a packet. Gunter plonked the gramophone on the vacant bench. 'Music to sooth the savage breast, as your Mister Shakespeare is wont to say.' He began to wind up the gramophone.

'Is Mister Shakespeare your father,' Kharos said, looking at Phillip.

Gunter bellowed out a laugh that shook his big frame.

Kharos lowered her head. 'Not really,' Phillip said, putting his arm round her. 'Dear Gunter has got things mixed up. Shakespeare is a famous English writer who lived a long time ago, but he never said 'Music sooths the savage breast', it was another English writer called William Congreve and he said, 'Music has Charms to sooth a savage breast, To soften Rocks, or bend a knotted Oak.'

'Oooh,' Gunter said, taking the packet from Ruth and unwrapping a shellac disc. 'The Good Knight, Sir Phillip, is riding to the rescue of the fair maiden, Kharos. Sorry, Kharos, I shouldn't have laughed, especially as I didn't know what I was talking about. Forgive me? Hug.'

Kharos gave him a hug.

Ruth gave Phillip a hug and a kiss on the cheek. 'Mmm. We are the bright one.'

Gunter carefully placed the disc on the turntable. He winked at Kharos and beckoned her over.

Kharos watched as Gunter lowered the arm onto the disc and the opening chords of the overture to *Parsifal* floated out from the conical horn. 'Music to inspire you,' Gunter said, and taking Kharos by the hands, swirled her round, dancing to the music.

Phillip beckoned to Ruth that she should follow him outside the barn.

They strode to the centre of the encampment and stood by the dead fire. Phillip told Ruth about Doctor Schmelter's visit that morning and what he'd heard. He added that he had learned at the university that she was connected with a eugenics programme funded by the Americans. He didn't say he'd been asked to translate documents that could help the eugenics programme.

'That is worrying,' Ruth said. 'We know Doctor Schmelter is connected with the Nazis. Gunter tried to stop her measuring and examining the Roma, but she had a permit from the Bavarian Government to carry out research into ethnic minorities.'

Phillip shook his head. Academia had sanctioned eugenics as a science, and politicians were using it to support their racist agendas.

'I'll have a word with Lena,' Ruth said.

As he watched Ruth plod across the compound, he felt guilty for having taken Kharos to the shop.

That afternoon as Phillip made his way to Lena's cabin, the tops of the hills were heavy with clouds as the horizon sank down, dragging the last light from the sky. Lights shone from some of the cabins, and in the fields patches of snow lay like islands in the gloaming. The fire blazed in the centre of the compound, but there was no sign of Gunter.

Phillip tapped on Lena's door. It was quickly opened and Kharos stood there beaming. Phillip stepped inside and was greeted by the smell of dried pigment. A tin with flat blocks of watercolours lay on the table, along with a sheet of paper that displayed a half-finished painting of the compound in daytime, with a sky interspersed with white clouds and blotches of different blues.

'I'm pleased to see you are wearing it,' Lena said, taking his coat and hanging it up. 'You must wear it all the time, especially when you go into Bayreuth. It suites you.'

'Thank you,' Phillip said. 'It's been a life saver.'

'Please, sit,' Lena said. 'Would you like a cup of tea or coffee?'

'No, I'm fine thank you.'

Phillip sat at the table. He leaned over and looked at the painting Kharos was working on. 'Would you like me to show you how to keep the sky all one colour?'

'Yes, please,' Kharos said.

'Right. What we need are three glasses of clean water.'

Lena took three glasses from the shelf and filled them with clean water. Phillip arranged them on the table. 'Now Kharos,' Phillip said. 'Always use one glass for one colour. There are three primary colours, red, blue and yellow, from which all other colours are made. If you use one glass for each colour to rinse your brush in, then you keep the colour pure. And, when you clean your brush, do it in a figure of eight, like this.' Phillip swirled the brush in the water with a serpentine action. He then tapped the brush on the edge of the glass. 'See. Perfectly clean. Do that and you will always have a true shade. And, change the water, often.'

'Ruth is right, you would make a good teacher,' Lena said.

'That's why I'm here. To get a masters so I can teach German.'

Lena stared at him. 'So, how are you getting on with the poetry?'

'Yeah, pretty good.' He rose and stood close to Lena. 'Do you think we could talk for a moment outside?'

Lena stared at him. She then turned to Kharos. 'I'm just going outside to show Phillip something. Back in a minute.'

Lena listened carefully as Phillip told her about the man in the shop and Doctor Schmelter's visit.

'Don't feel too bad about the shop,' Lena said. 'It's not the first time she's heard herself called those names.'

'But what about Doctor Schmelter asking all those questions?'

Lena shrugged. 'Ever since the Roma arrived a couple of months ago, she's been here measuring them. Perhaps that's what she wants to do with Kharos. But, of course, I won't let her.' Lena stared at Phillip for a long time. Then she nodded. 'Thanks for keeping me informed. Come on, it's cold out here. We need to discuss poetry.'

As they stepped inside, Kharos held up a painting.

'Very good,' said Phillip. He sat at the table and pulled books and a pad from his briefcase. He needed to pretend he didn't know much about poetry, since she had given him a nice coat and he could imagine she was a woman with strong views.

Lena reached out and picked up the book of sonnets. 'Ah, you are studying Shakespeare.'

Phillip took the book from her. 'Sorry. It's just that I've made some notes on the pages. Silly notes really.'

'Don't be ashamed. All budding poets copy and steal. So, are the notes for the dark lady who lives in our colony?'

Phillip kept his eyes down and put the book back in his briefcase.

'Sorry,' Lena said, 'I didn't mean to embarrass you.'

'No ... No. It's fine.'

'So, how far have you got? What are you finding difficult?'

'I think I'm making progress with George.'

'Oh, really?'

'Yes, I met Professor Kantorowicz and he explained everything to me. I actually met George at a ...'

Lena's eyes hardened. 'And you were captivated by him. Lots of the young, and not so young, who yearn for some mystical other world are in raptures over him, but in reality, he masks the face of Nazism.'

Phillip wasn't sure what to say. It was true the Nazis and their supporters, like Professor Muller, were trying to claim George as one of their own, just as Goebbels was trying to integrate the European Romantic Movement into National Socialist ideology, but they had nothing in common.

'Just like Eliot in *The Waste Land*,' Lena said. 'It's all just a metaphor for the so-called glories of the past. Eliot thinks the old ways are still there, but hidden, just like George's *Secret Germany*. Both reflect what many across Europe feel at the present time; a yearning for a glorious past that is dormant and waiting to be revived.' Lena's mouth was set and her eyes hard. 'Eliot's opening lines state that "April is the cruellest month" because it awakens buried memories by "stirring Dull roots with spring rain", and that winter had covered the "Earth in forgetful snow", so people had forgotten their glorious past. It's rubbish. Instead of looking at what is really happening now, and the real opportunities the modern world brings, George and Eliot are yearning for a past that never existed.'

'Of course it did. There's all the history books.'

Lena narrowed her eyes. 'The history books only tell about the rulers, not what it was like for ordinary people. It's wrong and dangerous to spend time saying how glorious the past was. Most people lived short, diseased lives. Those who glorify a nation's past are nationalists, and patriotism is just a cover for racism.'

'But there's nothing wrong with being patriotic, loving one's country.'

'Really? Love that fosters hate and rejection of other nations and their peoples, just because of their culture, or because the colour of their skin is different? As in the British Empire.'

Anger flared inside Phillip and he had to hold back. His mother had taught him the British Raj in India was a civilising mission, an undertaking to raise people out of poverty and ignorance, which is rampant in India, and to bring them the benefits of Western Civilisation, which was the finest in the world. He kept his voice in check. 'You're wrong,' he said. 'The British in India …'

Shouts and screams came from outside. Lena grabbed Kharos. Phillip's heart pounded. Lena opened the curtain a crack. 'The barn is on fire.'

Phillip scrabbled his books and notepad into his briefcase. What to do? What if the police had been summoned? He looked at the frightened face of Kharos. 'Don't worry. You stay here with your mummy.'

Phillip stepped cautiously outside. The roof of the barn was ablaze, the wet thatch crackling and spitting fiery flecks into the night sky, where they bloomed and died in the darkness. In the flickering light, he saw on the road an open lorry full of Brownshirts.

A whoosh rent the air as the barn roof collapsed inwards, spewing flames and sparks skywards. The Nazis shouted and gave the Hitler salute.

Phillip jumped. Two eyes of iron in a face with a fire-lit crimson scar bore down on him from the lorry. It was Major Drexler. Beside him was Wolfgang, pointing at him. Major Drexler stared at Phillip as the lorry sped away.

Had Major Drexler noticed him in the park when he was trying to trap the British agent? Would he make the connection?

He needed to find Max Schneider as quickly as possible and get out of Germany.

Chapter 20

The man was there again, waiting at the Bayreuth bus terminal.

Phillip sped towards the university.

It was the same man who had tried to follow him last time he was in Bayreuth. Who was he? He wasn't German Secret Service, since they would have just picked him up, interrogated him, searched his lodgings and no doubt found the codebook. Whoever he was, he knew Phillip came on the bus from Blue Ridge Farm. Was somebody at the farm tipping him off? Who? Was he a friend of Bluum's, or connected to the Communists who had killed the tramp? Whoever the man was, he was no good at tailing someone, and Phillip, now familiar with the narrow alleyways that surrounded the university, soon lost him.

The board outside Saint Mary's Church gave the list of services for each day. Being Monday, there was a nine o'clock mass and then confessions till midday. The afternoon was clear and so Phillip decided to come back after lunch. He needed to change his clothes and have a bath. He would head for the university in case the man was still following him and slip out the back entrance.

As soon as he stepped into the hall, Frau Weiser rushed out of her front room and held an envelope in front of Phillip. It was pale ivory with watermarks and sealed with red wax. 'It's for you from Count Koniger,' Frau Weiser said, her eyes shining.

'Thank you,' Phillip said, with feigned nonchalance. He turned and slowly mounted the stairs, aware that Frau Weiser was looking at him. He stopped at the top of the stairs. 'Oh, I forgot to book, but is it possible to have a bath?'

'Of course, of course.' She headed along the hallway towards the back of the house. 'Ready in thirty minutes.'

Phillip tore open the envelope. It was an invite from Countess Koniger to attend a soiree at her mansion the day after tomorrow. Who was she? Why had he been invited? Was it something to do with Max Schneider?

Drums echoed in the cold air as he reached the centre of town. Led by a man parading a swastika flag, a troop of young boys in brown shirts marched into Prince William Square. When they reached the centre they stopped and one of them placed a wooden box onto the ground. The man handed the flag to one of the young Brownshirts and climbed up onto the box. He tilted his head back and surveyed the square, waiting for the faithful to gather around him.

As Phillip passed by, the man on the box stared at him. Phillip pulled up his coat collar and his cap down and headed for the bridge across the Red River. He was pleased he was wearing his student cap, but it offered little protection from the weather. As he crossed the bridge, snow flurries wisped along the banks and settled on the surface of the water, blurring the line between river and land.

Set in a sea of white snow, Saint Mary's church looked peaceful and benign. As Phillip trudged across the snow, he thought someone in the church must know the man with the tin mask since he'd been reciting the rosary when they met, and so was clearly a practising Catholic. Also, he was the only one with a tin mask that Phillip had seen in Bayreuth, in Germany, come to that.

As he passed where the tramp had been killed he felt a stab of guilt, but deep down he knew it wasn't his fault – the man had brought it on himself by stealing the coat – but he also knew the tramp's actions had saved his life.

The church was warm and Phillip wondered if they kept the heating on all night. The pews were empty, aside from an old woman dressed in a black coat and dark veil, kneeling and praying in front of a statue of Jesus. A candle in front of the statue sputtered in a pool of wax as white smoke curled up from the black wick. The acrid smell of the spent candle rushed him back into his childhood.

There were no lights above the confessional cabinet, which meant confessions were not available. Pray for me, father, for I have sinned. My last confession was … he couldn't remember. If he lied and made up a time, would that invalidate the confession? If only he believed perhaps he could find peace from the guilt he felt about the tramp's death. But he could never be at real peace until he faced the truth about who he really was and stopped living with the fear of being exposed. He had once let his mind go down to the depths of his emotions, trying to resolve his anxiety and accept his real self, but his feelings had turned into pulses of panic, like the depression he had suffered in his late teens.

Should he tap on the sacristy door? Maybe that would draw too much attention. He began walking round the side aisles, looking at the plaster reliefs of the Stations of the Cross depicting Christ's journey to his crucifixion. Christ being condemned to death, then meeting his mother, then falling under the weight of the cross, then being stripped of his garments, then being crucified and finally laid in his tomb.

Phillip felt compassion for the persecuted figure who clearly suffered as an ordinary man, which made his pain even more poignant, since if Christ really were the Son of God, he had nothing to fear – his death was ordained, part of the plan, the final act before he rejoined his father in heaven – but Christ's suffering and death were all the more momentous because he wasn't divine, but an ordinary man who died for his truth. The priests told Christ he was a fraud, but he stuck to his truth, even unto death. Christ had lived an authentic life, unlike himself who hadn't the courage to tell people the truth, always driven back by anxiety and fear.

The sacristy door opened and a man dressed in a long black cassock emerged. He walked with a limp and started collecting hymnbooks from the pews.

Phillip went up to the man. 'Excuse me.'

The man drew himself up and fixed Phillip with a hard stare. The man was taller than he first looked, and Phillip felt intimidated by the man's penetrating eyes.

Phillip smiled. 'I was wondering if you know of a man who wears a silver mask on his face?'

The man stared at Phillip.

'That would be Kurt Schmidt,' said a soft voice, behind him.

Phillip turned. It was a priest. 'Manfred cannot hear you,' the priest said, nodding to the man with an armful of hymn books. 'He lost his hearing in the war.' The priest mouthed something to Manfred who then continued collecting the hymn books. The priest turned to Phillip and extended his hand. 'I'm Father Mayer. How may I help?'

'Oh, I'm Phillip. Phillip K … Fitzwilliam.' He shook the priest's hand.

The priest kept hold of Phillip's hand and looked at him quizzically.

Phillip felt his heart pound. Had the priest seen him in the church when the tramp was killed. Should he pull his hand from the priest's grasp and run out the church before he called the police?

'Englishman, but who went to school in Austria?' Father Mayer said.

'Ah, no. Well, yes. Englishman, but taught German by an Austrian teacher.'

'Well, you speak German beautifully. What can I do for you?'

'Well, Father, I was wondering if you knew how I could get in touch with him. With Mr Schmidt.'

'Ah. I'm not sure where he lives, but he usually comes to mass on Sunday. However, he wasn't here last Sunday. He's often around because he looks after three graves in the churchyard. I believe they were comrades of his in the war. He also has a special devotion to Saint Mary. You are a Catholic?'

'Yes.'

'Then perhaps we'll see you next Sunday, at mass?'

'If I can, Father.'

'Good. Welcome to the congregation.'

Phillip stood outside the church, trying to think of what to do next. Wait till next Sunday and hope Schmidt came to mass? What if he didn't? It would be a week wasted. Schmidt was definitely known at the Blue Lagoon where he arranged for the cocktail to be used as a password. Now he could actually ask for him by name, Schmidt. But the club only opened from Thursday to Saturday. Today was Monday. Tomorrow he had Stefan George's reading in the afternoon, and the day after, Countess Koniger's soiree in the evening. Should he stay in town or was the farm safer? He would stay in town. He would now go back to the Salvation Army Centre and see if they knew Kurt Schmidt and where he lived.

Only a few tables were occupied at the Salvation Army Centre and he was pleased to see the man who had tricked him out of the five dollars was not there. Perhaps he was avoiding the place in case Phillip was looking for him.

Phillip strolled up to a woman who was folding trousers on one of the tables. 'Excuse me. I don't know if you remember me, but …'

'Yes, of course,' the woman said, smiling into Phillip's eyes. 'I certainly do remember you.' She paused and let her eyes hold his. 'You were looking for the man in the tin mask. Did you find him?'

Phillip shook his head.

The woman looked away. 'Perhaps I should have warned you about Karl.' She hesitated. 'He can be a little ...'

'Yes.' Phillip shrugged. 'Perhaps he needed the money.'

She smiled and touched his arm. 'Very Christian of you.'

'Actually,' Phillip said, 'I now know that the man in the mask is called Schmidt. Kurt Schmidt.'

'Right, let me see if we have any record of him. We have a fund for those in real need, emergencies, so we might have helped him in the past.' She left Phillip and went out a door behind one of the long tables.

Phillip avoided looking around since he was aware that some people were watching him. He wondered what they were thinking.

The woman returned, holding a slip of paper. 'Yes, we have his address. But first, I have been told to ask that you do not use it to his detriment.'

'Oh, no. No. I met him at ... in Saint Mary's church. Also, a friend of his who ... is sometimes in the square with medals on his coat.'

She smiled. 'Nice of you to befriend those less fortunate than yourself.' She handed Phillip the paper.

Kurt Schmidt lived not far from the shop where Phillip had bought his army boots, in one of a string of old cottages that were in desperate need of repair. Primrose Cottage was at the end of the row. It looked in worse repair than the other cottages and had brown paper covering a hole in one window.

He knocked. There was a noise from inside and the door was pulled slowly open. A woman in her sixties, small, and bent over, with a floral apron stood and looked sideways at Phillip.

'Ah, sorry to disturb you …' he wasn't sure how to address her since there were no rings on her fingers. 'But is Kurt Schmidt at home?'

The woman eyed him. 'He's left.'

'Ah. Did he leave a forwarding address?'

The woman pushed the door closed.

Phillip wasn't sure what to do. Perhaps somebody else in the neighbourhood knew where Schmidt had gone. He looked around. Then he saw him. It was the man who had followed him from the bus terminus this morning, standing on the opposite side of the road looking at him. Phillip strode quickly along the road and headed for the university.

Phillip arrived at the university and then went through the foyer into a dingy corridor and out the back of the building. Rubbish bins were lined up against the back wall of the faculty and in front of him ran the Red River. He ran along the bank and then over a footbridge to a road that led to the main square.

The bus to the farm was there. He jumped aboard.

Chapter 21

'You will look for Christoph at George's reading this afternoon,' Ruth said, handing Phillip a cup of tea.

Phillip stretched under the bed covers and then sat up. 'Yes, of course.' He took the tea from Ruth. 'And, I've been invited to a soiree at Countess Koniger's tomorrow evening, so …'

'My, my, we are the toast of Bayreuth. A Stefan George reading today and Countess Koniger's tomorrow.' She gazed at Phillip and then sat on the side of the bed. 'Perhaps you will leave us for the high life.'

He snorted through his nose, but then thought that if this were England he would be pleased to be mixing with the elite. Or would he? His feelings towards the ruling class and the establishment were changing. The British Secret Service, which was part of the Foreign Office, had made it clear that he was expendable. They knew he was mixed race and suggested that changing his name would help him fit in. Fit into what? British society that as soon as they knew the truth would shun him, let him know his place.

'It's good you're going to Countess Koniger's,' Ruth said. 'Army officers from the right families go to her gatherings, and Christoph definitely belongs to that lot, being from the Hohenzollern dynasty.'

Phillip sipped his tea. He was not sure about attending Countess Koniger's party. The reason he was going to the George reading was to try to trace Max Schneider through Madam

Bernstein's contacts, rather than having to go back to the Blue Lagoon. He had thought of asking Ruth if she knew Max Schneider, but it might be dangerous. What if she went around asking people where he was? That could frighten him off and draw attention to himself. Also, being very bright, Ruth would ask questions.

Ruth stood up. 'If you see Christoph, you must tell him what Anna said about the baby. And if you meet any of his close friends, like Von Stauffenberg, tell them.'

Phillip's stomach dropped. The thought of being the one who said Anna would abort the baby filled him with abhorrence, especially telling Christoph's friends. What would they think of him? Christoph's side of the Hohenzollern family were Catholic. Did Ruth know that? Was Von Stauffenberg a Catholic? How could he tell them?

'He's a brilliant artist,' Ruth said. 'I wish I were half as good as he is. But, he's weak. Well, perhaps that's too harsh, but instead of following his vocation, he lets his family dominate him. What's so important about outward status if it crushes your inner being.'

'True,' Phillip said. What a hypocrite. He was the last person who should criticise others for not having the strength or courage to be themselves.

As Phillip headed for the bus stop, he could smell the charred wood. He had always loved the scent of wood smoke, equating it with Romantic poetry. From the cover of the trees Roma children stared at the scorched barn as if frightened they would be blamed for the

221

destruction. The sound of a tractor came from behind him. It was Gunter pulling a trailer full of corrugated iron to redo the barn roof. He waved to him. He reached the bus stop and saw the bus in the distance.

'Phillip?'

Phillip turned. It was Professor Ernst Kantorowicz, walking up the path to Madam Bernstein's house with a woman dressed in an evening gown. Kantorowicz wore a three-piece suit with a carnation in the lapel. He stopped in front of Phillip and bowed. 'This is my wife. And this is the young Englishman I told you about.'

The woman extended her hand, palm down. 'Nice to meet you.'

Phillip bowed and let his lips just touch the skin of her hand.

Kantorowicz leaned past Phillip and pulled the bell.

The gathering and atmosphere were different from the last time Phillip was there; now the room was filled with people speaking in low voices, as if in a church. The feeling of being somewhere sacred was reinforced by the lectern near the window and the two tall candles next to it. Not everyone was formally attired, but all were soberly dressed and the only cluster was around Stefan George who stood in the middle of the group smiling dreamily and speaking softly. There was no sign of Drexler.

Berthold Von Stauffenberg and a fellow officer were standing with Dr Krystal Schmelter and a man Phillip hadn't seen before. The man smiled at Krystal and she smiled back, touching his arm. Stauffenberg waved at Phillip and the Kantorowicz's.

'You join them,' Mrs Kantorowicz said. 'They always argue about politics and who will be the leader after we get rid of this Republic. I need a word with our hostess.'

Kantorowicz lifted two glasses of champagne from a tray. He handed one to Phillip and then they strolled up to Stauffenberg's group. They all bowed to each other. Stauffenberg waved his arm. 'This is Doctor Schmelter who …'

'Phillip and I know each other.' Krystal smiled at Phillip and kissed him on the cheek. She turned to her companion. 'Phillip, this is Professor Rodin.'

Phillip felt his stomach tighten. So this was Rodin who would head up the new Race Hygiene Centre. Rodin was tall and slim with a small block of a moustache below which was a stub of beard. He had a set mouth and hard eyes as if what he thought was too important for any other expression.

'I have told Professor Rodin how you are helping us.'

Rodin shook Phillip's hand. 'Good to have you with us.'

Von Stauffenberg put his hand on Phillip's shoulder. 'Don't let them mislead you, Phillip. Once we get rid of this Republic, Stefan George, or someone he chooses, is the next leader, not their Little Corporal. Only eternal figures have served Germany in the past; Frederick the Great created the First Reich, Bismarck created the Second Reich, and now George is calling, in his new book, for A New German Empire, a Third Reich.'

'The National Socialists are also calling for a Third Reich,' Krystal said.

Kantorowicz waved his glass at Von Stauffenberg and the other officer. 'We also agree we need a New Reich, since democracy is too weak to be the birth mother of the new Germany. Germany has a divine mission and trust me, when the Republic fails, the people will turn to those who express the true essence of Germany, Stefan George. A collection of people, no matter how large, is only a number of zeros, a row of noughts. Only when the number one is placed at the beginning of them are they a nation. Only when we have a leader who understands the celestial and the people, can we achieve the potential that is waiting for us, and George is that leader, is that one.'

Krystal smiled. 'You really think a self-appointed group of poets are more effective than a mass movement and organisation? Yes, George is inspirational and reflects what we all think, but he lacks the organisational means of achieving our goals.'

Von Stauffenberg clicked his heels and bowed. 'Please excuse us. I see we are called.' Both officers turned and headed to where George stood, surrounded by young men.

Kantorowicz peered across the room. 'I too need to talk to someone.' He bowed and moved off.

Krystal touched Phillip's arm, 'Well, Phillip, we must make sure you stay on the right path and are not ensnared by George. Also, you are becoming a bit of a celebrity. 'I understand you will be at Countess Koniger's tomorrow evening.'

'Well, it …'

Rodin stared hard at Phillip. 'I'll get another drink.'

Krystal moved close to Phillip. 'You must come tomorrow night, Phillip. It would create a scandal if an Englishman turned down the Countess. She is making a gesture. Two of her sons were killed in the war.'

'Oh, of course I'll come. It's just that I have nothing to wear. I mean I …'

Krystal laughed. 'Is that all. Come like you are now. Sports jackets and bow tie are very fashionable.'

A man came up to them.

'Ah, this is Doctor Eugen Fischer. This is Phillip. He's helping us with our work.'

'Good to have you with us,' Fischer said, shaking Phillip's hand.

Fischer looked around. 'George allows too many Jews into his circle. Look around, how could you tell who is a Jew? Did you realise Kantorowicz is a Jew?'

Phillip shook his head.

'Exactly,' Krystal said. 'That is why our work is so important.' She smiled at Eugen Fischer who smiled back.

Krystal turned to Phillip. 'As well as reading George, you must read Eugen's work. His book *Principles of Human Heredity and Race Hygiene* has become very influential. In fact, Hitler read it while he was in prison after the putsch in 1923 and used it for his book, *Mein Kamp*. Another book you should read.'

Fischer made a glum face. 'Indeed, Hitler did use my book and I didn't even get an acknowledgment. He was very quick to praise the Americans for their contribution to his writing of Mien Kamp. Hitler even wrote a fan letter to Madison Grant telling him his race eugenics book, *The Passing of the Great Race,* was his bible.'

Krystal touched his arm. 'Never mind, you'll get your reward when Hitler comes to power. After all, you are the director of the institute.'

Berthold Von Stauffenberg came up to them, clicked his heels and bowed. 'I'm sorry to interrupt, but I have been sent as an emissary to conduct our fair English cousin to the master.'

'Don't forget, Phillip,' Kristal said, 'the soiree at the Countess's tomorrow night. See you there.'

'Yes.'

As they headed for Stefan George, Phillip touched Von Stauffenberg's arm and they stopped. Then, as casually as he could, 'Is Max Schneider here, the actor?'

'Certainly not. His idea of art is dressing up as a woman and making obscene jokes. Why?'

'Oh, nothing. Just someone wanted to know when his next show was.'

'At Blue Ridge Farm, no doubt. I have to say they are not my cup of tea, as you English say, but Christoph seemed to like them, artists and all that.'

'Have you seen Christoph?'

'No, no, I haven't. Nobody has. Bit strange.'

'If you do, can you say Anna, his girlfriend, wants to see him urgently.'

'Will do. Now, I must take you to the master. The reading is imminent.'

George saw Phillip coming and reached out and grasped his hand. 'Ah, the seraph has returned.'

Phillip was unable to release his hand from George's grip. 'Thank you for inviting me, sir.'

George patted Phillip's ensnared hand. 'Don't call me sir. I'm Stefan. We are about to have a reading from the *Blätter für die Kunst*, the sacred book of poems that contain the essence of Secret Germany.' Phillip slowly slid his hand from between George's soft palms. George smiled at him and then floated away towards the lectern.

The room hushed and people began to assemble in front of the lectern. A book, bound in green leather inlaid with gold wreaths, was positioned on the stand and the tall candles next it lit.

Von Stauffenberg raised his hand. 'Shush.'

The room went quiet, the curtains closed and Stefan George stepped up to the lectern. The candle flame trembled as he opened the book. A shaft of light struck George through a half-closed curtain, highlighting his silvery hair and outlining his profile.

George, his eyes softly luminous in the yellow candlelight, stared directly at Phillip. His gaze passed through Phillip into a universe beyond the corporal, taking Phillip with him.

George slowly turned back to the book, parted his lips and spoke the opening lines of Holderlin's poem.

> *'Thus the sons of earth now drink in*
> *The fire of heaven without danger.*
> *And it is our duty, poets, to stand*
> *Bare-headed under the storms of God,*
> *Grasping with our own hand*
> *The Father's beam itself,*
> *And to offer the gift of heaven,*
> *Wrapped in song, to the people.'*

Phillip saw no one but George in the room – George speaking directly to him, revealing the world to be created. Despite himself, Phillip felt drawn into the vision George was defining, and felt the pull to belong to those select ranks, chosen to propagate the truth, to spread the word, the word made flesh in the coming kingdom of the poets, where Germany would attain its divine mission. George had grasped 'The Father's beam itself' and could now lead the people.

That evening, Phillip stayed in his room. He could have got the last bus back to the farm but then he would have had to face an interrogation about Christoph. But when he did go back to the farm, he could say he had spoken to Von Stauffenberg and asked him to pass on the message.

But what about the man who was following him when he arrived from the farm? He had taken precautions and gone the long way home, along Hofer Street and then down through the alleyways at the back of his lodging. No one had followed him.

He would see if the man was waiting tomorrow morning at the bus terminus. If he wasn't there, then somebody at the farm had told him he wasn't travelling in on the bus.

Chapter 22

So, it was somebody at the farm.

Phillip had checked that there was no one at the top of the lane that led to his lodgings, and then slipped out and ran through the alleyways to Hofer Street and then to the bus terminal via a side street. He waited till the bus from the farm arrived. The man never appeared. So, who was it and why? Were they after the document? They must be. Why else would they be following him? Why else would they be after Schmidt, watching his home?

He turned and made his way to the Italian café. He had grown to appreciate their coffee and pastries. He had plenty of time to kill before going to Countess Koniger's that evening and thought he would spend it in the university library.

As he stepped into the warmth of the café, someone waved at him from a table. It was Bluum. Phillip selected his cakes and carried them along with his coffee to Bluum's table.

Bluum gave him a friendly smile. 'Please join me.'

Phillip sat down and placed his coffee and cakes on the table.

Bluum leaned back. 'You think I'm a racist.'

Phillip shrugged.

Bluum stirred his coffee. 'Your Professor Muller and I were friends at university in Berlin. We both wanted to be poets, but, like most people, our dreams of capturing the muse faded with age. She gradually got more elusive and so we needed to earn money to live.'

He lifted his cup and smiled over it. 'Krystal Schmelter attended our university, studying anthropology, and was part of our gang that went to the nightclubs and taverns together. Her professor was Eugene Fischer, who became the head of the Institute for Anthropology. He helped get her the post here in Bayreuth.' He smiled at Phillip. 'I used to go out with her before she realised I was a Jew, but she stayed in my bed long enough to get what she wanted.' He winked. 'Small world.'

Bluum drained his cup. 'I'm not a racist. I'm a realist.' He leaned across the table as if what he was saying was top secret. 'After we have a viable state of Israel, whose doors are always open to Jews from anywhere in the world, I don't care who marries whom. But first, we must build a Jewish state that is able to defend itself.'

'From what I understand, the Jews are fully emancipated here in Germany.' Phillip held Bluum's stare. The last thing he wanted was for Ruth to go to Palestine. 'Lots of groups have been persecuted in the past, but things move on. I'm a Catholic, and Catholics were discriminated against in Britain in the last century, especially in Ireland, but not anymore.'

'That was all about politics and power. What is coming to Germany isn't like anything that has gone before. Yes, in the past the persecution of the Jews has been driven by political opportunism, economics or just plain envy or prejudice, but the German's are different. This is unique. They want to destroy us, wipe us out. There is a whisper in their blood that we are rotting their essence and destroying their ancestral bloodline, a murmur in their imagination that we are polluting their souls so they cannot unite with their true spirit, we are destroying their Germanness.'

Phillip was surprised at the eloquent language and wondered if Bluum had written a poem about it. He thought of Stefan George. Bluum would certainly fit in, being highly intelligent and sensitive to the times, and no doubt good company, like Michael and Axel, but he was clearly on a mission and had no time for frivolity, like a man who loved the good life but chose the austere to save his soul.

But Bluum was right. Germany had changed. He wondered if Bluum knew about Doctor Schmelter's eugenics programme. Given the way he had spoken, he must do.

'The same in America when Jews were included in the Immigration Act of 1924,' Bluum said. 'We are seen as inferior people who mongrelise the white, North European stock who are the only true Americans.' He looked away. 'That is the real world, my friend. And here in Germany, if we are infecting them like a virus and destroying their Volk, the only solution they have is to destroy and eliminate the disease. Us. The Nazis are not just political, they are a movement, that makes it irrational, like religion, and so its followers will do unspeakable things.' He leaned back. 'You should know all this. I heard you were helping Krystal with the translations.'

Phillip stayed silent. He was finding it difficult to get an angle on Bluum whose eyes twinkled but his lips were tight.

'Well, I must be off,' Bluum said. He stood up. 'But tell Ruth I will marry Anna and raise the baby. I've already asked Anna to marry me.'

The snow sparkled in the brittle moonlight.

It had fallen late in the afternoon and then froze beneath an open sky, creating a surface that crunched like icing as Phillip clomped across the bridge over the Red River.

His landlady, Frau Weiser, had been most accommodating and helpful when he asked her for directions to the Countess's residence. She no doubt gossiped and so it would give his credibility a boost in a small town like Bayreuth.

He came off the bridge and strode past Saint Mary's church. A single set of footsteps, outlined in the snow, lead up to the church doors. Who had made them? A penitent seeking forgiveness, a destitute looking for shelter, or the priest returning from visiting a sick member of his flock? Just past the church, Phillip turned onto an open road leading out into the countryside.

The town lights had ended, replaced by the moon's glow on the snow-covered fields. A large Mercedes rattled past, honking its horn. Phillip walked closer to the edge of the field. After about a mile, he saw lights. They appeared to hover above the ground, but as he got closer, he realised they shone from the top windows of a large mansion with high walls.

He strode beside the front wall and came to open gates, supported by stone columns. On one pillar was engraved River Hall.

Fear surged inside him. Halfway along the drive, two large dogs with pointed ears stood outside their kennels looking at him, their eyes balls of gleaming blackness. He would have to pass them to get to the house, but he couldn't move.

'Don't worry, they're chained,' a voice said.

Phillip turned and a dumpy man in full evening dress, top hat and a short cloak fastened by a silver chain from which dangled an insignia, stood in the snow. The man took his hat off and bowed. 'Count Rostov. I passed you on the road in my car. If I knew you were heading for here, I would have stopped.'

'Oh, Phillip Fitzwilliam.'

'Ah, the English poet.'

'Oh, no. Not really.'

Count Rostov entwined his arm with Phillip's. 'It's so sweet how you young English boys hide your endowments. You must let them flourish in this new Germany where all is permitted.' He led Phillip up the path.

The dogs growled as they strolled past them. Phillip held his breath.

Rostov pulled Phillip close to him. 'Oh, you poor thing, I can feel you trembling. Don't worry, you're safe with me.' He patted Phillip's arm.

The doors of the mansion house opened before they reached them, and a tall man stepped out and flung his arms wide. 'Rostov.'

Rostov released Phillip and fell into the man's open arms. They kissed each other profusely on the cheeks. 'And this is Phillip,' Rostov said, spinning round.

'Oh, we all know Phillip. The cherub from England.' The man smiled, clicked his heels and bowed. 'Count Koniger, at your service.' They shook hands and Count Koniger led the way into the house.

They gave their coats to a servant and then strode through a tiled hallway with Baroque arches and walls teeming with green and gold acanthus fronds that climbed to the ceiling. A servant in tails pulled open a white door with gold filigree, and they stepped into a dazzling room.

The ceiling was a manifestation of gold painted cherubs and nymphs cascading music onto the assembled guests. The walls were covered in gilt-framed paintings, beneath which stood richly upholstered chairs and sofas occupied by men and women in full evening dress. Phillip felt completely out of place in his bow tie. Professor Muller was talking animatedly to a group who suddenly burst out laughing. Muller looked at Phillip and raised his glass. Phillip smiled in return. There were no army officers present, or anyone he knew. He wanted to go home.

Krystal glided towards him, wearing a full-length ivory dress embroidered with gold, long white gloves and a gleaming diadem that clasped her blond hair, while diamond earrings sparkled drops of light. She looked incredibly beautiful. Phillip felt a tingle as she held him and kissed him on the cheek. 'So glad you could come.'

'I'm so sorry about how I'm dressed. I …'

'Don't be silly. You're our guest from England and so you dress how you want. Actually, you look great, like a stylish young Englishman. Bow ties are also becoming popular in Germany.' She patted his arm. 'Could you come to my office tomorrow morning, about ten. I …'

'Here,' said Rostov, coming up to Phillip with a glass of white wine. 'Have some of our wonderful Riesling.'

Phillip sipped the wine.

Rostov raised an eyebrow. 'Well?'

'It's very nice. Thank you. Thank you very much. Very nice.'

Rostov beamed. 'Good. We will make a German of you yet.'

Krystal linked her arm into Phillip's. 'I must introduce him to Countess Koniger.'

'Of course.' Rostov stepped aside and gave a low bow.

Krystal led Phillip to a woman sitting alone on a sofa. She had fine features and smiled as they approached, but her blue eyes looked sad. She wore a long black dress with a white lace collar. In her hand was a fan with an ornate handle. 'This is Countess Koniger, and this is Phillip Fitzwilliam from England.'

Phillip bowed and the Countess raised her hand, palm downwards. Phillip took her hand and kissed it. The Countess smiled. 'Well, Phillip, we have heard good things about you. Doctor Schmelter thinks you are the perfect Aryan specimen.'

Phillip blushed.

'Countess Koniger knew Madam Blavatsky in London,' Krystal said.

Phillip smiled, but he had never heard of Madam Blavatsky.

The Countess wafted her fan. 'The poor boy has no idea who you're talking about.' She patted the sofa beside her. 'Come, sit down and I will enlighten you, because you, young man, are a perfect example of what Madam Blavatsky sought to protect and foster.'

Phillip sat down.

The Countess settled herself. 'Now, you must read two books written by Madam Blavatsky. They are *Isis Unveiled* and *The Secret Doctrine*. I have both. I will lend them to you. Both are written in English.'

Krystal lent towards the Countess. 'Please do excuse me, Countess, but I must have a word with someone. Phillip, could you come to my office in the morning? About eleven o'clock. I need to talk to you.'

'Of course.'

'Have you heard of a place called Hyperborea?' the Countess said.

'I'm afraid not. I haven't been in Germany long and haven't seen ...'

The Countess smiled. 'Oh, you won't find it in Germany. Hyperborea was an ancient civilisation, incredibly advanced culturally, technically and spiritually, and Ultima Thule was their capital. Our society, The Thules, is named after Ultima Thule, which means the most distant north. It was mentioned by the Roman poet Virgil in his epic poem *Aeneid*. We believe it is where Greenland and Iceland are now. But many millennia ago, before the last ice age, that area supported life and that is where the true European Aryans come from.

'The Aryans originally came from Atlantis, just off the Greek coast. When Atlantis was flooded by the Mediterranean Sea, the Aryans moved to the mainland. Some stayed in Greece, while others moved north and made their home in the Himalayas. They were a white race and one of their sacred symbols was the swastika. Then they moved west and created Hyperborea. We, the European Aryans, are their descendants. Therefore, we have the sacred duty of keeping the blood true and pure so that once again we Aryans can rule the world.'

Phillip thought of all the places in India and England where swastikas had been carved into the portal of houses. But he had always thought it was just a good luck charm and represented the wheel of life in Hindu scriptures.

'The Aryans gradually moved south from Hyperborea,' the Countess said, 'and founded the German tribes whose descendants still live in Germany and England. The Aryans are the highest of the races and that is why we dominate the world in everything, from culture to science. But it is vital that the blood of the Aryans is kept pure, or the race will die out and become like the other races in the world who have achieved nothing.'

'So, the Aryans came to Europe from Northern India?'

238

'Yes, indeed. And Tibet.' She signalled to a man standing by the piano. The man came over to her. 'Another glass of wine for my young friend here and a whisky for me.'

Phillip wanted to say that his father was from Northern India and had given him a swastika. That the Nazis were corrupting the symbol, which was known as the wheel of life and was a sign for goodness.

The Countess watched the young man cross the floor and then turned to Phillip. 'But in India some of the Aryan's intermarried with the local natives, and so their pure blood became mixed and lost its vital essence. The pure Aryans that moved west to the Nordic regions kept their pure blood, but the mongrels left behind in India continued to intermarry. Their loss of the pure blood allowed them to be conquered and ruled by the British, which is absolutely right since it is the destiny of Aryans to rule over others.'

The young man arrived with the drinks.

The Countess drank half the whisky in one go. 'And, of course, the Aryan race continues to evolve and develop. That's why we need to protect ourselves and produce people like you, Phillip.' She patted his leg. 'And who do you look like? Your mother or your father?'

'My mother.'

'And what does she do?'

'I'm afraid she's dead.'

'Oh, I'm sorry to hear that.'

'So is my father.'

The tinny sound of metal tapping glass echoed round the room. The conversations faded to silence. 'Now, everyone,' Count Koniger said, in a loud voice. 'We come to the highlight of the evening. Karl will play for us.'

There was applause and then the room hushed. The young man who had brought the drinks to the Countess sat down at the piano.

'He's my son,' whispered the Countess to Phillip. 'I lost my other son in the war.'

As the music played, Phillip gazed round the room, but saw no one he could approach to talk to about Christoph. There were one or two in army officer uniforms, but how could he ask them about Christoph Von Allenbach and then say his girlfriend was willing to have an abortion and ask them to find him and tell him? If they were Catholics, as were many Germans, especially here in Bavaria, they would be outraged and he would be seen as someone promoting an immoral and illegal act. No, it was too risky.

He watched as Krystal stood in a gathering, laughing and obviously pleased that she was being admired. And yet, the people in this room held abominable ideas about other classes and races. They all looked so civilised and complimented him, but if they knew he was half Indian they would throw him out. He finished his glass of wine, located a tumbler of Cognac which he drank in one gulp, and then took his leave.

There was no point in going back to the farm tomorrow, Thursday. He had to see Krystal in the morning and then the Blue Lagoon in the evening to try to find Schmidt.

As he walked back towards the town, the grey clouds, moonlit with halos, sailed above, driven by a dark unseen wind. The alcohol, as always, made him hyper. He reached the bridge over the Red River and stopped and drank in the night air, savouring it like the after taste of good wine, and thinking of Holderlin's lines 'the fragrant cup, full of dark light'.

He felt too mixed up to go straight home. How could such cultured people harbour such wicked thoughts about other people? People they had never met, but were willing to condemn them to … what? How far would they really go? He thought of his father, one of the kindest and most civilised men he had ever known, and yet he would be … what? What would these people do to him?

He strode beside the dark flowing water, trying to make sense of it all. Words drifted into his mind – 'blood and soil', 'race is blood', 'blood is race'. Could it be true?

Where did that leave him? And what about Ruth, a Jew, one of the most naturally intelligent, wise and beautiful people he had ever met. And Kharos?

Chapter 23

Phillip arrived outside Doctor Schmelter's office just before ten o'clock.

She ushered him into her room. 'Now Phillip, I have two other papers I need you to translate. One is the synopsis of the minutes of the meeting we had in Berlin with our American cousins and patrons, which, needless to say is in English since it was their conference, and also the minutes of the Eugenics Conference in Washington, last May. If you do the work well, there could be a position for you here in the university in the languages department, and as my assistant.'

Krystal moved from behind the desk and stood facing Phillip, almost touching him. She smiled into his eyes. 'You could have a good future here, Phillip. At the university and possibly with the new Race Hygiene Centre. We need someone we can trust to help with our coordination with our American and British colleagues.' She held his arms. 'Everyone agrees you are the kind of young man who is the future.' Her eyes moved slowly over his face and lingered on his lips. 'You must choose where your future lies.'

Phillip stared at her.

Krystal walked back behind her desk. 'Or,' she said, 'are you being seduced by the black-haired Jew? Imagine, your babies would have dark skin, black hair, brown eyes and hooked noses.' She shuddered. 'Don't throw away your heritage, Phillip. You have beautiful blue eyes, fair skin and blond hair. You are a delight to look at and you enhance the world. Imagine a world without people like us, a world where everyone has coffee-coloured skin, thick lips, frizzy hair. That's what will happen if we do not defend the purity of our race.'

She stepped out from behind her desk and stood in front of him. 'It is our duty, your duty, to defend it. You say you were brought up by your mother; think what she would feel. It is our duty to protect and nurture the purity of our race. We …' The phone rang.

Krystal picked it up. She listened for a few moments, and then said, 'Yes. Hamburg. So her husband really was a poet. Probably got his rhythm and metre from the bongos.' There was a pause. 'Yes, her daughter is called Kharos.'

Phillip felt a stab of fear. 'Yes, good. As soon as possible. We need to show that we are in the forefront of developing the programme.' She listened. 'Yes, Applied Eugenics.' Krystal put the phone down. 'OK,' she said, handing the file to Phillip, 'if you could press on with the translation it would be a real help.' Krystal nodded and Phillip realised he was being dismissed.

As Phillip made his way back to his lodgings, fear spread through him. Why was Krystal was talking about Kharos? And what did she want done 'as soon as possible'? Should he tell Lena? And what was 'Applied Eugenics'? It was in the file he was meant to be translating.

He reached his lodgings, rushed up the stairs and found the eugenics file. He flipped through it to Applied Eugenics. His blood chilled as he read.

An approach has been put forward by Popenoe and Johnson in their textbook, "Applied Eugenics", published in 1920 by Macmillan & Co Limited. They advocate "Lethal Selection, through the destruction of the individual by some adverse feature of the environment, such as excessive cold, or bacteria, or by bodily deficiency." The Illinois Institution for the Feebleminded at Lincoln, Illinois, USA, took up this proposal and developed the practice of feeding inmates milk that had come from cows suffering from tuberculosis.

This resulted in a mortality rate of 40 percent. But this was recognised as not being efficient.

This reflects the findings of the Carnegie funded report of 1911 of the American Breeders Association, Committee of Eugenic Section. They were asked to: "Study and to Report on the Best Practical Means for Cutting Off the Defective Germ-Plasm in the Human Population."

In their report, they suggest euthanasia as a highly efficient method.

This has been the most commonly suggested method of eugenicide in the United States. The use of a "lethal chamber" or public, locally operated gas chambers. Again, from Popenoe's widely used textbook: "From an historical point of view, the first method which presents itself is execution . . . Its value in keeping up the standard of the race should not be underestimated."

Phillip flicked back through the report. The use of gas chambers to kill those whom society considered unfit to live was not only being advocated by George Bernard Shaw but also by other so called leading intellects. It was clear that using gas chambers to kill those deemed unfit to live was common thinking amongst those who promoted race eugenics.

He closed the file. His heart beat faster. He could hardly take it all in.

Was that what was planned for Kharos? That she would be incarcerated and then fed germ-ridden milk, underfed and left in the cold till she died, a victim of Applied Eugenics. How could it happen? But it was already happening, in America.

Seated at the table he'd occupied on his first visit to the Blue Lagoon, Phillip ordered a White Lady cocktail.

The waiter stiffened. 'Sorry, sir, we no longer do that drink. Perhaps a whisky?'

'Oh. OK.'

Why didn't they do a White Lady cocktail anymore? What had changed? Was the tramp's death anything to do with it? Without moving his head, he carefully scrutinised the patrons. The man in the tin mask wasn't there. How long should he wait? The response of the waiter when he asked for a White Lady cocktail worried him. One drink and then he would go.

A five-piece band was playing American swing music while a man, dressed in a sixteenth century French court costume and wearing a long curly wig, danced on his own just in front of Phillip. Phillip watched him twirl, swaying in his own pleasure, as if the clothes, the black beauty-spot on his alabaster cheek, the coat of golden brocade sparking with reflected light, were substance, and the man ethereal. The music ended and the man sashayed to Phillip's table and plonked himself down on the vacant chair.

The waiter returned with Phillip's whisky. 'I'll have my usual,' said the man to the waiter.

The man turned to face Phillip, his wig shimmering with light. For a moment, the sheer beauty of his face, enhanced by make-up, captivated Phillip.

The man smiled. 'You can look, but that's it. I'm not interested in sex, never have been, but I love dressing up and being admired. I suppose you think that's just vanity.'

'No. No. If it makes you happy.'

'It does. Besides, I have the feeling you're also not seeking the love that dare not speak its name.'

Phillip wasn't sure what the man meant. 'Um. Actually, I'm looking for a man who wears a tin face mask.'

'Ah, him.' The man shuddered, his wig rippling like shaken velvet. 'Ghastly features, poor man. Mind you some people like that sort of thing, lost limbs, deformed bodies. Arouses their Eros.'

Phillip leaned forwards. 'Have you seen him? Do you know him?'

The man laughed. 'My, my. Are you …?'

'No. No. Not at all.'

'No, I didn't think you were one of the flock. But some here fantasised you were, that you just needed the right push. Well, the man in the mask has only been here a couple of times. This place is not to his taste since he likes the rougher side of things, and so I'm not sure anyone here knows him, and besides, we tend not to reveal our real names, safer that way. I'm Louis, after the Sun God. You know the French …'

There was a scream, and a man in a dress burst through the entrance doors and ran across the dance floor, blood streaming down his face. Through the open doors, Phillip saw Brownshirts smashing clubs into people covered in blood.

Louis jumped up. 'This way.'

Phillip ran with Louis across the dance floor, past the toilets and out the back door into a yard. Ahead of them, people were clambering up steps. Phillip followed Louise up the steps and found himself in an alleyway. Screams and cries filled the air as people crashed out of the back door of the club and scrambled up the steps.

It was almost pitch black. To his right, at the end of the alley, Phillip saw a block of light that led to the main square. People who were running towards the square, suddenly stopped. Brownshirts, holding batons, appeared at the end of the alley, blocking access to the main square. The screech of whistles rent the air and the Brownshirts charged down the alley. The club-goers shrieked and turned like a flock of startled geese. Phillip felt terrified and ran beside Louis and others down the dark alleyway, away from the men with batons.

Screams and cries came from behind him but Phillip was too frightened to look back. Louis, who was running in front of him, stumbled and fell forwards in a heap. Phillip stopped and reached down, grabbed Louis's arm and yanked him to his feet, surprised how light he was. A bruising pain shot through Phillip as he was struck across his shoulders. Then came the sickening sound, like leather on marble, as Louis was struck on the head. Louise buckled to his knees. Phillip rushed at the dark form of the attacker, pushing him backwards onto the floor. People stumbled over the assailant, some falling on top of him.

Phillip pulled Louis up and dragged him forwards, making him run, but Louis wobbled and fell to his knees. Phillip lifted him up, slung him over his shoulder and began running. Phillip felt a couple of blows on the body he was carrying but kept running till he caught up with others fleeing along the alleyway, their clothes and shoes slowing them down. Phillip pushed his way through to the front and ran into the dark.

The alleyway seemed endless, but because no one was in front of him he could speed up. Behind he could hear cries as people were caught and beaten. He kept running and suddenly came out to a road with streetlamps. There was no one behind him. From the darkness of the alleyway, came the sound of faint cries. Phillip slid Louis from his shoulders and held him upright by the arms. Louis's eyes were closed. 'Are you OK?'

Louis opened his eyes. 'Yes. Yes, I am. Thank you so much for saving me.'

'Do you know how to get home?'

'Yes. Yes, thank you. I live near here. A house in the square. What is your name?'

Phillip hesitated. 'Phillip.'

'Well Phillip, you have saved me. Thank you. What about you getting home?'

'Not far.'

'Good. Well, at least you're not dressed as a queen.'

The sound of police sirens echoed over the houses.

'Late, as usual,' Louis said. 'Well, thanks again, Phillip, I will be eternally grateful. I'll be off. I don't want to meet any police.'

Phillip shuddered. What if the police picked him up? Asked for his papers? He looked around. Areas of deep shadow stretched away on the other side of the road. It must be open fields, which meant he was on the outskirts of the city. Which way to go? He turned right and trudged along the road.

There was the sound of water. The river. He followed a track into the darkness towards the sound of flowing water. Suddenly the blackness leaped over him as he slipped downwards and just managed to stop himself falling into the river.

He stood on the bank and looked left and right but couldn't get his bearing. He went right. The river's dark form flowed beside him like a malevolent companion. A large building bled out of the dark on the opposite side of the river. As he got closer, lights revealed it was Christoph's barracks. Phillip turned and walked back the way he had come.

The door to the alleyway beside his lodgings creaked and Phillip stopped. There was no sound inside the house. He retrieved the key from under the birdbath, unlocked the back door, slipped inside and relocked the door, then trod quietly up the stairs to his room, his body trembling.

He lay back on the bed and fought down the nausea. Pain spread across his back and shoulders. He sat up in fear.

His coat was back in the club. The paper with the details of how to contact the SIS agent were in the inside pocket.

Chapter 24

Should he go back to the Blue Lagoon?

The question had kept him awake all night. Did the Nazis have his coat with the note from SIS in the pocket? If the Nazis had stolen his coat and found the note, what would they do? Or, was it still in the club?

Phillip reached for his watch. A jab of pain shot through his shoulder. It was seven o'clock. Trying not to twist his shoulders, he rolled out of bed. There was no mirror so he couldn't see his injuries but even if they needed attention, he couldn't go to the hospital; they would ask questions.

When he drew the curtains, the sight of the back alley sent shivers through him. What happened to those who hadn't outrun the Brownshirts? If the attackers had blocked off both ends of the alleyway, he would have been caught and no doubt beaten. He had been lucky to escape.

The day was grey and overcast and a thin light struggled through the clouds. This time in the morning there wouldn't be too many people about, and the Munich police were unlikely to be watching the club since people only went there at night.

He turned from the window and started to dress. If he went by the Red River, the way he had come home, he could cut down the alleyway behind the club, as if he were heading for the main square, and knock on the back door. But he had to get there without a hat and coat – what if he was recognised?

He hurried across Bayreuth's main square. There were no police or Nazis around; perhaps it was too early or too cold. He left the square and strode down a street with tall houses towards Red River. The rugged sky was scattered with boulders of grey and white cloud, and a bitter wind drove snow flurries through the canyon of high buildings. His ears began to sting and his hands throbbed with cold. He came to the river, turned right and trudged through the snow towards the alleyway at the back of the club.

The alley was deserted and seemed shorter than he remembered from the previous night. When he reached the back of the club, the basement looked smaller and the downward steps narrower. His stomach churned when he saw dried blood on the railings. Without touching the railings, he went down the steps and knocked on the back door. There was no reply and he knocked again. Nobody came. He stuck his hands into his armpits to warm them and trod back up the steps.

At the top of the steps, panic hit him. In the entrance to the alley from the square, a man with a black leather coat stood staring at him. Phillip was about to run back towards the river when the man smiled, and called, 'The hero returns.' The man strode up to Phillip and extended his hand. 'I'm Jorgen. You don't recognise me because I'm not in my top hat and tails. Come, I'll make you some coffee, you look frozen. Your coat and hat are inside.'

Phillip followed Jorgen down the steps. His coat was still there, but was the note with the instructions of how to contact SIS still in the pocket? Without it, there was no way to inform them of developments. The pungent odour of bleach hit him as they passed the toilets. In the dancing area, the tables were set with tablecloths, vases of flowers and shaded lamps, as if the previous night's violence had never taken place. Phillip followed Jorgen across the dance floor, up onto the stage and through a red door behind one of the side curtains.

They climbed a small flight of stairs and stepped into a low-lit room. A window, draped with gold curtains, looked out over gardens to the main square. Rich oriental rugs covered a polished mahogany floor along with a white bearskin with curved yellow claws, pointed white teeth and piercing black eyes. Red flock wallpaper decorated the walls which were hung with Rocco mirrors framed with twisting vines. Jorgen brushed through a screen of brightly coloured beads into a kitchen. 'Sit,' called Jorgen, from the kitchen. 'I'll make some coffee.'

Phillip remained standing. 'Actually, I need to be going. I only came to get my coat. I have to be … I have an appointment.'

Jorgen emerged from the kitchen. 'Shame. Still, come back anytime. The man you saved last night is my brother. If there is anything I can do for you, just ask.'

'A man in a tin mask is sometimes here. I think he is called Schmidt. Do you know him?'

'Not really. We see him around. But he's … not our type. He had some arrangement with the waiters about meeting someone here, someone who would ask for a White Lady cocktail. All very mysterious. But then we live in interesting times, don't you think, Phillip?'

How did he know his name? Then he remembered he had told it to Louis, Jorgen's brother.

Jorgen handed Phillip his coat and hat. Phillip slipped on his coat, thrust his hand into the pocket and took out the note from Max.

Jorgen stiffened. 'Nobody's touched anything.'

'Oh … oh, yes, yes, I'm sure. It's just that there is an address I need to keep. And a date and time. I thought I'd lost it.'

Jorgen smiled and stuck out his hand. 'Indeed. Well, you must come and visit us again. And remember, if there is anything I can do, just ask.'

'Actually, you don't know someone called Max Schneider, do you? He sometimes calls himself Antonio Martini. You had a poster for one of his shows in the toilet.'

Jorgen laughed. 'Maestro Martini. Yes, he's a regular. He was here last night.'

Phillip couldn't believe what he had just heard. 'What? Really?'

Jorgen smiled and shrugged.

'Oh, it's just that I need to speak to him. Urgently.'

'Well, I don't know where he lives. And after last night we're closed for the time being. But he'll be here Monday afternoon. He's helping plan the tea dance.'

Phillip forced himself to stay calm. He didn't know what Max looked like. 'I wonder if I could have a private word with him.'

'No problem. You can use this room. Be here about three. I'll bring him up when he arrives.'

Phillip looked into Jorgen's smiling eyes. 'Thank you. Thank you very much.' He shook Jorgen's hand with both his hands. Jorgen laughed.

Phillip could hardly contain his excitement as he crossed the main square and headed for the Italian café. Perfect. It could all be tied up by the end of next week, and then he would be on his way back to England and safety.

When he arrived, the bus to Blue Ridge Farm was at the terminus. He would stay at the farm till Monday and then return to Bayreuth for the meeting with Max Schneider. Should he send a telegram to arrange a meeting with SIS for Monday afternoon or Tuesday? No, he would wait till he had the document.

Chapter 25

Phillip stretched beneath the duvet, luxuriating in the warmth as the morning sun seeped through the curtain.

Ruth lay beside him, softly snoring, as if everything she did was gentle. It was one of the many things that was so attractive about her. But would he lose her? Within days, his mission would be complete and he would be heading home. He hadn't told Ruth Bluum would marry Anna, even though she was carrying another man's baby. If Bluum persuaded Anna to go to Palestine, would Ruth go with her sister?

He slipped quietly out of the bed. He would surprise Ruth and start the fire in the stove, then make the coffee and bring her a cup in bed.

After breakfast, Phillip stepped outside. The November winds flurried the tops of the trees in the wood and patches of snow lay in the fields and along the sides of the cabins, but the day was mild and the sun warmed his face. It seemed the heavens were trying to keep winter at bay and had won the latest battle.

The repaired barn gleamed like a giant toy, red roof, white walls and a bright red door. The charred remains of the *Parsifal* scenery were still strewn in front of the barn. He looked where the lorry full of Nazis had stood and shuddered at the image of Drexler staring down at him.

The acrid smell of charred wood greeted him as he entered the barn and reminded him of cleaning out the fire grate at home. Corrugated iron panels were stacked along the back wall. The bench and metal vice were still intact and the tools were all there.

Gunter entered carrying a bundle of wooden slats on his shoulder. He walked up to Phillip and threw them down. 'There. Let's get cracking and show those Nazi bastards they can't defeat us. Up and over.' Phillip was surprised hear him use a wartime expression, but it was clear Gunter was angry. Gunter turned and marched out of the barn.

Phillip made good progress with the frames and was about to glue them when he heard a shuffle. Kharos was walking slowly towards him gripping a mug of steaming coffee. 'Mummy said she hopes she didn't upset you too much the other day.'

'Tell Mummy it's OK,' Phillip said, taking the mug. 'And say thank you for the coffee.'

'Can I stay and help you?'

'Of course. You can stir the gluepot.'

'Thank you, Phillip.'

He smiled at the way she said his name. He sipped his coffee and watched her carefully stir the pot. If he had children, he would want them to be like Kharos, well-mannered and talented. Anger surged inside him when he thought of what the race eugenicists would do to her and others like her. Perhaps to Jews like Ruth as well. Bluum said the Americans, in there immigration act of 1924 had identified Jews, along with Southern Europeans and other non-

Nordics, as the unfit and should be bred out of the population one way or another. And the German's were following the American lead in eugenics.

Should he tell Lena and Ruth they could be in danger or did they already know? Perhaps he would talk to Gunter and get his advice. He had somehow to explain what the Race Hygiene Centre was planning without revealing he was working for Doctor Schmelter. But if it got out and someone confronted Doctor Schmelter and it was traced back to him, he would be in trouble. They'd probably set the Brownshirts on him, perhaps even ...

The door banged open and Ruth ran into the barn. 'Kharos, quick. Come with me.' Ruth grabbed Kharos and rushed out.

Phillip crossed to the barn door. He jumped back when he saw two policemen, one with an Alsatian dog, standing by the cauldron, arguing with Gunter. One policeman was shouting that they had the right to search the property because they had a court order, but Gunter was arguing that the court order didn't include a search warrant. The policeman insisted they didn't need one and warned Gunter not to impede their search or he would be arrested, along with anyone else trying to stop them carrying out the court order.

Phillip's heart pounded inside him. Who were the police looking for? Him? No, it must be Kharos, which is why Ruth grabbed her. But what if the police questioned him? Asked for his papers. His passport. He had to hide. He looked at the pile of corrugated iron.

Ruth barged back into the barn, pushing a wheelbarrow with a tarpaulin over it. She manoeuvred the barrow into a corner of the barn. The tarpaulin was thrown off and Kharos sat up inside the wheelbarrow. Ruth pushed her back down and covered her with the tarpaulin. 'Kharos, please, please, darling, you must be very quiet and stay in the barrow. And keep covered. Uncle Phillip will be here.'

Phillip rushed up to them. 'The dog will find her.'

Ruth looked as if she were about to cry. 'What can we do. They have a court order for Lena to be committed to a mental asylum and Kharos to be taken into the care of her grandmother. God knows what will happen to them. We must save them.'

Phillip put his hands on Ruth's shoulders. 'Go to Gunter and get chilli pepper. The stuff he uses for cooking.'

'What?'

'Just do it, Ruth, please. Now. Remember, ask him for chilli pepper.'

Ruth rushed out.

Phillip ran over to the corrugated panels left over from when Gunter repaired the barn roof. He propped the sheets of iron lengthways against the wall, creating a tunnel.

Ruth ran in with the chilli power. 'They're searching Lena's cabin; perhaps we could make a run for it.'

Phillip took Kharos out of the barrow. 'Not with a dog chasing you.' He led Kharos to the corrugated sheets and helped her crawl into the tunnel.

'But won't the dog find her there?' Ruth said.

'Not with this they won't.' Phillip sprinkled the chilli powder on the floor around panels. He then lay down and slid himself into the narrow gap. He grabbed Kharos's hands. She was shaking. Phillip peered through a small screw hole in the sheet. He could see Ruth's feet and the floor up to the barn door. 'Ruth, you should leave.'

About ten minutes later, the barn door scraped open and Phillip saw two feet and four paws. The dog was panting heavily. Phillip began to sweat. Kharos gripped his hands tightly. He lost sight of the dog but could hear someone kicking the frames. Then he heard a muffled yelp and knew the dog had sniffed the chilli powder.

'Come here, come here,' shouted the policeman. 'OK. OK. We'll go outside.'

Phillip wasn't sure how long they were under the corrugated iron before the sheets were suddenly pulled away and clattered to the ground. Ruth and Gunter were standing in front of him. As Phillip stood up, Ruth grabbed Kharos and ran out of the barn.

Gunter patted Phillip's shoulder. 'Well done, Englishman. Here.' He thrust a mug of beer at Phillip.

Phillip swallowed it down. He was surprised how fast he drank it. Gunter took the mug. 'Come on. You could do with another one.'

Gunter led Phillip across the compound to his cabin. Gunter's cabin was larger than the others and had a cast-iron stove with an oven for cooking. Stacks of canvases, which occupied half the available space, were propped against the walls. An aroma of dried oil paint pervaded the room, reminding Phillip of the fine art studios at university. There was no furniture except for a wooden table and four upholstered dining chairs. Phillip sat at the table.

Gunter plonked a mug of beer in front of Phillip, and then sat opposite him. 'That was a good trick with the chilli powder.'

Phillip was shaking and held the mug with both hands while he drank. Gunter drank from a porcelain tankard, decorated with flowers. 'So, where did you learn the trick with the chilli powder?'

'I ... I read it in a book.'

Gunter leaned back and smiled. 'By the way, it's all right to be frightened. It's human. During the war, especially towards the end, we were all terrified. Alcohol and morphine kept us going.'

Phillip nodded and gulped down the beer. A warm numbness began to spread through him.

Ruth staggered into the cabin, carrying two duvets, clothes and an army rucksack. Gunter took them from her, dumped them on the floor and nodded to her to sit. He opened a cupboard and took out a bottle of amber coloured liquid with a cork wedged halfway into the neck. He yanked out the cork with his teeth, glugged a good measure into a tumbler and placed it in front of Ruth.

Ruth gave a tight-lipped smile and sipped the liquid. She licked her lips and turned to Phillip. 'Lena thanks you for saving Kharos. She wants to talk to you.'

Gunter poured himself a measure of the amber liquid and offered the bottle to Phillip. 'Peach brandy. Made here on the farm.'

Phillip shook his head. 'No thank you. I'm not into spirits.'

Gunter tipped a measure into a glass. 'This isn't your Scotch whisky.' He pushed the glass in front of Phillip. 'Try it.'

Phillip took a sip and liked the sweet mellowness. The alcohol was beginning to settle him.

Gunter poured another measure into Ruth's empty glass. 'I think we should explain to Phillip exactly what the situation is.'

Ruth took a deep breath. 'I think you know that Lena's husband, who was an African from German West Africa, was murdered in Hamburg by the Nazis. Lena then brought Kharos to Bavaria, to try to keep her safe. Lena first went to Munich, where her mother lives, but her mother, who supports the Nazis, rejected her and Kharos and told people Lena was mentally insane, which is why she married a black man. She said Lena should be put into an asylum and sterilised. That's what the court order was for.'

Sterilised – the word resounded in Phillip's mind. The programme Krystal was developing had already started. How could a mother reject her daughter and want her locked up and sterilised because she married a black man? His mother had married an Indian. But there could be worse to come, especially if Germany implemented what was happening in California and followed people like Bernard Shaw who wanted those unfit to live to be put into gas chambers and killed.

'That's the document they showed me,' said Gunter. 'The mother has a committal order, countersigned by two doctors and approved by a judge, to have Lena locked up in a mental institution and sterilised. The judge also sanctioned Lena's mother having charge of Kharos.'

'If that happened,' said Ruth, 'Lena's mother would also have Kharos sterilised.'

Phillip's mind was whirling. The alcohol and the escape from the dog heightened everything. Kharos, the girl he had held in his arms and kept safe from the police dog, to be incarcerated and sterilised. It was inhuman. 'But that's just wrong. The law shouldn't allow it.'

Ruth took a sip of the brandy. 'I've told you about the judges in Bavaria.'

Phillip clenched his teeth. The anger became resolve. He would fight it, fight to save Kharos and Ruth and others like them. He would not stand aside like a scared mouse, scared of what people would think of him for supporting Jews and mixed race people and the others that those in the establishment wanted cleansed from society, as if they were diseased and Race Hygiene Eugenics the disinfectant.

Ruth finished her drink and stood. 'Right. Let's go.'

Phillip followed her out of the cabin, carrying the two duvets. The weather had turned and snowflakes whirled beneath a grey, metallic sky, heralding worse to come. The whole landscape now looked bleak and foreboding.

Ruth led Phillip out of the encampment and across the main road into an open field. There was no path and Ruth led the way across the frozen pasture towards the foot of the hills. Iron-grey clouds hung low from the sky and a bitter wind drove a spiteful rain laced with ice into their faces.

Phillip tried to think why Lena would want to talk to him. They reached a stream, which they crossed by a wooden bridge. The floor of the bridge was slippery and Phillip had to grip the handrail, which sent a jolt of ice-cold through him. He needed to buy gloves. He was glad of his new boots.

They trudged alongside the river towards trees that looked to be the start of a forest. They slogged through the trees, along a path barely visible under the snow. Suddenly the wind died and the woods became eerily silent, like a snowstorm in a glass globe.

After about half an hour they came to a clearing. In the middle of it stood a large oil drum resting on a circle of stones. On one side of the clearing was a crude hut made of wattles with a thatched roof. Ruth headed for the hut. 'The hut belongs to a charcoal maker, but he's not burning at the moment,' Ruth said. 'But he'll be back next week, so Lena and Kharos need to be away before then.' She knocked on the wooden stanchion that supported the door. 'It's Ruth.'

The door was dragged open and Phillip could just make out Lena standing in the gloom inside the hut. He followed Ruth inside. The interior was grimy, with an earthen floor, an army bed with piles of blankets, a tree-stump for a table and one wooden chair. Strips of light penetrated through a wooden shutter. Kharos rushed up to Phillip and wrapped her arms around his waist, pressing her head into his stomach.

Phillip couldn't unwind Kharos's arms and so he placed his hands on her back. Ruth unpacked a thermos from the rucksack and then poured its contents into a cup. 'Here, Kharos. Some nice hot chocolate.'

Kharos held onto Phillip. Lena unfolded Kharos's arms from around Phillip. 'You drink the chocolate. Mummy wants to talk to Phillip.'

Ruth guided Kharos to the bed, while Lena took Phillip outside.

They strolled away from the hut and stopped at the edge of the clearing. Lena turned and held Phillip's gaze. 'You know why the police were here?'

Phillip nodded.

Lena stared at him, her eyes as sharp and penetrating as a bird's, making him feel threatened. 'And you still think you did the right thing by hiding Kharos?'

'Yes. Of course.'

Lena continued to hold his eyes. 'Really?'

She knew, thought Phillip, she knew what they would do to her and Kharos 'Yes. Absolutely.'

Lena gripped Phillip's hands. 'Deep down you are a good person, Phillip, but you have much to learn about people and the world. Not everyone is who they say they are.'

What did she mean, thought Phillip? She clearly wanted to tell him something. What?

Lena's grip tightened. 'Promise me that if anything happens to me, you will help look after Kharos. Save her from ...' Lena stepped up close to Phillip. 'Promise me you will not let her come to any harm. Even if you hear bad things about me.'

What did she mean? Hear bad things about her? 'Yes,' Phillip said. 'Of course. I will never let her come to harm. I promise you.'

It was unusually quiet as Phillip and Ruth arrived back at the circle of huts. Voices were low and Phillip wondered how many people knew why the police had searched the encampment, and what they thought about it. He didn't know many of the inhabitants, but presumed they were all liberal or left wing or nothing, and just wanted to be left alone to indulge their creative drives. But what did Lena mean about 'hearing bad things about her'? Why should that affect him? What was she trying to tell him?

Phillip sat at the table in Ruth's cabin, near the stove. 'So what's going to happen?'

'We need to get them out of Germany, but that means passports and they don't have any. The plan is to sit tight, wait a few days till it quietens down, and then smuggle them across the border to Alsace. We've decided we need to separate Kharos from Lena until they leave.'

'Why?'

'It was Lena's idea. She's desperate for Kharos not to fall into the hands of her grandmother.'

Phillip wondered how much Lena knew about the race eugenics programme. How much did Ruth know? Neither of them spoke about it. Perhaps they were unaware of it, like he had been, or thought it would never be allowed to happen in Germany, not like America. 'Where is Alsace? Switzerland?'

Ruth smiled. 'No. It's France. But it used to be part of Germany. Well, it was only German from 1871 and before that it was French. Anyway, after the Great War it was given back to France. Actually, I was born there.'

'Really.'

'Yes. My father wanted to remain German and so he moved the family to Berlin in 1919.'

'What do you feel?'

'Feel?'

'Yes, French or German?'

'I feel human. And hungry.'

Phillip was confused. Had he said something stupid? He'd always felt English and thought everyone belonged to one country or other.

Ruth got four bowls from the cupboard. 'I'll take some dinner to Lena and Kharos and then bring ours back.'

Phillip gazed into the flames of the stove and remembered the feeling of Kharos holding onto him when they were under the corrugated iron, and Lena's hands gripping his, as if pouring her need into him. There was no turning back, no going back to accepting the judgement of others. He would become who he was, who he really was. What came from within him would make who he is, not what others thought. He would keep his promise to Lena and protect Kharos.

But Lena had also warned him, just as Christoph had. What did they know that he didn't? Is it to do with the man who follows him when he gets off the bus from the farm? Did it have anything to do with his mission? It must have. But what?

Chapter 26

The clash of metal jolted him awake.

Had the police returned? It was Ruth raking out the stove. Phillip lay back in the bed. What if SIS sent him home before Lena and Kharos could be smuggled out of Germany? What if the police came back with more resources and made a thorough search of the compound and surrounding area and he was found without proper papers and questioned? He threw back the covers.

The living room was empty. A cup of coffee and a pot of porridge were keeping warm on top of the stove, and on the table a basket full of cheeses, meats and bread. Ruth barged into the cabin holding a canister of milk. 'I'm taking these to Lena and Kharos. Why don't you come with me?'

'Sorry, I can't. I have to go to Bayreuth.'

Ruth put the milk down and took Phillip in her arms. 'You must look for Christoph. I'm really worried what he might do. He always runs away from things and waits for them to go away.'

'Maybe he will come and live here with Anna and be an artist. You said he was really talented.'

'Yes, but that means making a decision and going against his family.'

'Of course I'll look for him. I met Von Stauffenberg at George's reading and told him to tell Christoph Anna desperately wanted to see him. He said he would, but he also said nobody had seen Christoph of late.'

Ruth shook her head. 'Did you ask him to tell Christoph Anna would abort the baby?'

Phillip looked down. 'There were too many people around. I …'

'It's OK. Anna's gone to Bayreuth to try to find him and tell him herself. You might meet her.' She kissed him on the cheek. 'OK. See you later.'

As he sat at the table drinking his coffee, he wondered why Ruth didn't ask what he was doing in Bayreuth.

Phillip strolled to the bus stop, gazing up at the black silhouettes of crows circling above the fields and wondering what they hoped to find on the frozen earth? As he reached the bus stop, he heard footsteps come up behind him. Gunter stood next to him at the stop. Ruth must have told him he was going to Bayreuth. Gunter peered down the road and then shook himself. 'I know, Phillip, you mix with lots of different people. And at your age it must be difficult to know who you really are, and what you believe in. Especially when people who wear red coats get killed outside churches.'

How did Gunter know? Who else knew? 'My coat was stolen.'

Gunter stared down the road. He then turned to Phillip. 'Why do you read the *Volkischer Beobachter*, a Nazi paper? There are lots of other papers.'

Phillip's heart pounded.

Gunter dropped his voice. 'Know your enemy?'

Phillip didn't understand. Did Gunter think he was a Communist? The green bus, topped with snow, was trundling towards them. Gunter touched Phillip's arm. 'I have to ask. You won't say where Lena is hiding?'

'Never. Why would I? You can't think ...'

Gunter put his arm round Phillip's shoulders. 'Sorry. Maybe I shouldn't have said it. But I had to ask. Lena says, deep down you are good and have promised to protect Kharos.' He took a piece of paper from his pocket. 'This is the farm phone number. If you need to get out of Bayreuth fast, call me.'

Phillip took the paper and stuffed it in his pocket. Gunter stuck out his hand. 'Be careful. And remember, be who you really are.'

Phillip shook Gunter's hand and nodded.

Phillip jumped as a fat man slumped into the seat beside him. He hadn't registered that the bus had stopped, his mind full of what Gunter had said. What did Gunter know? Why did Gunter think he bought the *Volkischer Beobachter* to 'know his enemy'? Who did

Gunter think he was? Did he suspect he was an SIS agent? If so, why did Gunter give him his phone number in case of trouble? And again, Lena saying deep down he was good, which meant … What did she know about him?

The man who had followed him on previous visits to Bayreuth wasn't at the bus station. But as he made his way across the square, he thought a different man was trailing him. Phillip resorted to the usual tactics and hurried to the alleyways around the university, where he soon lost whoever was trying to track him. Then again, it might have been coincidence, but it was best not to take a chance, especially as he was about to meet Max Schneider and make the exchange.

The back door of the club opened as soon as Phillip got to the bottom of the steps. Jorgen bowed. 'Right on time. Come in. It's nearly kaffee und kuchen time.'

Phillip knew this meant coffee and cake; a German custom similar to England's afternoon tea. Jorgen led the way up the stairs into his flat. On a small table next to the bearskin were two cakes, one a Black Forest Gateau and the other a caramel sponge with glazed nuts. There were two cups and plates.

Jorgen guided Phillip to the couch. 'Sit, sit.' He then pushed through the strings of beads into the kitchen. Moments later he returned with an antique coffee pot which he plonked on the table.

Using a silver knife with a filigree engraving, Jorgen cut a slice from each cake and put them on Phillip's plate. He then poured coffee into both cups and handed one to Phillip. 'The cakes are from

Gustav, my brother, who you saved. They're just for you. He makes them himself. I've told him he should open a shop selling them, but he thinks being a shopkeeper is beneath him.'

Phillip made short work of the two slices. They were delicious. Jorgen smiled and offered him more cake, but Phillip declined. Jorgen stood up. 'I'll just clear these away. I'll put the cakes in a box and you can take them with you. Maestro Max would eat the whole lot if we left them out.'

When Jorgen finished parcelling up the cakes in the kitchen, he returned with a clean cup and saucer. 'They're probably outside now. I'll go and check, you can't always hear the knock from up here. You can pour him some coffee. And, of course, for yourself.'

A few minutes after Jorgen left, there were heavy steps up the stairs. Through the door came a middle-aged man, half bald, with a protruding stomach. Phillip stood up. 'My name is Phillip Fitz … well, you know me as Kumar.'

'Never did get a good look at you. Are you Indian?'

'No.'

'But Kumar? That's an Indian name.'

'It's Scottish.'

'Really? How do you spell it?'

'C-o-u-m-a-u-g-h.' It was a lie he had told many times. But why did he do it? Why? What did he really care what this man thought? Why should he care?

The man frowned. 'How did you find me?'

'I asked Jorgen.'

'Oh. Oh, yes of course. You saved his brother. Luckily, I left before the Nazis arrived.' Max moved round the table and slumped down on the couch. He poured himself a cup of coffee. 'Mmm. Could do with some cake.'

Phillip thought of offering him some – after all, Jorgen had said the cakes were for him, but that might offend Jorgen who didn't want Max to have any. The overweight man who slouched on the couch making noises as he drank his coffee, seemed completely different from the bishop in the confessional. 'I have what you want.'

Max stopped with the cup in mid-air. 'What I want? Oh, the money for the document.'

'And the visa.'

'The visa? Oh, yes, the visa. Well, I'm sorry, Mister Kumar, but I am no longer part of the sordid game.'

'Sorry?'

'I am an actor, Mister Kumar, an actor, and I was asked to play a role – that of a priest, for which I would be paid. However, nobody said it would be dangerous and people would get killed. So I immediately resigned.' He gulped down his coffee and poured another one. 'And I never got paid. And another thing, you turning up at the stage door of the Cockatoo Club looking for me frightened everyone and so they closed the show. Thanks a lot.'

Phillip wasn't sure what he was hearing. 'But what about the visa and money for the document?'

'I don't need or want a visa. That was just part of the ruse to throw people off the scent. Make it look like I was leaving the country. I did it for the money, but I'd rather stay alive.'

'But where is the document?'

'No idea. I don't even know if the document exists. The only one who would know is Schmidt, and he's disappeared. Schmidt recruited me. Said it would be a simple job and we would do the exchange in the church. I'd do the exchange while he kept watch. Schmidt attends the church and knows when the priest is away. Just impersonate a priest, Schmidt said, while he kept lookout.' He sipped his third cup of coffee. 'At first you really did think I was a bishop, didn't you?'

'Yes.'

'And that woman confessed her sins. God, they were petty. But I did enjoy giving her a harsh penance. Six rosaries every night for a week.' He laughed and gulped down coffee.

'Where could I find Schmidt?'

'I think he's lying low in Munich.'

'Do you have an address? Where he lives?'

'No. But I know he goes to a place there called The Vikings.' He shuddered. 'It's a beer hall on Bismarck Avenue, a right den of a place, full of homosexuals who like to be manly. There are always fights. Police are involved but the Nazis get released. People have been killed in it, but that seems to add to its allure for some people. The SA men seem to have a death wish and wear silver skulls in their caps.' He put his cup down on the table. 'Well,' he said, standing up. 'If there's no cake, I'll be going.'

'By the way,' Phillip said. 'You were right. Kumar is an Indian name. My father is Indian. I'm mixed race.' He stared at Schneider.

Schneider dropped his eyes, shrugged and left.

Phillip leaned back in his chair. What had he just heard? Max didn't have the document and didn't know if it existed. What if it didn't exist and it was all a hoax? What should he do? SIS said not to contact them without the document. Without it, SIS would probably just abandon him, deny all knowledge of him; after all, Phillip Fitzwilliam didn't really exist. He would be stateless with a false passport. And if Major Drexler found out …

There was no alternative, he had to find Schmidt and get the document – if it existed.

Chapter 27

Phillip bought train tickets to Munich for the next day.

He planned to arrive in Munich late morning, watch the Viking Club entrance and catch Schmidt, who was easily identifiable, before he went in.

As he alighted opposite the farm, Phillip checked for police cars. There were none. Rain mixed with sleet drifted down. He pulled up the collar of his coat, drew down the brim of his cap and trudged through the slush to the cabins, pleased he had on his new boots.

Ruth smiled as he stepped into the cabin but Phillip could see she was upset. He took off his coat and hat and put his arms round her. Ruth hugged him and he felt a jolt of pain as her hands clasped his back. He gently untangled himself. 'Are Kharos and Lena OK?'

'Yes. They're both fine. Have you seen Christoph?'

Phillip shook his head.

'Have you made contact with any of his friends?'

'Sorry, no.' Phillip picked up two wooden bowls. 'Actually, I'm rather hungry. I'll get us some food.'

'I'm not hungry.'

Phillip tramped across the wet field to where Gunter stood beside the fire, seemingly indifferent to the rain.

Gunter smiled, scooped up stew and gently slid the food into Phillip's bowl. 'Just one bowl?'

'Ruth says she's not hungry.'

Gunter winked. 'I have a message for you.' He leaned forwards, close to Phillip's ear. 'Kharos wants to see you before she goes.'

'Goes?'

'We're leaving tonight. Ruth is coming to the farmhouse at eight to say goodbye. You come too.'

Phillip felt elated as he walked back to Ruth's cabin. It would all be OK. Lena and Kharos would be safe.

The lower half of Gunter's farmhouse was built from cut stone, while the upper part consisted of planks of dark oak, oiled and weathered to a deep honey colour. An enormous thatched roof lay over the building like a giant rug, through which poked a terracotta chimney with a weathervane resembling a bird in flight. All the windows had wooden shutters, painted green.

Gunter opened the front door and Ruth and Phillip stepped into a large room with a roaring log fire, above which towered a stone chimneystack. Large black beams ran across the ceiling, supporting dark wooden planks. An imposing staircase, with carved banisters and spindles, ran up the left side of the room.

Gunter took Ruth's and Phillip's coats and hung them on pegs. 'Follow me.'

They climbed the stairs to a landing and then followed Gunter into a large room with a double bed, on which sat Kharos and Lena. Kharos jumped up and ran to Phillip and hugged him.

Phillip peered over Kharos's head at Lena who remained sitting. She stared back at him, as if looking into his soul, as if she knew what he had read in Krystal Schmelter's eugenics papers. Phillip lowered his eyes.

Gunter tousled Kharos's hair. 'Show Phillip the drawings you've made for him.'

Kharos unravelled herself from Phillip and went to an antique writing desk where she gathered up sheets of foolscap paper.

'Lay them out on the bed,' Gunter said.

Lena rose from the bed and kept her gaze on Phillip. Phillip thought Lena looked smaller than normal. Her shoulders sagged and she looked tired. He viewed the paintings spread on the bed and was surprised at how competent they were. They all depicted Phillip in the barn making the frames. Phillip picked out one showing him holding a chisel and striking it with a mallet. He was impressed by the way it captured his mental concentration and physical movement. 'These are brilliant. When you grow up you must go to art school. You must keep these to show people how good you are.'

Kharos beamed. 'No. They are for you.'

Silence.

Kharos stopped smiling. 'Don't you want them?'

'Oh, yes, yes, yes. But they are so good I was just thinking … OK. I would love to have them. I will show them to people in England.'

Kharos gave a little jump and hugged Phillip.

Gunter looked at his pocket watch. 'Sorry to be a drudge, but we must get ready to go. It's almost dark and we have a long journey ahead of us.'

Phillip let Kharos give him more cuddles and promised to keep in touch with her via Gunter.

Lena followed Ruth and Phillip down the stairs and out the front door. The sky had cleared and a quarter moon hung in the cold night air, sharp and pure but too weak to dim the stars. Lena touched Phillip's arm. He turned and Lena's eyes bore into him with almost savage intensity. 'Remember what you promised. To look after Kharos if anything happens to me.' She gripped Phillip's hands. 'Remember Phillip, Kharos is the innocent one, no matter what you hear about me.'

'Yes, of course.'

'Be careful when you go to Bayreuth. Perhaps you shouldn't …'

Ruth came up to them. Lena turned and went back into the house.

On the way back to Ruth's cabin, Phillip kept playing Lena's words in his mind. It was clear she wanted to tell him something. Was it about the man following him whenever he arrived in Bayreuth? Was he in danger? He excused himself and headed for the communal toilets. He had wanted to pee when they first arrived at Gunter's, but wasn't sure they had indoor toilets, and now the cold added urgency.

As he left the toilet, Phillip jumped as a figure detached itself from the shadows and stood in his way. Bluum. Phillip felt scared as Bluum's features became more distinct and he could see he was angry. 'We need to talk.'

'Well, why don't you come to the cabin?'

'No. You must not help Anna kill her baby. You are a Catholic. You know it is a crime. A mortal sin.'

'Yes, well …'

'You know I have offered to marry Anna and bring up the baby as mine. The baby is Jewish because Anna is Jewish. The Jewish line comes down through the mother, so the baby is a Jew and so Palestine is its real home.'

Phillip was silent.

Someone coughed in the night. A dark form was moving towards the toilets. Bluum stepped up to Phillip so his breath was in Phillip's face. 'Do not help them kill the baby. If you help kill a Jewish baby, I will kill you.' He turned and marched towards the road.

Phillip felt afraid as he made his way to Ruth's cabin. Solid darkness enclosed the compound. Was Bluum watching him from outside the perimeter? If Bluum was staying in the village, he could be prowling around the encampment at any time, especially when it was dark, like now. What should he do? He had always believed abortion was a mortal sin, it was taking a life, but Christoph and Anna needed help.

But if he did tell Christoph, and Anna had the abortion, would Bluum try to kill him?

Chapter 28

Someone was at the foot of the bed.

The room was pitch black. Was it Bluum?

'Sorry,' said a voice from the dark. Ruth. 'I'm trying to find my shoes. Sorry to have woken you.' A dark form rose from the end of the bed and went silently out of the bedroom.

Phillip lay back. Lena had left the country with Kharos so they were both safe, but he still had to find Schmidt and that meant going to the Viking Club in Munich.

Light slanted into the bedroom through the half-open door, and then came the sound of Ruth raking the burned cinders in the stove. Perhaps he should help her, but he didn't want to talk about Christoph or commit to finding Von Stauffenberg and discussing abortion. What if Von Stauffenberg and Christoph were practising Catholics? Also, there was Bluum who had threatened to kill him if he helped Anna abort the baby.

He eased himself out of the bed, the pain in his shoulders more intense than before. He'd kept his vest on to hide the bruises, and when Ruth had reached for him in the night, he didn't respond. She had lain awake for some time and he wondered if she was thinking that he had rejected her and there was someone else, or was she thinking about Kharos and Lena? Or Anna and Christoph? The front door opened and then softly closed.

He sat up and pulled back the window curtain. The sky was murky milk, and the dark earth sleeked with ice as if giant snails had left trails of frozen slime. The compound was deserted; not even Gunter's fire was lit. Was Bluum somewhere out there, hiding, watching the cabin? Bluum's commitment to Zionism was obsessive – as if there were no moral or ethical constraints that could hinder the realisation of the Zionist dream. Would Bluum really try to kill him? He would need to be careful, never be on his own, especially at night. The cabin door opened and then came the sound of plates and utensils. He finished dressing and went into the living room.

Ruth was standing by the stove, measuring coffee into a saucepan. Phillip put his arms around her. 'So Lena and Kharos got away safely?'

'Looks like it. Gunter isn't back yet. I don't expect him till this afternoon. It's quite a journey to the border.' She finished measuring in the coffee and put the saucepan on the stove. 'Please don't take this the wrong way, Phillip, but only you, Gunter and I know about Lena and Kharos going to France. It would be best if we didn't tell anyone. Some of the people here support the Nazis.'

'Really? I thought everyone here was …'

Ruth closed in on him, wound her arms round him and kissed him on the lips. 'As Lena says, you have a lot to learn about people.'

Phillip winced as Ruth touched the bruises on his back. 'I fell over in the snow.'

Ruth stepped back. 'You should have said so. Gunter has liniment for bruises and strains. I'll get some.' She moved in closer. 'I'll put it on for you.' She smiled. 'Any excuse to rummage that body of yours.'

Phillip shook his head, but was pleased Ruth was so open about her needs.

'I told Gunter I would stay here and keep an eye on things till he got back,' Ruth said. 'But we need to find Christoph quickly. He is very emotionally based and so we need to get to him before he does something stupid. Anna is in Bayreuth looking for him, but you'll carrying on looking for him as well?'

'Sure. However, Bluum says he will marry Anna if she keeps the baby.'

'I know. But he wants to take her to Palestine and live in a desert. She'd die there.'

Phillip sat at the table. 'Bluum feels very strongly about her not having an abortion. He knows what you've asked me to tell Christoph.'

'How?'

'I don't know. But he threatened to … he threatened me not to tell Christoph or … he'd kill me.'

Ruth handed Phillip a cup of coffee. 'He's all bluster. Anyway, when was this?'

'Last night. He stopped me on my way back from the toilet.'

'You didn't tell me.'

'Well …'

'Anyway, Bluum is a fanatic and is always trying to bully Jews to go to Palestine and build the Zionist dream. About a quarter of the people here are Jews, so Bluum sees it as a pool of potential settlers in Palestine. Gunter has banned him from the encampment so he shouldn't be here. Don't worry, I'll have a word with Gunter when he gets back.'

Phillip looked at his watch. 'I need to go.' He was catching the eleven o'clock train to Munich.

The bus drove cautiously through the snow and slush – each time the wipers cleared the glass, a veil of soft sleet covered the windscreen. Phillip wiped the condensation from his window and looked at the bleak fields. He felt snug in the warm bus. A woman shouted to the driver that he had gone past her stop. The driver pulled over and said sorry but the woman complained as she bumped her way from the back of the bus. A male passenger said in a strange accent that it wasn't the driver's fault. The woman told him he was a foreigner and to mind his own business.

Phillip turned and looked at the passenger who had spoken. He had a waxed moustache and sat upright with an imperious air that suggested he was used to giving orders. Phillip's heart jumped. Sitting behind the man was Bluum, glaring at him. Phillip turned quickly and stared out the window.

Was it just coincidence that Bluum had got on the bus before him? Or had Bluum been watching the camp? If Bluum was living in the village, he could keep surveillance from the woods. Is that what he had done? Seen Phillip head for the bus stop and then got on the stop before the farm.

Phillip moved to the edge of the seat, ready to hop off the moment the bus reached Bayreuth.

The bus swung into the terminus.

As soon as the doors opened, Phillip jumped off. The man who usually followed him wasn't there. He hurried towards the university but the narrow alleyways didn't prove as useful and Bluum was still behind him when Phillip turned down a narrow lane and slipped into the bookshop next to the Arts Faculty. As he browsed the books, he kept an eye on the door and window.

He reached for a copy of George's poems. Next to it was a booklet with the Swabian Hohenzollern crest on the front, the same one as on the pouch Christoph had. The brochure was a potted-history of the Swabian branch of the Hohenzollern dynasty, which had split from the main branch of the Hohenzollern's, who embraced Protestantism during the reformation in order to continue to practise their Catholic faith. Christoph was Catholic. He would never agree to an abortion.

Phillip replaced the booklet and sauntered up to the window. There was no sign of Bluum. Perhaps it was mere chance that Bluum was on the same bus as he was. No, he didn't believe that. Bluum was a fanatic, totally driven – someone for whom the ends justified the means.

Phillip stepped out of the bookshop. He glanced up and down the road. Bluum was nowhere in sight.

When he got to the university, Phillip sped through the ground floor and out the back door. If Bluum was still following him he would think he was studying somewhere in the faculty.

Dead on twelve noon, the train pulled into Munich railway station. It reminded Phillip of Waterloo in London with all the platforms adjacent to the concourse and the line of gates each manned by a ticket collector. And, like Waterloo, it had shops along with bars offering alcoholic drinks. Tall colonnades ran along the exit which came out onto a cobbled esplanade. A city map on the wall showed that Bismarck Avenue, the street that hosted the Viking Club, was not far from the station.

As Phillip strode through the town, he was amazed at the mass of political flags draped from windows and party posters plastered on lampposts. It seemed that all the political parties were parading their insignia, as if they all thought an election was imminent. They were all represented, The Communist Party of Germany, Social Democratic Party, Centre Party, German National People's Party and the National Socialist German Worker's Party, the Nazis. In England they only had Labour, Conservative or Liberal, and if supporters wanted to display political elegances, they put small posters in their windows.

Bismarck Avenue had a predominance of Nazi flags, with one or two red flags fluttering high up on blocks of flats. On one building, the black flags of the anarchists fluttered in the wind like dancing Jesuits.

Along the curbs, men stood with wooden barrows and boxes stacked with old clothes or used household items. Here and there stalls sold hot soup and bread. Men and women, along with small children, stood on the front steps of the houses, the men in old clothes with shiny sleeves and elbows, and the women in bulky brown coats. A fine drizzle was seeping from an overcast sky as a cold wind blew the steam from the soup cauldrons into frenzied patterns.

A beggar with a crutch stood precariously on one leg and stared at Phillip. Phillip dropped a coin into the man's hat and gave him a smile, but the beggar said nothing and just glared at him. Phillip was going to ask the beggar where the Viking Club was, but decided against it.

The sound of military music echoed along the street and a parade, led by a small brass band, came into view. Behind the musicians marched men in smart clothes. One of them held a flag with horizontal stripes of red, white and black, which Phillip recognised as the German National People's Party. They marched past in orderly silence – the men on the pavement watched them, some with dead eyes, others with looks of deep hatred.

Phillip reached the end of Bismarck Street without finding the Viking Club. He crossed to the other side of the road and walked its length, but still couldn't locate the club. A plump woman selling soup, her cheeks red from the cold, smiled broadly when he asked for directions to the club, and then pointed across the road to a drab frontage with brown shutters and a big front door. There were no signs on the building to say what it was. Phillip bought soup and bread from the woman and then strolled along the road till he was opposite the club.

Despite the weather, men sauntered along the road and entered the Viking Club dressed in just trousers and shirts, some with their sleeves rolled up, showing their bulging biceps. A policeman strode by and glanced at Phillip.

Over an hour passed and there was still no sign of Schmidt. Some of the stallholders were giving him looks of suspicion. Phillip crossed the road and pushed through the club's doors. The interior was huge, like a church hall, the air heavy with smoke and noise, while the sound of an accordion wafted above the babble of voices. Tables and chairs were scattered round the sides of a wooden floor, which was packed with men standing in groups, talking and drinking. Many wore brown shirts with swastika armbands. Phillip felt scared. There was no sign of Schmidt, but it was too crowded for him to see everyone.

Phillip threaded his way through to the bar that ran along one wall. Just before he reached it, a man bumped into him. 'Oh, sorry, sorry,' Phillip said. The man stood facing Phillip. Phillip went round him. The man snorted.

At the bar Phillip ordered a beer. As he waited his anxiety rose. He was sure the man had bumped into him on purpose. If he were attacked there was nothing he could do. What if he was taken to hospital? Interrogated by the police?

He paid for his beer and then sipped it while keeping his eyes on the rows of bottles behind the bar. If he left before finishing his beer it might draw attention, but he would leave as soon as he had drunk it. There had to be some other way of finding Schmidt. Possibly spend a few nights in Munich and watch the club and catch Schmidt before he entered.

Someone pushed against him. He moved along the bar without turning round, but the pressure against his back followed him. Could he turn and, without looking at whoever was pushing him, make it to the door? If he moved quickly and then ran once he was outside, maybe he could make it to the station. The pressure on his back increased. 'Do they serve White Lady cocktails here?'

Phillip turned and looked into the bloodshot eyes of Schmidt. Relief made him laugh nervously. 'I don't think so. Can I buy you something else?'

Schmidt nodded to the barman who poured a tumbler of white liquid and put it on the bar in front of Schmidt. The barman looked at Phillip. 'Oh, I'll have another beer, thank you.' Phillip paid and Schmidt nodded towards the tables on the far side of the room.

They sat at a vacant table and Schmidt lit a brown cheroot. He leaned back in his chair, blowing smoke from the side of his mouth like a train letting out steam. 'Well?'

'Well, actually, I was speaking with Max Schneider and …'

'That piece of shit. Ever since we were kids he was a pussy, frightened of his own shadow. Made sure he never got called up to fight in the war. Acting is just right for him.'

Phillip waited for Schmidt to finish speaking. He then leaned forward. 'Actually, I wanted to talk about the document.'

'Don't lean forwards. Makes it look like we're conspiring. Just smile and speak softly. I may not have much of a face, but I still have good hearing.'

'Oh. Sorry. Well, I have … I have money for the document.'

Schmidt drew deeply on his cheroot. 'I don't have the document. But for a price I can tell you who can help you get it.'

Phillip felt exasperated. All the contacts seemed to be go-betweens. 'For sure?'

'For sure. The man who hired me.'

'How much?'

Schmidt looked out at the backs of the men standing in the centre of the hall. 'Well, we were going to get two hundred US dollars. But since Max is not in, shall we say one hundred.'

'OK. When can I have the document?'

'I told you, I don't have it, and I'm not going back to Bayreuth. But there's someone there who will help you get the document. He's the man who hired me and is in direct contact with the man who has it. I know they are still very keen to give you the document.' He drank most of his glass. 'But I'm staying clear. There's too much heat at the moment after that tramp was killed.' His eyes twinkled despite the bloodshot whites. 'Meant to be you, wasn't it?'

Phillip said nothing.

Schmidt drained the last of the drops from his glass. 'Anyway, I'm staying in Munich. But for one hundred US dollars I will tell you who hired me. He will then arrange for you to meet the man with the document, who is, as I understand it, high up in Bavarian society and so doesn't want to be seen to be involved.'

'Hence all the go-betweens.'

Schmidt shrugged. 'Do you know what's in the document?'

'No.'

'Neither do I. But it must be incredibly important if people are being killed over it. Anyway, one hundred US dollars and I'll tell you who to contact so you can get it.'

'I don't have the money on me.'

Schmidt snorted. 'Yes, well, I suppose it would be taking a chance to bring that kind of money to a place like this. OK. Meet me at Munich railway station tomorrow at noon. I'll be in The Flag Bar on the station forecourt.'

'OK.'

Schmidt stood up. 'Sorry I can't buy you a drink in return, but I'm broke. I haven't yet been reduced to begging, but it's not far off. Fight for your country and then they shit on you.'

Phillip watched Schmidt merge into the crowd of standing men. It seemed Schmidt's loyalty and allegiance had been worn away by the fight for survival, now everything had a price.

Phillip had almost reached the door when a man blocked his path. It was the man who had bumped into him earlier. Phillip felt rigid with fear but knew he mustn't stop. He dummied to one side and then stepped past the man. The man grabbed Phillip's coat and pulled him back. As Phillip was yanked round, the man let go and slumped to the ground like a sack of potatoes.

Schmidt was standing over the man, his fists clenched. He nodded to Phillip who rushed out the door.

Chapter 29

Phillip ducked back from the bus window.

Police cars lined the road next to Blue Ridge Farm.

Using the bus for cover, Phillip slipped off, ran into the field opposite the farm and hid behind bushes. The bus pulled away but Phillip couldn't see any activity within the encampment. He crossed the road and skirted round to the woods where the Roma were camped.

There was no fire and the caravans were dark.

Phillip crept to the edge of the woods, knelt behind a cluster of holly bushes and scanned the encampment. Despite the deepening gloom, most cabins had no lights, and the encampment looked deserted, aside from the figures by the fire – Gunter and three policemen. One policeman was waving his arms while Gunter stirred the pot. From beyond the cabins came the sound of barking dogs. How many policemen and dogs were there? Judging by the number of cars, the police had come in force.

He looked at his watch. The last bus back to Bayreuth was in fifteen minutes. Should he take it or continue to hide? The barking grew louder. Had the dogs sensed him? His sleeve was jerked and he jumped up in terror. It was Kharos.

His heart pounded and for a moment couldn't register what was happening – he'd thought the pull on his sleeve was a dog.

Kharos put her fingers to her lips. She wore only a short-sleeved dress. Phillip cupped his hand around Kharos's ear. 'Where's your mummy?'

'I don't know. Gunter told me to run away and hide in the woods.'

'Does anyone know you're here?'

Kharos shook her head.

The sound of the dogs was getting closer. Phillip grabbed Kharos's hand and ran back through the woods

He raced with Kharos along the main road to Bayreuth till he got to the next bus stop. They were now out of sight of the encampment. Phillip took off his coat and wrapped it around Kharos, but it was much too big for her small frame. He slipped his coat back on and then enfolded Kharos inside it, holding her close to his body as he felt her shiver.

Ten minutes later, headlights arced into the main road and the bus rumbled towards the stop.

The garden was pitch black as Phillip groped his way to the birdbath.

He found the key and then led Kharos to the back door. The door's glass panels showed no light in the hallway. Before anyone heard them, they had to get in and up the stairs to his room.

Phillip unbuttoned his coat. He lifted Kharos up and got her to hold him round the neck so she clung close to his chest. He then wrapped his coat around her, holding the front closed. He knew he looked odd, but it was his only chance to get Kharos into the house and up to his room without her being seen. Hopefully, if Frau Weiser came out of her room, she would see only his back climbing the stairs.

The door opened with a slight creak and he stepped inside. He waited. Nothing, all was quiet. He coaxed the back door shut and locked it. There was no sound. Treading softly, he reached the foot of the stairs. The stairs would creak, as they always did, and so he braced himself and ran up two at a time. As he reached his room, he heard the parlour door open. He fumbled in his pocket for his room key. Where was it? He slid Kharos to the floor. He searched his pockets frantically. The key was in his jacket pocket. He unlocked the door, pulled Kharos into his room and closed the door.

He waited. There was a knock on the door. His heart jumped and he pointed under the bed. Kharos slid under it and Phillip draped his coat on the bed so she was hidden. He opened the door. Frau Weiser stood on the landing.

'I've been waiting to find you in,' she said, giving him a steady stare.

'This letter came for you. It is marked urgent.' She handed Phillip a white envelope with his name written in beautiful handwriting along with urgent underlined.

Phillip took the letter and bowed.

Frau Weiser smiled and nodded. Then turned and clomped down the stairs.

Since she had seen his invitation to Countess Koniger's soiree, she had been most deferential to him, even suggesting he could have a bath anytime he wanted.

Phillip helped Kharos out from under the bed. She was shaking. He hugged her to him, her hands cold as ice.

He filled the kettle and lit the gas ring. While the kettle boiled, Phillip held Kharos's hands near the jetting flames. He pulled off his pullover and slipped it over her, and then slid off her slippers and wet socks. He warmed her feet in his hands, and then found a clean pair of his socks in the wardrobe and put them on her, pulling the tops up to her knees.

Kharos looked frightened and was shivering. Phillip put his arms round her and whispered. 'You are safe now, but we must be very quiet.'

What had happened at the farm? What about Lena? Had the police captured her? Is that why Kharos was alone in the wood? Where was Ruth? He didn't want to question Kharos.

Making the tea, Phillip realised he had no milk or sugar. 'Do you like honey in your tea?' he whispered.

Kharos nodded.

Phillip found the small pot of honey he had bought in the market but the jar was empty except for residue at the bottom and streaks down the inside. He emptied a cup of tea into the jar, swilled it around and then poured it back into the cup. 'It's what we do in England,' he whispered. 'Makes it special.' He handed her the cup. 'As I said, we must be very quiet. In fact, we mustn't speak. Is that OK?'

Kharos nodded.

Phillip touched her cheek. How could anybody want to harm a child? Was that really what Krystal and her programme would do? Surely not, not if she met Kharos. But she had met Kharos and she still intended to do her harm.

It was lunacy, this set of ideas that some people were special and so had to protect themselves by only breeding with their own kind. But there was not different 'kinds' of humans. It wasn't like cats and dogs who were different species. And the idea that Western Europe was special and superior was nonsense. Long ago, when the Europeans were living in caves, painting themselves blue and throwing rocks at each other, the East had houses, palaces, reading and writing, forms of government and were highly civilised.

And that story Countess Koniger told him about the Aryans migrating from Atlantis was rubbish. CUBE. But how near was he in supporting similar ideas? If he were honest, the British establishment, especially the Conservatives, all believed in such ideas and he had supported them. But that was because he wanted to belong, not to be seen as an outsider. But the people he loved were outsiders; his father, Ruth. And what about Kharos who sat beside him, her body pressed to his as if attaching herself to him would keep her safe. Well, it would. He had promised to protect her and he would, no matter what the consequences.

He opened the letter the landlady had given him. It was from Kantorowicz asking to meet him the Italian café next day at two. It was signed it urgent. What had happened? Was it about Christoph?

Kharos finished her tea and he took her cup. Perhaps she was hungry? There was no food in his room and he couldn't leave her while he shopped. Besides, at this time of night there wouldn't be anywhere open.

What if someone had seen them? What if the police had interrogated people at the farm and were now tracking his address? He couldn't escape with Kharos out of the window. They must leave first thing in the morning when it was still dark and get the first bus back to the farm. They could hide in the woods if necessary or find their way round to the back of Gunter's house. Whatever happened, he would not abandon her.

Phillip found a jumper in the wardrobe and put it on. It would be a long night.

Phillip saw Kharos was still sleeping as the grey dawn light began to seep through the curtains.

Once in the night, Kharos had got up to use the chamber pot and he had wanted to step outside, but Kharos had begged him not to leave her. He would have to empty it before they left. They would need to start soon. The first bus back to the farm was at six. It would still be fairly dark, so there was a good chance they wouldn't be seen. He felt in his pocket for the back door key.

He had to be in Munich at noon to meet Schmidt, which meant getting the ten thirty train from Bayreuth station. Perhaps Gunter could drive him back in. But what if the police were still at the encampment, or were watching the cabins and surrounding area?

They got off the bus one stop before Blue Ridge Farm and crept into the strip of poplar trees in the field adjacent to the farm.

Phillip searched the cabins and the open area where Gunter lit his fire. All seemed quiet. He wrapped Kharos inside his coat and pulled up the collar around her face. 'You stay here. I'll be back in a minute. I just want …'

'No. Please, don't leave me.'

Phillip scrutinised the encampment. They mustn't be seen, but already smoke was snaking up from one or two cabins. He slipped his coat back on and enveloped Kharos in its folds. They stumbled across the field to the road that ran adjacent to the farm.

They stopped and Phillip peered at the encampment. There were no signs of police cars. Shambling along with Kharos inside the folds of the coat, they crossed the road and laboured as quickly as they could up the track to Ruth's cabin. The door was unlocked and he dashed inside, almost tripping over Kharos.

Ruth rushed out of the bedroom, flung herself down on her knees and hugged Kharos. Ruth's body pulsed with sobs.

Ruth ceased crying and Phillip touched her shoulder. 'What happened?'

'They were stopped at border and turned back,' Ruth said, wiping the tears from her face. 'Then yesterday afternoon, a police unit from Munich arrived. We didn't see them till we heard the shouting. They had come in from the other side of the forest, surrounded the hut where Lena and Kharos were, and smashed down the door. Only Lena was there, Kharos was here with me. I'd left her to go to the shop and I asked Gunter to keep an eye on the cabin. When the police came, Gunter told Kharos to run to the woods behind the barn. The plan was he would delay the police till I came back and could collect Kharos and hide her. You got to her first. Thank God.'

'How did they know where Lena and Kharos were hiding?'

'The Roma.'

'Bloody bastards.'

'No. It wasn't their fault. The police arrested one of the men and threatened to charge him with sexually assaulting a German child if he didn't tell them where Lena was. You could imagine what would happen, what the local Nazis in the police would do to him.'

Phillip sighed. 'I think Kharos would like something to eat.'

Ruth gently levered Kharos away from her. 'We need to get her somewhere safe first.' She held Kharos's face in her hands. 'Will you stay here with Uncle Phillip while I go out for a minute?'

Kharos nodded and reached out for Phillip's hand.

Ruth went into the bedroom and emerged moments later wearing socks. She threw a coat over her red pyjamas and put on boots. 'Lock the door behind me and take Kharos in the bedroom.'

Phillip locked the door. 'OK. You go in the bedroom and I'll make some tea.'

The stove was hot. Ruth must have been up all night.

Ruth returned fifteen minutes later. She knelt down, dressed Kharos in a coat and wrapped a scarf round her head. Kharos coughed. 'Sorry, sweetheart,' Ruth said, unwrapping the scarf from Kharos's mouth. 'But we don't want people to see you.'

'I could be under the coat.'

'Under the coat?'

Phillip put on his coat and Kharos slipped inside its folds. 'It's how we got in and out of Bayreuth,' Phillip said. 'We are the masters of disguise, aren't we, Kharos.'

Kharos nodded inside the coat.

Ruth stood up. She smiled at Phillip, her eyes full of tears. 'Our saviour. OK. I'll walk beside you. We are heading for the road.'

As they made their way along the track to the road, it was the quietness that struck Phillip. No voices echoing over the chilled ground. One or two people were carrying water to their homes, heads bowed and not making eye contact. A murky pall hung overhead as if the dense clouds were too heavy to rise above the hills.

They reached the road. Gunter was sitting in a black Citroen car, the exhaust pumping vapour into the air. Phillip and Ruth shielded Kharos with their bodies while she slipped into the back seat and lay down. Ruth climbed in the back and put her coat over Kharos. Phillip got in the passenger seat. Gunter drove up to the main road and turned left towards Munich, the opposite direction to Bayreuth.

They left the main road, drove through country roads for about half an hour and then turned onto a rough track. They bumped along the track and came to a large building which Phillip recognised as the back of Gunter's farmhouse. They scrambled out the car, making sure Kharos was shielded from sight.

Gunter held up his hand. 'Phillip, you stay here, and keep an eye out. We won't be long.'

Minutes later Ruth emerged from the farmhouse. 'Gunter wants us to come back in a couple of hours' time,' Ruth said. 'Kharos wanted you to stay, so Gunter promised her we would come back in two hours. Then …'

'I have to be in … in Bayreuth for an important meeting. It's vital I be there. Could you look after Kharos while Gunter drives me in? It's incredibly important. I'll be back this afternoon. I promise.'

Chapter 30

Phillip alighted from the bus as soon as it reached the Bayreuth terminus.

He checked he wasn't being followed and hurried to his lodgings. The exchange on Munich station had taken only a few minutes. Schmidt was nervous and as soon as he had the money, he said Count Rostov was the man who hired him and then quickly left the bar. Although surprised that the comical little man he'd met at Countess Koniger's was mixed up in espionage, Phillip was pleased it was someone he knew, and who didn't seem threatening.

He rushed into his room, grabbed Count Rostov's card from his bedside cabinet, and then ran out. He had to meet Kantorowicz in the Italian café at two. Phillip's watch showed it was nearly two.

As he headed for the café, he considered going to Count Rostov's after he had seen Kantorowicz, but he had promised to return to the farm in the afternoon and he wasn't sure where Rostov lived and how long it would take to get there. He would get an early bus back to Bayreuth tomorrow morning.

The café was, as usual, full of people talking animatedly. Professor Kantorowicz was sitting with a young man at a table. When Kantorowicz saw Phillip, he said something to the young man who rose and went past Phillip without acknowledging him. Phillip crossed to Kantorowicz's table and sat down.

'Would you like a coffee?' Kantorowicz said.

'No thanks. I have to get back to … I have an appointment.'

Kantorowicz looked steadily at Phillip. 'Only one thing can serve the Germany of today and the Germany of tomorrow, Phillip, and that is clarity and an unshakable faith in the eternal figures of this land and their promise.' Kantorowicz took a sip of coffee. He slowly lowered the cup into the saucer. 'George is the poet Fhurer. The high priest of the spirit and therefore must be obeyed. He cannot be challenged. He is in a state of grace and so embodies, physically, the German Volkish ideal, the divine mission of the German people, their eternal calling, which they can only glimpse, but which George sees clearly. Therefore, he cannot be questioned, he can only be obeyed.' Kantorowicz leaned forwards. 'Only when poets, such as George, give guidance, thereby raising political thought to the level of the sacred, can a nation find its true destiny. In this day and age, Stefan George is the only one who can do this and is therefore in a state of grace and beyond criticism. He must be obeyed and all must conform to his teachings.'

Kantorowicz leaned back and stared at Phillip.

'I ... I agree with you,' Phillip said.

Kantorowicz jerked forwards, his eyes blazing. 'Then why did you write what you did? Your essay on George's translation of Shakespeare's Sonnets is ... is blasphemous.'

'But ... it's just my ...' How had Kantorowicz seen and read his critique? Muller must have given it to him. Why? How dare he.

Kantorowicz turned his empty cup round in the saucer. 'I'm sorry, but I'm instructed to tell you, you cannot be admitted to the reading on Saturday. In fact, never.' He stood up. 'You are not the first one to underestimate Stefan George, and you won't be the last.'

'Look, I'm sorry. But …'

'So am I. I like you, Phillip, a lot. You're highly intelligent and, I believe, a gifted poet, but I have my instructions.' He sat down again. He took an envelope from his pocket and held it in his hand, gazing at it. 'This is a letter for Ruth Kaplinski. It was written by Captain Christoph von Allenbach who asked me to give it to you to pass to Ruth.' He paused. 'That was before Christoph was found hanged in the woods just outside Bayreuth.'

Phillip's mouth went dry and he felt the nerves in his stomach tingle.

'Some say it was suicide,' Kantorowicz said. 'His family refuse to believe it. They are Catholic and it would mean he couldn't be buried in sacred ground.' Kantorowicz fingered the envelope. 'Stefan George said I should destroy this letter. The police are investigating von Allenbach's death and are asking questions from all who knew him.' He looked at Phillip. 'They want to talk to someone who followed Christoph to his barracks one night.'

Phillip's knees shook.

Kantorowicz stood up. 'I know he was deeply in love with Anna, who I believe is Ruth's sister.' He looked away, his eyes glowing with water. 'Christoph showed me Anna's portrait he'd painted, and the poems he wrote about her.' He breathed in. 'That's why I'm giving you this letter.' He threw it on the table. 'But we must never meet again.' He turned and walked out.

Phillip picked up the letter. It was addressed to Ruth.

There were no police cars.

Phillip snuck off the bus, darted into the field opposite Blue Ridge Farm and hid behind bushes. The bus pulled away and he searched the compound. All looked normal, with people walking to and from the toilets and shower block.

'We have to see Gunter, urgently,' Ruth said, as Phillip stepped into the cabin.

'Is everything OK?'

'Yes, but we need to act quickly. It's not safe for Kharos to be here. Come on.' Ruth stopped by the door. 'What's wrong?'

'Christoph was found hanged in a wood just outside Bayreuth. It looks like suicide.'

Ruth stepped back into the room and slumped on a chair. She held her head in her hands and silently wept.

Phillip placed the letter on the table in front of her.

Ruth smeared the tears across her face and picked up the letter. She opened it slowly and then read the contents. She sank back in her chair. 'Christoph worked for the Abwehr, the Military Secret Service. He was asked to infiltrate the Artist's Colony because Gunter had been involved in the Communist uprising here in Bavaria in 1919.'

Phillip sat in the chair opposite Ruth. 'Christoph must have told them where the sets for *Parsifal* were.'

Ruth held his gaze with water-filled eyes. She wiped her face and sniffed, then stood up. 'You must say nothing about this to anyone, especially Anna. Not until I have had a chance to talk to her.' Ruth picked up the tin of cakes. 'Now, we must help save Kharos.'

Instead of going straight across the fields to Gunter's farmhouse, they did a detour through the woods. Phillip kept alert but there was no sign of Bluum. There was also no Roma, only charred sticks in pools of blackened earth where fires had been. Either they had been told to leave or fled for fear of reprisals.

Ruth led Phillip out of the woods and then took a circuitous route, through fields and across lanes, till they came in sight of the back of the farmhouse. The chained dogs barked and strained on their leads. Phillip stood still. Suddenly the dogs stopped barking and went into their kennels. 'Gunter must have seen us,' Ruth said. 'He has a dog whistle. He's positioned dogs at the front and back of the house, so if the police come we will be alerted.'

Phillip tensed as he passed between the kennels – the dog's heads just visible inside their lairs. The back door of the farmhouse opened, and Gunter stood aside while Ruth and Phillip hurried in. As Phillip followed Ruth up the stairs, he heard Gunter locking and bolting the door.

Gunter joined them on the landing, and then led the way up a narrow flight of steps to a small wooden door, which he pushed open and they all filed in.

The room was a tiny attic with a sloping ceiling, walls of painted wood and a small skylight. Kharos was sitting on the bed wearing a woollen coat and bobble hat. The room had no fireplace. Kharos rushed up and hugged Phillip. He let her embrace him for some minutes, and then sat down on the bed beside her.

Gunter put his hand on Phillip's shoulder. 'I'll bring some coffee. And then we need to talk.'

Ruth handed Kharos the box of cakes she had made. 'Mustn't eat them all at once.'

Phillip helped Kharos open the tin. 'Why don't you do what we do in England? Eat some of them after lunch, and then again after your dinner in the evening.'

Ruth gave Phillip an approving look. Phillip smiled and shrugged.

Gunter arrived with a tray holding a pot of coffee and three cups. The tray was placed on the floor. Gunter poured the coffee into the cups and handed them round. From his pocket he produced a bottle of orange juice and gave it to Kharos. Kharos put the bottle on the bed. 'Can I go to the toilet, please?'

Ruth stood and took Kharos's hand. 'Of course. I'll take you.'

'Use the chamber pot in my room,' Gunter said. 'I'll empty it later.' He turned to Phillip. 'All go well in Bayreuth?'

Phillip held his gaze, but Gunter's eyes revealed nothing. Phillip shrugged. 'Just things I needed to deal with. Concerning my being here, in Germany. There's a problem over my certificates, they …'

The dogs outside started barking. Footsteps came running up the stairs and then Ruth burst into the room with Kharos. 'Police. At the front and back.'

Gunter jumped up. He pressed both hands on the wall near the head of the bed and slid a wooden panel sideways, revealing a dark hole. 'Quick. Kharos. Inside.'

Kharos stepped back. 'It's dark. I'm afraid.'

Ruth squeezed her hand. 'I'll come in with you.'

'No. I will,' Phillip said.

Gunter and Ruth stared at him. Loud banging came from the front and back of the house.

Phillip grabbed Kharos's hand. 'I need to.'

Gunter gave him a smile. 'OK. In you go.'

Phillip squeezed into the opening and then Kharos edged in. The panel was slid back into place. Phillip crouched on his haunches, while Kharos squashed into him with her head on his chest. Phillip hoped Kharos couldn't hear his heart pounding. There was the muffled sound of receding footsteps and then silence. A thin streak of light ran down the side where the panel didn't quite close. Could anyone see in? If they were caught, he would be charged with trying to conceal a fugitive.

There was a noise.

Someone was stamping up the stairs.

The attic door banged open and someone stepped into the room. Footsteps plodded round the room and then stopped. The bed creaked as it was lifted and then dropped. The wardrobe door was opened, followed by the sound of clothes being swished. There was a short silence, and then the sound of boots retreating down the steps.

To Phillip, it seemed like half an hour before the panel slid away. He handed Kharos out to Gunter and then eased out, his knees unfolding painfully as he stood up.

They sat in silence for some minutes, with Kharos on Phillip's knee.

Gunter passed round the cups of cold coffee.

Phillip said the reason he needed to avoid the police was that there had been a mix up with his certificates coming from England. This meant he wasn't officially registered, and so shouldn't be in the country and would have to return to England soon. He stressed that his passport was not in order because it didn't have a residency stamp.

Gunter observed Phillip. 'I thought you were here to study for one year?'

'I am. I plan to come back with my certificates.'

Kharos hugged Phillip's arm. 'But you'll be back?'

'Yes, of course.'

When they were sure Kharos was asleep, Ruth and Phillip crept downstairs and joined Gunter in the living room. He was sitting in a chair next to the fire with a drink in his hand. Two other chairs were in front of the fire along with a small table with a bottle of peach brandy and two cut-glass goblets. Phillip and Ruth sat in the vacant chairs.

Gunter poured two measures of brandy and handed one to each of them. He took a big swig from his glass. 'OK. We need to plan what to do. Kharos cannot stay here, or anywhere on the farm. Too many eyes.'

'Or anywhere in Germany,' Ruth said.

Gunter nodded. He drained his glass. 'True. Lena's mother is behind it all, and she has the backing of the Munich police and the Bavarian courts.'

'Not only Lena's mother,' Phillip said. He then told them what he'd read about the proposed Race Hygiene Centre and Doctor Schmelter's phone conversation.

'My God,' Ruth said. 'And now the Nazis are the second largest party.'

'They'll never get into power,' Gunter said. 'The majority of Germans are too wise to fall for that kind of bullshit.'

There was silence.

'But still,' Gunter said, 'getting Kharos out of the country is the only option.' He refilled his goblet. 'I cannot take her. I have no passport and I'm banned from travelling abroad.'

Phillip stared at Gunter.

Gunter smiled. 'I come from a long line of smugglers. My father bought this farm with the proceeds. Where you and Kharos hid is where we used to keep the Cognac we smuggled in from France. Since 1920, France has put an embargo on German imports of brandy and champaign until the war reparations are paid. I got caught three years ago smuggling both into Germany.' He raised his glass. 'My passport was taken away and I was banned from ever entering France. However, I thought I could slip Lena and Kharos across using one of the old smuggling routes, but the French are now watching all the roads, which is why I was stopped. Luckily, they didn't see Kharos and Lena who were hiding under coats in the back. They just turned me away.'

Ruth sipped her brandy. A log tumbled onto the hearth. Gunter scooped it up with a shovel and slid it back on the fire. Phillip felt the tension but didn't know what to say.

'I can't get a German passport,' Ruth said, 'because the Bavarian Government classify me as a French Jew. They say because I was born in Alsace, which is now part of France, I should apply for a French passport.'

'So can't you get a French passport if you were born in Alsace?' Phillip said.

'The French say I'm now a German citizen. It will take months or years to get one.'

Gunter leaned over and filled Ruth's glass. 'They'll never give you one. The French don't want any more Germans living it Alsace. They want all Germans out and only Frenchmen in Alsace. They want to hang onto it forever. That is until the next war.' Gunter poured brandy into Phillip's goblet, even though it was still half full. 'Which leaves you, Phillip. You are the only one with a passport.

You could take Kharos across to France and then down to Cognac where I have a house.'

'I have relatives in Alsace,' Ruth said. 'They might help till I manage to get across the border.'

Gunter snorted. 'The French will shoot any German trying to cross illegally into Alsace. The best bet is to head for my place in Cognac.'

Phillip took a drink of brandy. He thought of Kharos upstairs asleep, of her frightened body pressed against him in the cubbyhole, of her trust when she had slept in his bed in Bayreuth and he had watched over her. He had to meet Rostov tomorrow, then find who had the document and then get it to SIS. He leaned back in his chair. There was a way he could save Kharos and be with Ruth. But everything would need to fit into place. 'I can't do anything for the next three or four days, so we will need to hide Kharos till then.'

'Then?' Ruth said.

Phillip leaned over and kissed her. 'Then, we escape Germany.'

Gunter looked at him and smiled.

Ruth hugged him.

Phillip sat back and took a deep swig of brandy. Even if they were caught and his plan failed, he would have done what he knew was right.

Chapter 31

Phillip scanned the bus.

Bluum was not on board. Two of the passengers nodded and smiled at him. He had seen them before on the morning bus to Bayreuth. He took a seat at the back, where he would be able to see if Bluum got on.

Phillip changed buses and travelled west out of Bayreuth.

He told the driver to let him off near Welf Hall, Count Rostov's home. A man on the bus informed Phillip that the family of Welfs were an ancient dynasty that used to rule this part of Bavaria and had connections with the British Royal, family dating from the early eighteenth century. This surprised Phillip since he assumed Count Rostov was a Russian *émigré*.

Rostov had hired Schmidt, but whom was Rostov working for? Schmidt said it was someone high up in Bavarian society, the kind of people Rostov mixed with.

The driver called out and Phillip got off the bus.

Welf Hall was set back from the road, surrounded by fields and had the appearance of an English manor house. Phillip pulled a long chain at the side of the front door and heard chimes inside the house. Moments later the door creaked open and an elderly woman, clasping the door with both hands as if for support, squinted at Phillip.

Phillip raised his hat. 'Could I speak to Count Rostov, please?'

'Name?'

'Phillip. I met Count Rostov at Countess Koniger's.'

A smile wrinkled the woman's face. She shuffled the door closed. Phillip stood waiting for some minutes, but the door remained shut. He wasn't sure what to do and was about to ring the bell again when the door slowly opened. The woman gestured Phillip to enter.

The entrance hall was cluttered with fine porcelain objects, some on shelves, others on side tables. Portraits of people in royal dress gazed down from the walls. Phillip followed the woman across the hall to an ornate wooden door. The woman opened the door and Phillip stepped into the room.

Count Rostov was perched upright on an upholstered chair, wearing a silk dressing gown, cravat and slippers. He rose with the grace of a dancer and came to Phillip, hand outstretched. His eyes looked bleary and bloodshot. 'How kind of you to visit me, Phillip.' He clasped Phillip's hand and kissed him on both cheeks. 'Come, sit, sit, and bring comfort to a distressed soul.' He ushered Phillip into an upholstered chair opposite him. 'I have ordered tea. If you're cold I can ask Maria to lay a fire.'

'No. No. I'm fine, thank you.'

Rostov dabbed his eyes with a lace hanky and then let out a long sigh. 'Thank you so much for coming to visit me, Phillip. You have brought sunshine into a house full of sorrow.'

Phillip didn't know what to say. He wondered if Count Rostov was a friend of Christoph's family and was upset about his desertion. Or perhaps a relative had died.

Rostov leaned forwards and patted Phillip's knee. 'The world is full of the wicked, Phillip. They triumph everywhere. Never give your heart away; they will trample on it and destroy it.' He drew a deep breath and leaned back. 'Well, Phillip, what brings you to the home of a crushed soul?'

'Actually, I was told by Mister Schmidt that you know the man who has the document.'

Rostov gave a little start. He stared at Phillip. 'My understanding is that the agent's name is Kumar. And that's an Indian name.'

Phillip hesitated. He was about to say no, it was Scottish, and give the made-up spelling. No more. He would be who he was and who he could become; helping save Kharos had given him the courage. He thought of the lines of Keiler's poem: 'I am who I am, made from all who love me'. 'Yes. My father is an Indian.'

The door banged open and Maria struggled in with a tray. She wobbled across the floor, the teacups rattling. Phillip started to get up to help her, but Rostov touched his knee and shook his head. Maria clattered the tray onto the side table.

Rostov bowed and smiled. 'Thank you so much, Maria.'

Maria bowed and tottered out of the room. Rostov clasped the teapot. 'She's too old to be a servant but she insists on doing her duties, as she calls them. She was the housekeeper for a local farmer but when she got too old to do the work, he threw her out. She has no family or relations, so I took her in.' He dispensed two cups of tea and handed one to Phillip. The tea was black and had a piece of lemon floating in it.

Rostov sipped his tea in silence.

Phillip tasted his tea, which he found rather nice. He had always refused black tea with lemon when Ruth offered it to him, but now he realised he liked it.

Rostov placed his cup and saucer on the table. 'So, you are the British agent. Well, well.' His eyes smiled. 'You do it very well. I would never have dreamt … but who is who they say they are. Who is true? Who is constant like the North Star?' Rostov gazed at Phillip. 'Well, you are still beautiful, no matter where you come from, and beauty is all that matters, inside and out.' He stood up. 'I will make a phone call and we will see. The person who has the document is a very private man and one of elevated rank.' He glided out the room.

Phillip felt pleased. He had admitted who he really was and had been accepted, not shown the door as an unwanted outsider, someone from an inferior race. But more than that, he felt strong, empowered. The truth had set him free, made him untouchable by others, their judgements of him irrelevant. He could become who he really was – a teacher, poet, someone who fought for the rights of others regardless of their background. He knew his education and intellect was superior to most, but he would use it in the service of others and to fight the racism that was emerging all over the Western world.

A few minutes later, the door opened and Rostov strode into the room. He settled on his chair and picked up his tea. 'Would you like another cup, Phillip?'

'No, thank you. It was very nice.'

Rostov sipped his tea with his eyes half closed. 'I have arranged for you to meet the man who has the document next Sunday evening.'

'This coming Sunday?'

'Yes. In three days' time.'

'Thank you. Thank you.'

Rostov placed his cup and saucer on the table. 'But before I tell you the time and place, you must do something for me.'

Phillip nodded. 'Yes, of course.'

Rostov smiled. 'I want you to come to a tea dance on Saturday afternoon.'

Phillip blinked. Max Schneider had been at the Blue Lagoon to organise a tea dance. Was it the same one?

'I want you to dress in your best attire and meet me at three o'clock on Saturday afternoon, next to the fountain in the main square. You will then accompany me to the dance as my partner.'

'But ... But I'm not ...'

'A homosexual? No, I don't think you are. Well, maybe ... But that is not the point. I need a partner for this tea dance. Everyone will be there, and he who was to be my escort, my hope for an untroubled future, has shown himself a viper and is going with someone else. Perfidy. Treachery.' He dabbed his eyes.

He reached over and patted Phillip's knee. 'Don't worry, I will look after you. All you have to do is have one dance with me.' He rose and waved his hand, his eyes glowing. 'We will arrive late, when everybody thinks I am not coming and I'm at home lying bleeding from my soul.' He curved his hand through the air. 'Then I will enter with you on my arm, have one dance, and then sweep out.' His eyes were shining. 'Please, Phillip. Don't make me beg.'

Phillip almost laughed. 'OK. Why not. And you have definitely arranged for me to meet with the person who has the document?'

'Yes. Trust me. On Sunday evening.'

'OK, then. I'll come to the dance.'

'Fantastic. Thank you, Phillip. Then, after the dance, I promise I will give you the time and place where you will meet him.'

Phillip stepped out of the post office. He had sent a telegram to SIS requesting a meeting, in the church outside the farm, tomorrow afternoon. He would tell them he was collecting the document on Sunday evening and wanted a new passport to be ready for him on Monday.

SIS had said they could have a new passport for him in twenty-four hours, but there would be changes to his passport that needed to be agreed before he would hand over the document.

The British Government had seen him as expendable, someone who was insignificant in the scheme of things, but he was sure that if he were pure Anglo-Saxon and middle-class, they wouldn't have treated him that way. Well, no more. Gunter and Ruth were endangering themselves to save a child, acting with true principles, and he would stand with them.

As he turned into the square, he saw the bus to the farm was about to depart. He ran across the road, causing a car to swerve to avoid him. The driver tooted his horn as he drove off.

As Phillip watched the bus trundle away, he felt a presence behind him. He turned. It was a policeman. The officer looked Phillip up and down. The policeman was shorter than Phillip and had on a thick military-style coat with lots of buttons. On top of his plump face was a peaked cap whose rim glistened. 'Did you not see the car?'

'No. Sorry. I needed to catch …'

'Papers.'

'Oh, papers. Well, actually, I'm English.'

The policeman stared at him. 'Passport.'

'Oh, I'm a student. My passport is at home. I was told not to carry it about in case I lost it.'

'Who told you that?'

'My professor.'

'Well, he was wrong. Where do you live?'

Phillip stammered out his address. The policeman wrote Phillip's name and address in his notebook. 'Just a few streets away.' He glared at Phillip. 'Let's go and get it, Mister Englishman.'

The policeman waited at the front door while Phillip ran up to his room and returned with the passport. The policeman looked at it. 'You need to come with me to the station.'

Phillip was marched to a room with just a table and two chairs. The walls were dark brown and there were bars at the window. The policeman ordered him to sit, and then left.

The building echoed with footsteps and voices. There were only supposed to be three police officers in Bayreuth. The station must be full of officers from Munich. The door opened and a uniformed officer with stripes on his sleeve stepped into the room. He was thin with hollow cheeks, bright eyes and black hair. He was holding Phillip's passport. He paused for a moment and then sat down opposite Phillip.

The policeman glared at Phillip. 'Where do you study?'

'At the Arts Faculty.'

'Who teaches you?'

'Professor Muller.'

The policeman's eyebrows moved. He tapped Phillip's passport. 'You have not registered for residency.'

'Ah, yes. You see my certificates …'

'You cannot be in Germany unless you are registered.'

Phillip tried to keep his gaze steady. 'I was thinking of going back to England to get them, but Doctor Schmelter asked me to do some special work for her.'

'Doctor Krystal Schmelter?'

'Yes. We were at Countess Koniger's party.'

The policeman tossed Phillip's passport onto the table and leaned back in his chair, all the time staring at Phillip. 'When were you last in Saint Mary's Church?'

Phillip put his hands under the table. 'I visited it when I first came here. I'm a Catholic. Unfortunately, because of all the work I need to do at the university, I haven't ...'

'Were you there on Tuesday, the 26th of November?'

'No. I only ...'

'When you arrived in Germany, did you have a red coat?'

Phillip shook his head and squeezed his hands together.

'A man ... a tramp, was killed just outside the church and he was wearing a red coat. The coat was English. From a shop in London.' The policeman flipped open Phillip's passport. 'You are from London.'

'Yes.'

'There were also leather gloves and a scarf found.' The policeman leaned forwards. 'All made in England.'

The policeman stared at Phillip. 'We are also looking into the death of an army Captain. Christoph Von Allenbach. You knew him.'

'Well, sort of, I ...'

He leaned forwards. 'Did you, some days ago, follow him back to his barracks at night.'

'No.'

Phillip breathed through his nose as the policeman stared at him. 'The priest told us a woman who attends his church saw a young man with blond hair wearing a red coat sitting in the pews, just before the tramp was killed. She said she would recognise the young man again if she saw him.'

Phillip pressed his hands into his groin. He desperately needed the toilet.

'We have sent an officer to the church to find the woman and bring her here. When she arrives, we will hold an identity parade. We believe the person who wore the red coat was there to meet a man dressed as a bishop. We say dressed as a bishop because he wasn't a real bishop. The priest said no bishop was in the diocese at the time. We believe the young man in the red coat was there to meet the person impersonating the bishop. You must wait here till the witness arrives.'

The policeman rose slowly and strolled out of the room.

Why hadn't he said he was in the church and his coat was stolen? But then they could think he killed the tramp because he stole his coat. They knew about the bishop, that he wasn't real. What else did they know? What if they called in the German Secret Service? Drexler.

Twenty minutes later the door was unlocked and the policeman with the stripes on his arm strode into the room. 'Unfortunately, the woman has gone to Berlin, to her sister's funeral. He said she should be back next Monday. You are to report back here next Monday at two o'clock.' He waved Phillip's passport. 'We will keep your passport till then. Do not leave the area.' He glared at Phillip. 'You understand?'

Phillip nodded, and the policeman strode out of the room.

Minutes later, the policeman who had brought him to the station marched in. 'Follow me.'

Chapter 32

Next morning Phillip boarded the first bus to the farm.

It was still dark and there was hardly anyone around, and no policemen. If stopped, he would claim the Artists' Colony was in the area of Bayreuth and he had to collect an essay he had been working on for his studies. Tucked in his shirt were the visa, money and the new codes. Carrying them was risky, but the police might search his room.

All was quiet as he slipped into the cabin, Ruth must be still asleep in the bedroom. He wondered if she had told Anna that Christoph was dead.

'We were expecting you last night.' Ruth was in the doorway of the bedroom in her red pyjamas.

'Yes, I had some trouble. The police have got my passport.'

'That means you cannot get Kharos out of the country.'

'I'm getting a new one.'

'What's going on? Why have the police got your passport? And how can you just get another one?'

Phillip stared at the stove. Should he tell her or wait till his plan was in place? The silence became palpable, like another person in the room.

'So, Gunter was right,' Ruth said. 'He said you aren't just a student.'

Phillip slumped into a chair beside the table. 'I'm here to collect something and take it back to England. My real name is

Phillip Kumar. My father is Indian and my mother white English. I was sent to Germany by the British Government to collect a document.'

'What document?'

'I don't know. Nobody knows.'

'Somebody must know what it is or the British Government wouldn't want it.'

Phillip breathed out and looked at the table.

'I think you need a drink,' Ruth said. She pulled the cupboard door open and grabbed the bottle of peach brandy. She poured liquid into two glasses, placed one in front of Phillip and then sat beside him.

'I've found who has the document,' Phillip said, 'and will get it … well …' he took a deep slug of brandy. 'Better you don't know. But later today I will be meeting someone and arranging for a new passport. The passport will be for Mr and Mrs Kumar and their daughter, Kharos, retuning to England from a holiday in Germany.'

Phillip stared straight ahead while he felt Ruth's gaze upon him. He gulped down the remaining brandy and then turned to her. 'That is, if you would agree to marry me.'

Ruth plonked her glass on the table and threw her arms round him, crying and kissing him repeatedly.

They had just finished lunch when Anna stepped into the cabin.

Phillip thought she looked deadly pale. She must have had the abortion. Ruth went up to her and put her arms round her. 'How was the funeral?'

'I wasn't allowed in the church. People who were my friends, we ate in each other's houses, went on holiday together, and now they attacked me and spat on me, knowing I am pregnant and called me a dirty Jew.'

She still has the baby, thought Phillip. Good.

Bluum entered and stood behind Anna. He stared hard at Phillip.

'We are going back to Berlin, to Mum's,' Anna said. 'I'll have the baby at home.'

'And then to Palestine,' Bluum said.

Ruth held Anna and gazed into her eyes.

'My child won't go through what I have gone through,' Anna said. 'And everyone says it will get worse when the Nazis come to power.'

'Who says they will?' Ruth said.

'Even if they don't,' Bluum said, 'Germany is no place for Jews. You should come to Palestine as well.'

Ruth held Bluum's stare. 'Kharos as well?'

Bluum looked away.

'I'll walk you to the car,' Ruth said.

Phillip wanted to say to Ruth not to say anything about them escaping from Germany with Kharos.

Ten minutes later Ruth returned with Gunter and a woman with a nurse's uniform on under her coat. 'This is Rachel,' Gunter said, shutting the door behind them. 'She is a nurse in the institution where Lena is being held. This is Phillip.'

The nurse gave a tight smile. 'I am a Christian woman. Wrong things are happening.'

They stood in silence, not looking at each other.

The nurse clutched her handbag. 'Lena Maharero is a patient at our hospital and she asked me to pass on a message to both of you.'

'How is she?' Ruth said.

The nurse looked at Gunter who lowered his eyes. She then turned to Ruth. 'She ... she has been sterilised.'

Ruth put her hand to her mouth. 'What?'

The nurse stared at her woollen gloves. She pushed up the fingers, like stockings that had fallen down.

Gunter stepped forward. 'Lena was forcibly sterilised and has been committed indefinitely, and Lena's mother has obtained a court order giving her wardship over Kharos.'

Phillip felt his stomach drop.

The nurse wiped tears from her face. 'Lena is terrified that her mother will have Kharos sterilised as well. She says she heard one of the doctors talking about it.'

Or even Applied Eugenics, thought Phillip. The thought of Kharos being slowly murdered by deliberately being fed germ-ridden food and receiving substandard care, filled him with deep anger. How could they?

'Did you hear this as well?' Ruth said.

The nurse looked away.

Gunter touched the nurse's arm. 'There's nothing the nurses can do. It's all official.' He squeezed the nurse's arm. 'It was very brave of you to come here.'

The nurse nodded. She turned to Ruth and Phillip. 'Lena said I had to tell Ruth and Phillip they must save Kharos. That's what she said. That's what I had to tell you.'

'We will not let any harm come to Kharos,' Phillip said. 'I swear. Tell Lena I will take Kharos to England where she will be safe.'

Gunter looked at Phillip and smiled. He then turned to the nurse. 'You must not say that to anyone. In fact don't tell Lena until …' he looked at Phillip.

'Until six days' time.'

The nurse nodded. She gathered herself together. 'I have resigned from the hospital, so I will get a friend to pass on the message in a week's time.' She hesitated. 'Also, Lena said to tell you, Phillip, not to wear the coat she gave you when you travel to Bayreuth.'

'Why?' Phillip said.

The nurse looked at Gunter who nodded. She turned and left.

Phillip looked at Gunter.

'Don't wear the coat Lena gave you,' Gunter said. 'Here.' He threw a navy herringbone overcoat at Phillip. 'And wear this hat. Lena wanted to tell you what she had done, but she thought you would abandon Kharos. After all, she had put your life in danger.' He stared Phillip. 'I only learned from a letter the nurse gave me when she arrived just now. Lena wanted me read it and then to ask you to forgive her.'

Phillip held Gunter's eyes. 'So it was the Communists who killed the tramp wearing my red coat.'

Gunter nodded.

'And so Lena set me up to be identified and ...'

Gunter pressed his lips together.

Phillip turned to Ruth.

'Ruth knew nothing of this,' Gunter said. 'None of us did. Both Lena and her husband were active in the Communist Party in Hamburg. They were on a march that was attacked by Nazis and her husband murdered.'

Ruth went up to Phillip and curled her arm round his waist. 'Please don't judge her. The Nazis murdered her husband. Nobody was ever charged. She obviously wanted revenge.'

'And,' Gunter said, 'she thought she was helping stop them taking over Germany.'

Ruth squeezed Phillip. 'Kharos is the innocent in all this.'

Phillip sighed. 'Yes, yes, she is.'

Chapter 33

A band played military music in Bayreuth's main square, while Nazis waved swastika flags and gave out leaflets.

Phillip folded his newspaper under his arm so that the title, and the red swastika printed next to it, were clearly visible. It was Saturday and many people were out and about with shopping bags.

Phillip wore the coat and hat Gunter had given him. Underneath he had on his best checked shirt, a paisley cravat with a gold tiepin, a green sports jacket, fawn trousers and brown brogue shoes. The clothes suited him and gave him the appearance of an English gentleman.

Rostov was posing next to the fountain dressed in a long black cloak, fastened at the neck with a gold chain. On the left-hand side of the cape, just below the collar, was a resplendent badge, embroidered with green, gold and blue threads. A black fedora, one side of which was pinned with a silver broach holding a bird's feather, was perched on his head at a jaunty angle. His regal air impressed the Brownshirts who showed due deference by saluting him as they passed. When he saw Phillip he raised his cane and smiled.

Phillip thought he would be safe in Rostov's company.

Rostov kissed Phillip on both cheeks. 'Thank you so much for coming.'

Rostov led Phillip across the square to the alleyway that ran behind the Blue Lagoon. 'We need to go in the back way.' Rostov took Phillip's arm. 'Don't worry, we have a tacit agreement with the police chief that if we slip in through the rear entrance, he will turn a blind eye to our little gathering, just for today. Mind you, his son will be there so it's not just for our benefit.'

At the top of the steps, Phillip peered down at the young man who was standing at the back door of the club. He was wearing a long coat with an astrakhan collar and a Russian fur hat. As they descended the steps, the young man raised his eyebrows at Phillip and then smiled at Rostov. He bowed and opened the door.

Next to the toilets, freestanding rails were filled with coats. Rostov slipped off his cloak. He had on full evening dress with a white bow tie and a red rose on his lapel, tied with a silver pin. Phillip took off his coat and hung it with the others.

Rostov brushed fluff from Phillip's shoulder. 'You look gorgeous, Phillip. Thank you so much for making the effort.' He leaned up and slightly adjusted Phillip's cravat. 'Would you mind terribly if, when we went in, you put your arm through mine? Just to show them there is someone who wants to be with me.'

'Of course,' Phillip said, thinking it was like a pantomime.

'Thank you so much, Phillip. You really are a kind person,' Rostov said, pulling Phillip a little closer. 'And just one other thing, when we walk in, stop and stand with me while they all look at us. I'll pretend I'm looking for our table.'

They went through the doors and stopped. All the guests were seated at tables and dressed in full evening wear or long gowns.

A quartet played chamber music. There was a hush and then a ripple of soft chatter as Rostov and Phillip stood gazing at the assembly.

Phillip felt himself going red as they stood there.

Rostov sailed forwards and escorted Phillip to a vacant table with a card in a silver holder – Reserved for Count Rostov and Guest.

A waiter came up to their table and served them with Earl Grey tea and small sandwiches with the crusts cut off.

Rostov sipped his tea, his little eyes darting about from under his hooded lids as he raised his cup to his lips. His eyes were shining.

Despite not having had breakfast, Phillip couldn't eat or drink. He had to get back to the farm and try to figure out what to do. He was collecting the document on Sunday evening, after the last bus to the farm, which meant he would have to spend the whole night in Bayreuth. Then what? If he didn't turn up at the police station the next day, Monday, they would come looking for him. He had to flee Bayreuth Monday morning. But what if the police were watching his lodgings?

The music changed and couples got up and began to waltz round the dance floor. Rostov put down his cup. 'Tell me, Phillip, how are you at dancing?'

'Oh, not bad. I learned the quickstep and the waltz at school.'

'Wonderful. We will dance the next waltz, and then, when the music stops, we do not come back to the table, but walk to the back door without looking back.'

'Sure.'

They waited for the music to end. The next tune was a slow waltz. Phillip rose with Rostov and stepped onto the dance floor. Rostov led and Phillip was swept around the room with exaggerated turns and pauses. The music captured Phillip and he floated effortlessly across the floor. It didn't seem to matter he was dancing with a man.

The music stopped and Rostov bowed to Phillip. He then slipped Phillip's arm into his and led the way out of the room, his head cocked back.

When they reached the main square, the Nazis had gone. They stopped by the fountain and Rostov patted Phillip's hand. 'Thank you so much, Phillip. You are a good person. Be careful, we live in dangerous times. Here, this is the address and the instructions on how to enter. Be there at eight o'clock tomorrow night. This is the key to the garden door.'

Phillip took the paper and key. Rostov kissed him on each cheek, and then turned and walked away, swinging his cane in an exaggerated manner.

Phillip hurried back to his lodgings. Everything was now in place. When he got home, he would pack so that Monday morning he was ready to leave. He would stay in Bayreuth tonight and collect the document tomorrow night.

Wolfgang stepped out in front of him as he reached the top of the lane that led down to his lodgings. 'Enjoy the dance?'

Phillip stood his ground. Wolfgang had shown himself no fighter.

Wolfgang sneered. 'So, you are a pervert as well.'

'As well as what?'

Wolfgang glared at Phillip. 'That's what we are going to find out, Mister Englishman. Find out who you really are. I never trusted you from the beginning. You are not one of us; you don't want to keep the race pure. You mix with Jews and gypsies and communists.' His eyes narrowed. 'Maybe you were you involved with Christoph von Allenbach's murder?'

Phillip stepped up close to Wolfgang. He was at least six inches taller than Wolfgang.

Wolfgang stepped back. 'Doctor Schmelter says all the papers on eugenics must be returned. You are under police investigation and so must not have anything to do with the programme.' He stared at Phillip. 'What were you doing in the park last …'

'Watching people sail their boats.' Phillip held Wolfgang's glare. 'Yes, we British are a maritime nation. In fact we have the largest navy in the world so most of us have an interest in boats and ships of all sizes.' He knew this would hit home since the German Navy, under the terms of the Versailles Treaty, was restricted in the scope of their fleet and the size of their ships, and this was felt as a national humiliation.

'Just make sure to return the documents and papers,' Wolfgang said, and then walked away. He stopped and then turned. 'And don't try to run for it. We will find you, Englishman.'

Chapter 34

Next evening at nine o'clock, Phillip located the door in the wall surrounding Count Koniger's estate.

Phillip unlocked the wooden door that led into Count Koniger's grounds. He hesitated. There were dogs in the grounds. What if they were near the summerhouse where he was headed – or were roaming around and came across him? He took deep breaths to calm himself and then pushed open the door. Should he lock the door behind him? No, in case he needed a fast exit.

A cold, three-quarter moon lit the gravel path that lead to the summerhouse, a stylised Bavarian cottage whose windows cast squares of light onto the grass. Phillip trod cautiously up the path, trying not to crunch the gravel and so alert the dogs. He reached the summerhouse. Through the window he saw Count Koniger sitting by a log fire with a drink in his hand. Faint notes of Beethoven could be heard. Phillip tapped on the door.

Count Koniger pulled open the door, smiled broadly and motioned Phillip to enter. He pointed towards a vacant chair. 'Take off your coat and sit by the fire. What would you like to drink? Whisky, cognac?'

'Oh, thank you. Whisky, thank you.'

Count Koniger poured whisky into a cut-glass tumbler. As he handed it to Phillip, shards of light sparkled within the glass as it passed in front of the fire. Count Koniger resumed his seat and raised his glass. 'Well, you certainly had me fooled. When I met you at my sister's gathering, I thought you a rather gauche young man. Here's to you.'

Phillip raised his glass and took a sip. 'Actually, I'm not really a … an agent. I just …'

'Got roped in. Yes, it happens. A smart move by British Intelligence. Nobody suspected you.'

Phillip took a sip of whisky and felt the warmth seep down into his stomach. He began to relax. The whisky was smoother than any he had tasted before. Should he speak or wait for the Count to say something?

The Count tossed a log onto the fire. 'Do you like Germany?'

'Yes, yes, I do. Very much.'

'Would you live here?'

'Yes, yes I would. In fact, I was planning to do so, after … but …'

The Count smiled. 'Good.' He took an envelope from his pocket. 'This is the document I want the British Government to have. I am doing this for the good of Germany. The evil monster that is Hitler must be stopped.' He placed the envelope on the arm of his chair and then took a sip from his glass. 'Here in Bavaria, in 1919, Hitler sided with the Communist uprising when he thought they might win and was part of the Bavarian Soviet Republic they set up. The Communists rounded up members of the Thule Society and shot them. One of those murdered was my brother.' He swigged from his glass.

'After the Bavarian Soviet was crushed, Hitler switched sides and joined the German Workers' Party which had been set up by the Thule Society. He lied about his involvement in the Soviet Council that had shot my brother.' He drank down the liquid in his glass. 'Hitler corrupted the German Workers' Party and turned it into the National Socialists, a blend of Socialism and Nationalism, trying to appeal to the masses. He always smells the wind, looking for what makes the herd move in a certain direction.' He got up and poured himself another drink.

'Sorry, Phillip, I forgot my manners. Another one?'

'No, thank you.'

'You sure?'

'Yes, honestly, I'm fine.'

The count slumped into his chair. 'I'm telling you this because I want you to be clear about my motives. I love Germany and its history and culture. Hitler had no real ideas until he discovered the American's obsession with eugenics, breeding – as if you can breed a great people, like you can cattle. That's why leading Nazis claim they are biologists. It's rubbish – a nation is great because of its culture and its spiritual awareness. Hitler is a peasant farmer, he's too stupid to be anything else.

'Tell any animal in the farmyard they are special and you will have them eating out of your hand, and more than happy to see the other animals going to the slaughterhouse.' He drank from his glass. 'Hitler read the American books on race and eugenics in 1924, when he was in jail for that stupid Putsch in 1923. He just stole the

American's ideas. Hitler says what people want to hear. The Jews are to blame, the stab in the back by politicians, only pure Germans should be in Germany, anything to rouse instinctive prejudices driven by emotion and not fact.'

Koniger gazed into the fire.

'The problem with us Germans is that we believe in the spirituality of a nation, which makes us vulnerable to corrupters like Hitler.'

Silence.

The count held out the envelope. 'The Nazis are now the second largest party and could win in the next election, so make sure this gets to the British Government. They must be stopped.'

Chapter 35

Phillip checked under his pillow.

The envelope from Count Koniger was still there. It was half past seven in the morning. The faculty library opened at eight. Time to get ready.

Most of his clothes were at the farm; those that weren't he would leave – he didn't want to be seen carrying a suitcase, not when was supposed to present himself at the police station at two p.m. He had written a note for Frau Weiser which he would leave on the washstand. It said he was called back to England on a personal matter.

He finished dressing and opened the curtains. The sky was clear and the snow gone.

In his new life, he would never be as strong as he wanted to be, but he knew that being with Ruth would sustain him. He would never hide Kharos the way he had concealed his own identity. Cages had opened inside him. He was free. He knew he would be tested but as long as he had Ruth he could be strong.

He picked up the two library books. If anyone was following him it would look like he was going to the university to do some work. His plan was to return the books and then go down the back stairs and slip out the back door of the faculty, make his way to the terminus without going through town, and catch the nine o'clock bus.

The police were expecting him at two, but by then he would have his new passport, with Ruth and Kharos on it, and on his way out of Germany.

The library assistant stamped the books and asked Phillip if he was taking out any new ones. Phillip said no. He thought of handing in his library tickets but decided not to. Now all he had to do was to get the bus out of Bayreuth and he would be safe.

As he left the library Phillip stopped. A woman had pushed open the door to Krystal's office, and through it he saw Kharos sitting in a chair with a skull-measuring device on her head. The door closed. Phillip's heart pounded as he stepped back into the library. What had happened? How had they caught her?

He ran down the stairs to the phone boxes near the registry.

Gunter answered. He told Gunter what he had seen. Gunter said he must get Kharos out of the building. He would be waiting with a car outside the back of the faculty, on the other side of the river. He would be there in three quarters of an hour.

Phillip ran back up the stairs to the library. He positioned himself so that he could see Krystal's office door. He had no idea how he would rescue Kharos.

An hour passed, but Krystal's door stayed shut. Gunter must be outside by now, waiting. And the police? It was now half past nine. In four hours' time, they would be out looking for him. Phillip steeled himself. The next time the door opened he would charge into Krystal's room and grab Kharos.

Fifteen minutes passed, then the door opened. Phillip jumped up. The woman who had gone in earlier emerged holding Kharos's hand. The woman led Kharos down the stairs.

Phillip followed them down.

The woman stopped at a door marked 'Female Staff Toilet'. Kharos went inside and the woman guarded the door. Phillip went back up the stairs. He took a deep breath and then ran down the stairs.

'Ah, you're with Kharos,' Phillip said, to the woman waiting outside the toilet.

'Yes.'

'Doctor Schmelter asked me to say she wants you back in her office immediately. She wants me to bring Kharos back up to her office.'

The woman stared at Phillip.

Phillip took her arm and led her to the stairs. 'Doctor Schmelter says it's an emergency and you must go right away. I'm her assistant. Phillip Fitzwilliam.'

The woman peered up the stairs. 'Make sure you bring the girl straight back up to Doctor Schmelter's office.' She started up the stairs.

Phillip pushed the toilet door. It was locked. He tapped on the door. 'Kharos. Kharos. It's me, Phillip. Open the door. Quickly.' The door opened and Phillip grabbed Kharos and ran down the stairs.

When they reached the ground floor, he pulled her out the back entrance, along to the footbridge and over the river. He bundled her into the back of Gunter's Citroen, and the car roared off. 'Keep your heads down,' shouted Gunter. Ruth was beside him in the passenger seat.

They drove through the countryside for about an hour. Gunter explained that he'd hid Kharos in the secret cubbyhole up in the attic and locked all the doors, but when he got back, she'd gone. 'I know who it was,' Gunter said. 'My brother. He sold his half of the farm months ago and lost it in some speculation. He collected a reward for betraying Kharos and has now run away to Berlin. He knew about the cubbyhole in the attic from our smuggling days.'

The car stopped. Phillip raised his head. They were outside a small cottage surrounded by woodland. They all scrambled out and ran into the cottage. Inside, Ruth threw her arms round Kharos and sobbed. 'We thought we had lost you.' She slid her hands over Kharos's head.

Gunter shook Phillip's hand. 'You are a real hero. If you want, I will present you with one of the medals they gave me during the war.'

Phillip burst out laughing – and then wanted to cry.

'Steady, Mr Kumar, you now have a wife and child,' Gunter said. 'When do you collect the passport?'

'At twelve o'clock.' He thought of the police expecting him at two.

Gunter looked at his watch. 'Half an hour's time. Where?'

'In the village church.'

'OK,' Gunter said. 'Then slight change of plans. Ruth will drive all three of you in my car to the church. She knows the way. Then you'll drive to Cheb, just across the border in Czechoslovakia.' Gunter then explained that in Cheb they would be met by one of Gunter's friends who would then drive them to Prague. There they would get the train to Milan, then on to France and then England. 'The only danger,' Gunter said, 'is that they will be watching the Bavarian borders for Kharos. A mixed-race girl.'

'And me,' Phillip said. 'No doubt Doctor Schmelter has alerted the police that I took Kharos from the university.'

Silence.

Ruth hugged Kharos. 'Then we will disguise her as a boy.'

'Good idea,' Gunter said. 'And Phillip, when you drive my car, Ruth and Kharos can sit in the back as mother and son. The border guards will not question an English family travelling around Europe. And with a name like Kumar, they will think she is an Indian boy.'

'What if I dye my hair?' Phillip said. 'They will be looking for a blond Englishman called Fitzwilliam. I can say my name is Kumar, true, and I'm an Indian living in England. Also true.'

Gunter stared at Phillip.

'I have some hair dye,' Ruth said.

Kharos was making a sketch as she sat beside Phillip on a bench in the Milan Railway Station.

Phillip watched Ruth step out of the telephone booth. The call seemed to have taken a long time. She strode back and slumped down beside him. 'The document has been destroyed,' she said. 'Gunter was in Bayreuth on his way to the post office when the police tried to arrest him. He escaped and ran and threw the letter in the river.'

Phillip shook his head. 'What happened to Gunter?'

'He denied everything. Said he never saw you or Kharos. There was no evidence and so they eventually let him go.'

Perhaps it was just as well, thought Phillip. If the document were published in the *Munich Post* newspaper, then SIS would know he had double-crossed them and read the document then replaced it with a blank sheet of paper. Ruth's skills as a graphic designer had helped him reseal the envelope he had given to SIS in the church.

They had opened the envelope because Count Koniger had made it plain the document was to be used to harm Hitler, but Smythe said it must not see the light of day. This meant the British establishment were trying to protect Hitler and the Nazis. The envelope contained a letter from Hitler, written in 1910, asking to be admitted to the Vienna Art Academy because he had a Jewish grandfather and knew the academy favoured Jews.

There was also a letter from Count Koniger confirming that Maria Schicklgruber, Hitler's grandmother, gave birth to Alois, Hitler's father, while she was single and working as a cook for a rich Jewish family named Frankenberger. The count knew the

Frankenbergers and confirmed that one of their relatives was the father of Maria Schicklgruber's illegitimate baby, Hitler's father.

The train to Milan entered the station.

Phillip stood up. 'Let's hope the Germans see the Nazis for what they are, and not vote for them next time.'

*

Phillip was sat at the window as the train pulled into London's Liverpool Street station.

People on the platform peered into the carriage at the dark-skinned girl - some observing with sympathy, some turning until the carriage passed, some staring with hatred and fear at the child who carried the threat of otherness.

Phillip reached over and took Kharos onto his knee.

END

Printed in Great Britain
by Amazon

15766121R00202